A QUICK KISS

"What did you promise Angelica?"

Theresa grimaced. "A white pony and riding lessons. She so wants to ride, James, but you won't let her because you worry about Jacob wanting to ride, too. But I think Jacob *could* learn to ride. He has been so much better lately, don't you think, and . . ."

He did the only thing he could, under the circumstances. He pulled her to her feet, wrapped his arms around her, and kissed her.

Theresa thought of all the poetry she had ever read, all the romances describing in ecstatic detail a first kiss. It did not begin to compare. James was clearly a master of the craft, if she was to judge impartially.

He stopped. She stared at him for a long moment. Doubt creased his forehead and he took a step backward.

"I'm terribly sorry."

"Are you?"

"Yes. I mean, I'm sorry if you didn't like it, but you looked so adorable and I was tempted beyond caution."

"Adorable?"

"Yes. You were pleading Angelica and Jacob's case, and the only way to shut you up was to kiss you."

"Shut me up?"

"So I could tell you . . . I love you . . ."

From *A Father's Love,* by Donna Simpson

A MATCH FOR PAPA

Maria Greene
Victoria Hinshaw
Donna Simpson

ZEBRA BOOKS
Kensington Publishing Corp.
http://www.kensingtonbooks.com

ZEBRA BOOKS are published by

Kensington Publishing Corp.
850 Third Avenue
New York, NY 10022

All Kensington titles, imprints and distributed lines are available at special quantity discounts for bulk purchases for sales promotion, premiums, fund-raising, educational or institutional use.

Special book excerpts or customized printings can also be created to fit specific needs. For details, write or phone the office of the Kensington Special Sales Manager: Kensington Publishing Corp., 850 Third Avenue, New York, NY 10022. Attn. Special Sales Department. Phone: 1-800-221-2647.

First Printing: May 2003
10 9 8 7 6 5 4 3 2 1

Printed in the United States of America

CONTENTS

THE MOST UNLIKELY PAPA

Maria Greene

One

"This is a most foolish idea, Mrs. Rutherford," Rose said with a peevish grimace on her face. "You're about to give birth any second now, and I have palpitations just thinking about it. I don't know how I'll cope with a crisis like that. I'm not as young as I once was." She fluttered her hands over the strands of gray hair sticking out of her mobcap, and two red spots glowed on her cheeks.

"Don't take on so, Rose. You shan't have to do a thing. I don't expect more of you than to take care of my clothes when we get to Bath. We'll arrive at my brother's before anything happens at all. For all the precariousness of this situation, I wouldn't miss the chance to see him . . . before . . ." Allegra dabbed at her burning, teary eyes with a lace-edged handkerchief. "I couldn't live with myself if I didn't go to his side in his time of dire need. You never know. . . . He's my only brother and I love him dearly."

Rose nodded. "I understand, ma'am, but to put your own safety in jeopardy . . . well, your family shouldn't expect it of you."

"They don't, but if Reggie dies from that bullet wound—it would be just too much to bear." She glanced at her maid, so uncomfortable on the seat across from her in the swaying carriage. Rose was old enough to be retired, but how do you tell a loyal retainer that they're no longer needed? You just didn't; you had to repay that loyalty.

The rain beat relentlessly against the windows of the coach. It had been raining for days even if the month of June was well underway. The weather resonated well with the heavy feeling in her heart as she thought about her brother, whom she'd loved for as long as she could remember. Reggie had always been there to support her through her awful marriage, and now he needed her support—in the eleventh hour of her pregnancy, well maybe in the eleventh-and-a-half hour.

She touched her round belly uneasily. The baby had been moving with great vigor and had changed position since they left Shorecliff, and she sensed that her time had come. She begged the wee one to hold off until they arrived at her brother's house in Bath. The family, meager as it was, would be there to assist, a doctor at hand.

"Dear God," she murmured as perspiration dampened her forehead. She didn't feel very well at all.

Rose made a strangled sound, her worried blue gaze riveted to the large mound under Allegra's voluminous black gown. "And you without a husband to look after you," she murmured. "Mr. Rutherford would never have allowed you to make this trip."

Allegra nodded. "You're right; but he's not here to dole out his icy commands. As you know, he ruled the household with an iron fist, causing me many tears and much heartache. A more miserly and miserable man you couldn't find!"

"Hush," Rose hissed in outrage. "You can't speak so bitterly of someone deceased. He was your *husband.* You must revere and obey—"

"Balderdash!" A flare of anger burned through Allegra. "He lived for creating misery for everyone around him, and deviousness was his game. You might as well see the truth as it is. He did you no favors."

"A gentleman of great standing nevertheless, a pillar of the community. You should be grateful to have married a gentleman of such importance. Your guardian, the esteemed Mr. Mansfield, had only your best interests at heart when he negotiated a liaison with Mr. Rutherford."

"Mr. Mansfield had only his eye on the settlement." Allegra flung out her arms in outrage. "Jebediah Rutherford was twice as old as I and cold as an icicle. Pillar of the community? Robber's more like it, but no one realized his duplicity. How could I ever have hoped to form a romantic attachment to a man like him?"

The storm outside matched the one going on within her at the mention of her deceased husband. "My parents, had they been alive, would never have allowed my marriage to Mr. Rutherford."

Rose looked pained. "You may be right on that score. They were gentle and caring people, but you can hardly remember that. I can vouch for the fact that they would've preferred a love match for you."

Allegra fought back the prickly emotion rising within her. These last nine months had changed her. Never had she been so moody and prone to tears. Then there had been the ambiguity within her when she found out she was *enceinte* whether she'd wanted to carry Mr. Rutherford's heir.

She would never wish any offspring of hers to pass on the mean traits of Mr. Rutherford, but she could teach the child caring and consideration. That inner struggle had brought on waves of guilt, but with time she'd come to love the little being now ready to enter the world.

The road had potholes and as they bounced through a particularly deep one, she moaned as her back jarred with the impact. Clearly the horses were struggling with the muddy tracks as the coach leaped forward, then slowed down. She leaned sideways to look out the water-streaked window. The rain had abated some and the trees lining the lane looked washed clean and vibrant green.

"We're traveling through a wooded area. It's beautiful, don't you think, Rose?"

The maid shivered and made a strangled noise. "Highwaymen abound," she said hoarsely.

"Don't be a goose," Allegra scoffed. "No highwaymen linger to be drenched by rain in full daylight."

"You never know," the maid said direly.

"I for one have never met one, and I wouldn't be above telling them—"

"Ack, it's that high-spiritedness that always brought you into trouble," Rose said, her voice brimming with remembrance. "You and your daft brother both."

" 'Tis no crime surely to want to experience some adventure before one turns staid and old."

Rose pruned her lips and said nothing. Just as well, Allegra mused, tired of lectures. She had barely finished the thought when the coach lurched to a sudden halt, then tilted alarmingly as if about to tip over. Automatically, she braced herself against the leather squabs and remained seated.

Rose struggled not to lose her balance and fall against the door. The sound of the driver's curses cut the air, and the horses stamped restlessly, sawing at the bits, no doubt. The shackles prevented them from bolting.

After a breathless moment, Billy the coachman opened the door and stuck his grizzled head inside. "I apologize, ma'am, but one of the wheels 'as come orf. 'Tis this perishing weather. The roads are nothing but mud troughs."

Rose clasped her hands to her bosom, her face pale. "What are we going to do?" she squeaked.

"Have faith," Allegra said with a conviction she didn't feel. "We'll find transportation to the nearest inn, and we'll wait there until the wheel can be repaired."

"Ma'am, I don't want to frighten you, but on this lonely stretch of road, there are no inns," Billy said.

"Don't we know someone who lives close by?" Allegra wondered aloud, peering through the trees lining the road.

No one replied, and she realized they were far from any friend's estate. Most of her cousins lived in Yorkshire and two aunts in Sussex. Her friends were scattered across the country, but none lived in Somerset.

With the help of the coachman, she got out of the carriage.

"Ma'am, 'tis slippery and wet out here. Ye'd better be careful."

"I'm not an invalid, Billy." She looked at the wheel and the axle mired in the mud.

Billy went to release the horses from the tilted shackles and led them to a copse of trees where he tied them. Rose joined Allegra and wrung her hands in distress as she viewed the damage.

"Neither the wheel nor the axle are ruined, but we need help to put 'em back together." Billy glanced down the road. "For now, all we can do is wait."

Allegra shook her head. "You must ride to the nearest hostelry for help, Billy. We can't tarry here. There's no telling how long we'll be stuck. I need to get to Bath posthaste."

"Aye, that I know," Billy said, scratching his neck. He eyed her rotund belly furtively and Allegra knew he worried about her condition. She pulled her black cloak more closely around her.

"Everything will be fine. I shan't have the babe in the road."

"I begged you to bring outriders," Rose commented peevishly.

"There was no time for all that," Allegra said. "Even as we stand here, Reggie might breathe his last." A wave of sadness came over her at the thought, and she fought back her tears. She gave Billy an imploring look. "Please hurry. "

He hastened to obey, and Allegra watched wistfully as he rode off, praying he would return without delay. She sat down on a mossy tree stump by the side of the road and stared at the lopsided carriage. The moss, dampened from the rain, soon made inroads on her cloak, and she stood, knowing she would be wet through in minutes.

"We'll be here all night," Rose said gloomily as she surveyed the gray clouds overhead. "And we'll have another downpour, you mark my words."

Allegra gave an incredulous laugh. "Your comments are so very uplifting, Rose. Don't you ever see any bright possibilities?"

Rose sniffed, clearly annoyed. "If I were younger it wouldn't bother me to hare across the county at breakneck speed, but my aching joints protest too much."

Allegra had nothing to say to that. Rose had always spoken her mind and certainly wouldn't change now. "If it starts raining, we'll climb back into the coach, and we certainly don't have to worry about breakneck speed." She glanced down the road where the trees filtered the light to a soft green dusk. Mist hung among the branches and above the mossy rocks. The vista was beautiful in its own way, she thought just as a vicious spasm of pain went through her back and abdomen.

Dear Lord, she thought and pressed her hand to her belly. Dear Heavens, had the baby decided that this was the moment to start its entry into the world? It couldn't be.

Allegra winced and threw a cautious glance at Rose. She would have to keep the pains a secret for as long as possible, as she could not cope with any hysterics from her maid at this juncture in their adventure. She prayed that Billy would arrive posthaste with another coach.

Another forceful spasm went through her, forcing tears to her eyes. *Oh no, not now, please not now! Slow down, will you.* She stroked her hands over her abdomen, knowing in her heart that the birth would go fast. That was just her luck.

To her relief, she heard the fast approach of a horse. Billy! Thank God he'd found someone to help them that quickly.

But it wasn't Billy. The gentleman approaching them rode an enormous dappled gray with ease. He carried himself with style and elegance, decidedly a man of the world. She strained her eyes to see if he was someone she knew, but another contraction went through her, and a short bout of panic set in.

She noticed a coach behind him. He, or whoever was in the coach, might be able to help.

Rose ran into the lane and waved at him to stop. He reined in sharply, sending a searching glance over the tilting carriage and at Allegra sitting on the stump, onto which she'd reseated herself when the pains were washing over her.

He must have caught her grimace as she almost fainted

with the pain that rolled through her in another spasm. The last thing she knew, she looked into deep brown beautiful eyes, filled with concern. Somewhere, sometime, she'd seen those eyes before.

Two

"Where am I?" she asked, feeling nauseated as if on a ship in strong winds.

"At Fairleigh, my estate," a male voice responded far away.

A contraction tore through her, and she wanted to scream. "Where?" She'd never felt this much pain before. It ripped through her body and left her devastated. She suspected she was being torn apart and would never survive the ordeal.

"Fairleigh."

"Dashed if I know where that is," she said between gritted teeth, not caring about her language. Through her pain she wanted to shout worse things.

"In Somerset."

She remembered her brother as another pain slashed through her. "Reggie?"

"No. Jack . . . James Hollister."

She could not connect the name with anything, but she recalled the coach and the missing wheel, and the gentleman on a horse, and a very elegant woman. Then everything had become a blur of pain. Under her, she felt soft sheets, and a mountain of pillows propped up her head and her shoulders.

A cool hand touched her perspiring brow, and after a particularly powerful contraction, she heard his soothing voice right by her ear.

"There . . . there, just breathe and push," he said, sounding commanding and gentle at the same time.

She liked his velvet-deep voice, but why should he be talking to her? Where were the women? Where was Rose?

"Rose?" she croaked through cracked lips.

She heard a soft wail and someone placed a cold cloth on her forehead. Looking up, she noticed Rose standing by the bed, deathly pale. "This is what I feared, ma'am. Not a soul to help us except this gentleman, and . . . and some woman." Rose threw a fearsome glance toward the end of the bed, but Allegra couldn't see beyond her pulled-up knees.

"Is Reggie your husband? Where is he?" the man asked.

Allegra moved her legs under the sheet, as there was a lull in the pain. "No, he's my brother, and I need to be at his side."

She noted the stranger's beautiful wavy dark brown hair, his very broad shoulders, and his capable-looking hands, now busying themselves awkwardly with a washcloth and a basin of water. He glanced over at her, and their eyes locked.

He had the face of a fallen angel, and she remembered seeing him once at a gathering before she married Mr. Rutherford. Jack Hollister had been the center of attention among the ladies, and probably still was the darling of the London society matrons, and possibly still a Lothario of the worst kind.

At this moment he was lifting the sheet covering her, and she realized that he could see her in all her glory. A wave of embarrassment washed through her, and in its wake, another devastating spasm.

He smiled. "Almost there."

Oh my God, she whispered to herself as she succumbed to another violent contraction.

Jack thought he was moving through a strange dream. During all of his escapades he'd never been involved with anything so delicate, so frightening, so exhilarating, so sacred as the birth of a child.

"Minerva," he addressed the woman beside him. She looked so out of place with her elegant pearl gray silk dress and her painted face, and the diamond necklace he'd given her for Christmas. "Dash it all! You'll have to help me."

"I refuse to touch her," she whispered fiercely. "I have no experience in childbirth, and all that blood makes me sick. What do you expect of me anyway? Why would you bring her here?"

"What else could I do? She's in dire need of our help."

He forgot about the mother's plight for a moment as he watched the tiny head poking through, and he wondered what to do. He had taken part in some foalings, but this seemed more momentous. He'd sent old Tom, the only retainer left at the estate, for the doctor. Why, of all days, did this have to happen on the day when all the servants had the day off to celebrate the wedding between the first footman and one of the upstairs maids in the village?

He hadn't the first clue of how to deliver a baby, and the maid, Rose, just stood there wringing her hands, and he suspected she might faint at any moment. Minerva would never soil her manicured hands, but that's what could be expected from her. He had hoped for more though.

His white shirt clung to his back with sweat as he washed his hands thoroughly in another basin with hot water, and went to grip the slick head of the baby. He held his breath and winced as the woman screamed with pain and pushed hard. His thoughts floundered as he held on. What would happen next? He felt a lot of movement and a rush. Within seconds, he had the tiny slippery being in his hands.

"It's a girl," he cried out, for one moment jubilant at the momentous event, until his nerves got the better of him. He noticed the tiny hands and feet and the beautifully formed little mouth and nose. "She's perfect. Looks just like her mother," he added with more confidence than he felt inside. His hands shook terribly as he held the tiny girl, not knowing what to do next.

His heart pounded with fear and awe, and he swallowed hard as the baby let out its first wail, lying right in the cup formed with his hands. She flailed her tiny fists, and he laid her down on a pile of towels he'd spread on the bed. What now? He glanced helplessly at Minerva, who had the audacity to look annoyed, then at Rose. "Is this . . . ?"

Rose only moaned in response, placing her hands on the sides of her face and rocking back and forth as if in agony.

Beyond nervous, he gently wiped the baby and viewed the umbilical cord with suspicion. It would have to be cut. No such gargantuan responsibility had ever been placed on his shoulders before, and he worried he would do something wrong. Where were Tom and the doctor? he wondered irritably.

Minerva stomped out of the room, slamming the door, and he was glad to be rid of her.

The woman in the bed produced the afterbirth and there was no time to wait any longer. Exhausted, he watched. It seemed that he'd been struggling with this birth for hours, and he would have to finish his task. He knew he had to tie off the umbilical cord, but how close? Guessing, he made the two tight knots with cotton ribbons and cut the cord before he lost his nerve.

"Miss!" he ordered the maid sharply. "Pull yourself together and make sure your mistress is clean and comfortable. Now!"

The maid scurried to comply—thank God—and he busied himself with cleaning off the tiny wiggling body in his care. Before long, he had given her a gentle sponge bath and wrapped her in a soft towel. She had downy hair, the same chestnut color as her mother's. Only her little red face peeped through the folds, and he took the precious bundle to the head of the bed.

The woman looked peaceful and half asleep, her cheeks pink with the recent exertion. She had a beautiful oval face, her brown hair a tangle of rioting curls. Her eyes were a clear blue, her nose held a spattering of freckles, and her plump lips expressed a hint of willfulness. He found this stranger very attractive, and wondered why Fate had sent her literally into his arms on his very own birthday.

Once he had escorted Minerva to the coast as he'd promised, he had planned to celebrate his birthday in peaceful solitude—to the likely disappointment of his cronies—but that's what he'd wanted. He'd been excessively tired of the din and glitter of London. Well, his wish hadn't been granted.

Uncertain, he looked down at the woman's closed face, and then at the tiny one among the towels. Something stirred in his heart, something akin to a flutter of wings, and he felt as if some door—hitherto closed—had been opened. A trembling sigh escaped from his chest, and he swallowed convulsively. How could this wee thing have such power to stir him this deeply?

"Here she is," he said hoarsely and waited for the woman to open her eyes. He'd never felt this uncertain in his life. Nothing that he'd ever experienced had prepared him for this moment.

The woman opened her eyes with difficulty. She must be exhausted. They lit up with thousands of sparkles and she struggled to sit up against the pillows, and then eagerly stretched out her arms. He handed over the baby but found that he was reluctant to do so, as if by the act of delivery he had somehow become entitled to keep her in his arms forever.

"Does she have a name?" he asked, not knowing what to do with his empty hands. He placed them behind his back.

She admired the baby, touching every finger and the tiny nose, one after the other, then looked at the toes.

She smiled, and he found his breath catching in his throat. How beautiful, how unspoiled and fresh, he thought, comparing her to the hard-as-diamonds females he knew in the capital, Minerva among them.

"Beatrice Elizabeth Allegra, after her grandmothers and myself." She held out a slim hand toward him. "I owe you an enormous thank-you and an apology for thrusting myself upon your charity in this manner."

He shrugged. "Don't mention it." Feeling embarrassed, he smiled at the memory of the labor. "It was a frightening but very profound experience."

"I'm Allegra Rutherford, and this is my abigail, Rose." She motioned to the maid, who had somehow collected her wits and busied herself with cleaning.

"And your husband? Where is he on an important day like today?"

Mrs. Rutherford's smile faded. "Presumably in Heaven, but I highly doubt it."

Rose made a suppressed squeal, and Jack was somewhat

taken aback by the force of Mrs. Rutherford's statement. "I see," he said, even if he didn't see. "I suspect he would've been a proud father all the same."

"I would like to think so, but his entire world revolved around himself." She sighed. "I'm sorry. There is no call for speaking in this manner to you, and I don't know what prompted me to do so."

"You're vulnerable after your ordeal," he offered as an explanation, and found himself strangely relieved that she had no husband to claim ownership of the baby, or the mother. "Is it long since he passed?"

"About eight months."

That explained why she'd been wearing black from head to toe. "It must be a most difficult situation."

" 'Tis the past, and all I'm worried about now is my brother, Reggie, who succumbed to a stray bullet in France. Last I know—yesterday?—is that he hovers on the brink of death."

"I brought you here this morning," he explained. " 'Tis now four o'clock. My servants should be back from the wedding shortly, and I'll dispatch one of the grooms to your brother posthaste."

"I will have to go to him in Bath, tonight if possible," she said, urgency evident in her voice.

"You cannot travel right now," he explained patiently. "I understand your concern, but your body needs to heal before you can travel. I'm certain the doctor will second that, and he should be here shortly." Jack wondered if Tom had managed to get hold of the physician, but since it had taken so long, it didn't look promising.

She nodded, her eyes bright with a film of tears. "Reggie is my best friend besides being my brother," she explained and cradled the baby closer.

Those tears were his undoing. "I shall find someone right now to ride into Bath and carry the news about Beatrice's birth."

"Thank you." She leaned back tiredly and the baby started to cry. "She's hungry."

Knowing that was her hint for him to leave the room, he

complied. Feeling strangely protective, he wanted to put someone by the door to guard it, but how ridiculous! Nothing would befall his guests at Fairleigh.

He was imagining things. His whole world had been turned topsy-turvy from the moment he'd laid eyes on the beautiful Mrs. Rutherford.

Overcome with the sense of the miracle, Allegra fed Beatrice. Here lay the most perfect little being in her arms. She had produced Beatrice from her own body, a fact that filled her with even more amazement. Exhausted from the ordeal and the awkwardness of her position, she nevertheless experienced a great happiness that flowed out of her every pore.

"Isn't she wonderful?" she asked Rose.

The maid hovered by the bed, busying herself with folding towels and cleaning up the last of the afterbirth. "You should be under a doctor's care," she replied gloomily. "There's no telling what will happen."

"Don't be such a misery, Rose. Didn't you take at least one peek at her?"

Rose nodded. "She is beautiful," she admitted grudgingly. "But that doesn't remove the fact that we're in a highly compromising situation, with only a bachelor and a dubious woman in attendance. A *notorious* bachelor at that!"

"What do you mean?"

"The man who assisted us is the Earl of Roche; he has the reputation of a gambler and a womanizer, and the woman—"

"Oh?" Allegra interrupted. She didn't want to admit that she'd remembered who he was as he stood holding out the baby to her. Rose was right; he *did* have the unsavory reputation. It pained her to some degree that a notorious rake had delivered her child, but in her desperation what choices did she have?

"That he is assuredly. His reputation travels before him."

Allegra shrugged. "Be that as it may, he behaved with complete decorum in my time of need."

"But he was in *here*—with you."

"Without him we would've had a very difficult situation. You don't like the sight of blood, for one."

"It makes my nerves all fluttery," Rose said in an apologetic tone.

Allegra gave up the conversation and settled in among the pillows, Beatrice sleeping at her breast. A great feeling of peace came over her, and she refused to look at the impropriety of the situation. Everything would work out to complete satisfaction, of that she had no doubts.

The only cloud in her sky was the condition of her brother, and as she drifted off to sleep she sent out a prayer that Reggie would be whole and hearty again. After all, he now had a niece that he had to meet.

Jack opened the door cautiously and looked at the sleeping mother and the baby clasped in her arms. Rose had tucked a blanket over them both, and they looked happy and peaceful. The maid was asleep in a wing chair, snoring slightly.

He tiptoed inside to take another look at the infant, whose rosy face struck him with great awe once more. How completely innocent, how trusting, he thought. *Presumably I was once like that. When did I lose those qualities in life?* he wondered.

These two females had brought new life to Fairleigh in one quick sweep, and he knew his life had changed forever. One can't come face-to-face with the divinity represented in a newborn child and remain oblivious, he thought. In that perspective, his life looked tawdry and bleak. It may have all the flash of superficial gaiety, but somewhere he'd lost the depth of who he once was.

He stood by the bed staring at Allegra innocently resting in his best guest room, but what would she say when she discovered his identity? Would she be filled with horror and leave in disgust? And what if Minerva decided to act out her jealousy as she often did when other women came close to him? Not that it mattered anymore, but he wanted to protect Allegra from any kind of confrontation, or even scandal. He shied away from the word, but the situation had the potential of great discomfort for her.

As if she felt his presence, she opened her eyes and looked right at him. Her sleep-filled gaze made his heart turn over, and he felt his cheeks redden.

"I sent someone to Bath to inquire about your brother," he whispered. "I just wanted you to know."

"Thank you," she said. "I'm so worried about Reggie. Tomorrow we need to continue on our journey."

"Only if the doctor agrees."

She stretched and glanced down at the sleeping infant. "Where is the doctor?"

"I ask that same question. Most likely he got delayed with some other patient."

He stood next to the bed, not knowing what to do. Officially he should not be in this room due to the impropriety, but he couldn't make himself leave. He threw a guarded look at Rose, and Allegra chuckled. "I could read those thoughts going through your mind."

" 'Pon rep, the one about my wish that she were to leave the room?"

"She sleeps very heavily. Anyway, she's only protective of me, and she informed me about your vile reputation, and I doubt I can get any more compromised than what we've already gone through. No one needs to know that a Lothario of the worst kind delivered my child."

"Ah." He took a deep breath. "Every word is true, alas, but I daresay my touch did not taint the girl."

"I believe she's protected from the likes of you," Allegra said with a small smile.

"Thank you for your vote of confidence." He sat down gingerly on the very edge of the bed. "I've been thinking a lot lately."

"I beg you not to strain yourself."

"Ha, ha. Sarcasm does not fit you." He gave her a baleful

glare. "I have no reason to tell you what's been going through my mind."

"Don't put yourself out. I'm quite happy with the status quo, and any confessions you need to make, find a clergyman."

Exasperated, he stared heavenward. "The point is that Beatrice's birth confirmed that my thinking has been sound."

"Oh." She raised her already imperious eyebrows and gave him a challenging stare.

"I've behaved abominably in the past, but before I returned to Fairleigh, I'd decided to change my life. It has become very tedious as it is. Mayhap I have finally come to see reason." He inclined his head toward Beatrice. "She and I have something in common."

Allegra raised her eyebrows once more, her gaze tinged with amusement. Evidently his reputation didn't frighten her.

"Really?" she asked.

"Today is my thirtieth birthday. Perhaps the birth signified a new beginning for me and definitely for her."

"A new start? I daresay." Allegra gave him a glance full of doubt, and he could understand her reservations. "Happy birthday."

"I know that you're thinking that a leopard can't change his spots."

"I thought no such thing. I can't understand why you would confide such a personal decision to me, and at this point in time."

"Because of the earth-shattering events of this day. A miracle happened to me today, and I'll be eternally grateful."

Her expression softened. "To me as well."

"We share that on the deepest level."

"Possibly." She sounded noncommittal as she tucked the blanket more closely around the sleeping infant. Beatrice worked her mouth. A perfect bubble of spittle hung on her lower lip, and Allegra gently wiped it away with her fingertip.

"Are you hungry or thirsty?" he asked, cursing silently the fact that the servants were away.

"Yes . . . thank you for your concern. A glass of water would taste wonderful."

He smiled, feeling on safer ground. He had something on which to focus his scattered mind. "I'll return shortly."

Allegra watched him leave, noting the broad back under the striped waistcoat and the immaculate shirt into which he'd changed. His step rang purposeful on the polished floor, and for the first time since the birth, she really noticed her surroundings. The massive carved furniture was from the previous century and the patina showed the care of loving hands over time. Lots of beeswax had gone into keeping up the shine of mahogany and walnut.

Old portraits and Oriental carpets lent further accents of ageless grace to the room. Despite the heavy furniture, the room held an inviting quality. Fairleigh seemed to be a friendly, accessible sort of house, old as the ages, no doubt. If the rest of the estate held the same air of care, a person would feel a great deal of comfort in these surroundings.

The Earl of Roche. Fairleigh. As far as she knew, the name was worth a great deal of wealth, but mayhap the earl had squandered most of his riches at the gaming tables and that's why he planned to change his life. It wouldn't be the first time a peer of the realm ruined name and fortune.

But somehow she sensed that he was far too shrewd to let that happen to him; he had a great deal of pride, but carried it well. She detected no pomposity in his character, only open curiosity where she was concerned. And he had an abundance of charm and self-confidence, traits so attractive to the female heart. But not to *hers*.

He'd been very instrumental during the greatest moment of her life, and for that she was eternally grateful. However, that's as far as it went. After this was over, she would never set eyes on Fairleigh and its owner again.

Three

Dr. Bainbridge came with his instruments and his air of friendliness and pronounced Allegra hale and hearty after listening to her heart and examining her. He also proclaimed that Beatrice had a pair of lungs that would make her proud in the future. "You must rest for a few days, Mrs. Rutherford. The earl informs me that you're eager to continue on your travels, but I forbid you to do so until you've recovered your strength."

"But my brother?" Allegra said, and closed her dressing gown. "I must go to him."

"And jeopardize your own life and possibly that of the child? I think not," the doctor said with force. "The earl has graciously offered you his house until you recover, and his aunt Georgina, will keep you company. She arrives tonight, and I've known her for a long time. There will be no gainsaying her."

Allegra felt trapped, but there was nothing she could do but obey, at least for another day. Truth to tell, she felt rather like a wet rag and her spirits were low despite the miracle of the birth, all due to her worries about Reggie. "Very well, I trust your judgment, Doctor Bainbridge. I was fortunate that Lord Roche happened to arrive on the road just when I needed him."

The doctor chuckled. "The experience must've rather unnerved him."

"I doubt that," Allegra said, knowing there were few situations that would throw the confident earl off keel.

"'Twill be a unique story he can tell for years to come—one I'm sure none of his cronies can top." He closed his bag with a snap. "Rest is the best remedy, and you seem remarkably strong despite your ordeal, Mrs. Rutherford."

"I don't see childbirth as a reason to appear the wilted lily. 'Tis a natural occurrence, after all."

The doctor left and Allegra nursed the baby. Little Beatrice rarely cried, spending peaceful after peaceful hour sleeping. Rose claimed it to be a great blessing, and Allegra tended to agree as she struggled to stay awake. A young maid had been allotted the role of nursemaid until Allegra would leave Fairleigh.

She slept the rest of the evening, and as the sun set beyond the fringe of trees in the park around nine o'clock, she got up, sore but needing to move around. Dressed in her nightgown and her robe, she slowly walked out onto the balcony that went the length of the house at the back. The wind had died down, making way for peace and quiet.

A pale moon was rising over the horizon and she inhaled the misty evening air with pleasure. Looking up at the sky streaked with pink and orange, she prayed that Reggie would recover from his wound. A wave of anxiety came over her that she was not at his side, but she vowed to be shortly.

The sound of steps came to her ears, and she turned. The earl was walking toward her from the other end of the terrace. He must've come from the master suite, or some other bedroom, whose door must open toward the terrace. He looked handsome—if indecent—in a white shirt open at the neck and buckskins, casual as if he'd been grooming horses in the stables. He looked comfortable and relaxed, very far from the image of stiff aristocracy. In fact, he looked incredibly attractive, his hair tousled and a faint streak of dirt on his chin.

"Good evening," she said, momentarily distracted. She glanced down at her robe. "I'm not really dressed for . . ."

"It's a bit late for modesty now," he said with a wry grin.

She blushed to the roots of her hair. "I suppose—"

"I didn't know you could blush," he said, scrutinizing her face. "You appear so very much in command of yourself."

"You hardly know me, my lord."

"I know you enough to realize you're brave, adventurous, determined, and loving. I noticed how tenderly you held your little daughter."

She felt another wave of red suffusing her face. Never had a gentleman spoken to her in this manner, so understanding, so intimate. She didn't know how to handle it. Recriminations and strictures had been her daily sustenance from Jebediah. Peace had only arrived after his demise.

"How could I but hold Beatrice tenderly? She's the greatest gift that has ever been given to me. It's difficult to describe the feeling. Life changed in the moment she arrived, never to be the same again."

He leaned his elbows on the balustrade, his gaze directed at the mist rising among the trees to meet the moon. "The event touched me deeply."

"Doctor Bainbridge said you would have the greatest story to tell for years to come."

He gave her a quick glance. "That would sully the memory of the occasion. No, I believe it would be a mistake to make a spectacle of Beatrice's birth. Besides, the *ton* does not need to hear about it. There's enough gossip going around as it is."

"Yes. And thank you for assuring me that I won't become the next name people bandy about in their eagerness for scandal."

He nodded, staring at the moon. It was almost full, and the silver-gold beauty against the velvet blue sky invited intimacies and confidences. She moved farther away from him, as she feared the powerful attraction he exuded.

"I want you to know the servant returned from your brother's residence in Bath with a message." He pulled out a folded missive from his waistcoat pocket. Her hands trembling, she broke the seal and read it quickly in the light from the open door.

"It's from my sister-in-law, Evelyn." She drew a sigh of relief as she scanned the cramped lines. "My brother is over the worst. The doctor believes he has a good chance recovering from the wound. The fever has broken and the infection has subsided. He's not going to die. Thank God!"

"I'm pleased to hear it."

Her legs trembled from the wave of panic that had washed through her as the earl handed her the note. She sat down on the wrought-iron bench outside the door, feeling weak. "I'm so grateful; I have been so worried."

"Now you can truly relax and regain your strength. No need to run yourself ragged because of these worries." He came to sit next to her. "I know what it's like to worry about siblings; my younger brother sought adventure on the Seven Seas at eighteen. He's in India at the moment, and I have to trust that he'll survive, as there's nothing I can do about it."

"You didn't feel an urge to venture forth to other lands?"

He shook his head. "No, I rather like this green turf." He swept his arm to encompass the estate.

"But you live all alone in this rambling mansion with only the servants?" She wondered what he would reply. His reputation went before him, but she could not detect any air of dissipation about him. He looked to be in splendid health.

He looked thoughtful as he nodded. "Yes."

When he didn't elaborate, she prodded, "It must get rather lonely."

"I don't lack friends, or hangers-on for that matter. Sometimes I like the solitude that Fairleigh offers."

"What about the future, what about children?" Her own daring surprised her. She had no right to ask him such intimate questions, but it was as if all the polite rules had been nullified at their unusual first encounter. By the event of Beatrice's birth, there would always be a special connection between them.

"I have pondered the question," he said, his face honest and open. "When I held your daughter in my arms I felt for the first time I lacked a connection with the future. With such a gift in your arms, all other gifts seem tawdry in comparison."

Allegra nodded. "Yes. I never realized the enormity of the blessing until I held Beatrice for the first time."

They sat side by side in silence and looked out over the peaceful park. A lone owl hooted in the distance, and a soft breeze rustled in the leaves. The scent of flowering roses sweetened the air. She heaved a deep sigh as contentment filled her. The nagging worry about Reggie had eased, and the pain and discomfort from the birth had abated.

"I think I'll enjoy motherhood," she said simply.

He laughed. "You'll be the perfect mother. Anyone could see that, and Beatrice will be a stunning beauty, just like you." His gaze caressed her, and she looked away quickly.

"You're stepping over your bounds, my lord." She moved away from the bench.

"Call me Jack, and truth to tell, I don't like to call you by the stiff and proper Mrs. Rutherford."

"My name is Allegra."

"As in 'joy.' That is a beautiful and fitting name. Your husband must've been proud to bring you along on his arm to any function."

Allegra remembered the monotonous, miserly, and gray days of her marriage. "There were few occasions where we went into society. My husband did not hold with frivolous pursuits and expenditures."

"But as most ladies, you must love fripperies and the fallals of fashion."

She didn't detect any scorn in his voice. "Yes, I'm no different from other ladies on that score. My husband was a very religious man and looked upon worldly adornments as sinful."

"How could it be sinful if it brings joy?"

Allegra agreed with that, and she breathed easier. The earl had common sense besides that great dose of charm. "Thank you for those words," she said simply.

"I rather shower my wife with fripperies if that would make her happy," he said.

"But you don't have one, so you don't know what you would actually do. Perhaps you base that on how you treat your female friends."

He shrugged. "Possibly."

"Tell me"—she smiled conspiratorially—"as we sit here in deepest confidence—why aren't you married?"

He leaned his chin against the heel of his hand and stared out into the purple blue darkness. "I don't know. There have been plenty of opportunities, but I've never felt drawn to any of the ladies. I've never met one whom I wanted to marry."

"I'm baffled at that statement. There must be any number of interesting ladies in the capital."

" 'Pon rep, the city is positively overrun with them," he teased.

"All putting out their snares, no doubt," she replied in kind.

"No, usually their mothers do. It takes great vigilance to stay unattached, since some of them stop at nothing to compromise a gentleman into marriage. I stay away from any kind of snares."

"That's prudent." She sat back down and patted his arm. "You have nothing to fear from me. I've decided I'm never going to wed again. My freedom is much too dear to me now, and I'll never bow to the will of some ogre husband. That would be utter foolishness on my part as I've thoroughly learned my lesson. I'm free now."

He nodded. "Yes . . . in your case I would feel the same, but I find it hard to believe that someone won't come along and try to court you."

Allegra squared her shoulders and lifted her nose into the air. "They can try."

"But you've made up your mind," he added with a chuckle. "At least you don't have problems making decisions."

"Hard-won experience always makes those decisions easier."

"Not one romantic bone in your body, eh?"

She shook her head vehemently. "Not even a sliver."

"You have no hope?"

"None."

"But don't you want more children? Bea will need brothers and sisters, or she'll end up a spoiled princess."

"Her name is Beatrice, and no, if I have to make the sacrifice of not having future children, so be it."

"You're rather bitter for one so young."

"Be that as it may, my armor has no chinks, and the brick

walls around my heart are solid. Weakness is for romantic fools."

He chortled. Evidently he found their conversation vastly entertaining. "We're one of a kind then. However, I'm not bitter, only jaded and prudent."

"There lies another difference between you and me; you would never lose your freedom if you got married. The gentleman, no matter how addlebrained, always keeps the control of the household, the woman loses all of hers."

"Not all gentlemen are dimwits."

"I daresay you have to defend your species, but that makes no impression on me at all."

"You can't hold such a narrowminded judgment. You'll frighten off prospective suitors."

"You must not have heard anything I said," she cried and moved away from him on the bench. "I don't care if the gentlemen don't give me a second glance. The fewer glances, the better."

He moved a few inches closer, his expression devilish in the light from the open door. She kept inching away, and he followed, all the time looking at her with great admiration. If it hadn't been for that impish gleam in his eye, she would've thought he was flirting with her.

"Desist," she said wearily, and refused to move any farther. His arm touched hers, and she felt the heat of him through the layers of her robe and gown. "Your teasing won't affect me." She swept her hair back from her forehead, knowing he had much too much an intimate view of her.

"But I do it so well," he said softly.

"It doesn't surprise me, but you'll have to seek more susceptible prey."

"A challenge this monumental has more appeal to me."

She looked at him, aghast. "You can't be serious! If you are, I shall remove Beatrice and myself posthaste. I will not suffer this kind of treatment from anyone."

He shook his head and grimaced with mock chagrin. "I daresay you're safe from me. Truth to tell, I don't see much of a challenge. In the end, you members of the fair species always succumb."

"Succumb?" Allegra's ire rose by the minute.

"To my charm." He said that so softly she doubted she'd heard correctly.

"Of all the arrogant!" She stood, shaking out her robe as if feeling the need to get rid of any speck of his presence on herself. "I've heard enough."

He threw his head back, laughing. "I knew that would get your goat, Allegra. The first tiny chink in the armor."

"Nonsense! I've never heard such a silly notion." She stared down at him, anger boiling under the surface. "Why would you make such a fool of yourself?"

He gave her a startled look, his eyes narrowing. "Fool? It's called light conversation, dallying, trifling."

"I don't play games like that, not with you, not with anyone else."

"I daresay Mr. Rutherford has made his presence known here and now. Such a pitiful legacy to leave behind—teaching you to fear fun, fear attraction. And most of all, swearing off all interaction with gentlemen. 'Tis most sad; Mr. Rutherford won in the end, even from beyond the grave."

"You are stepping over your bounds, my lord. I know I can't expect better from a man whose reputation has traveled far and wide, but I don't see a need for me to become a victim of your distasteful attention, especially under these vulnerable circumstances."

"I apologize if I have offended your tender sensibilities," he drawled, not sounding the slightest bit contrite. "I did not expect your prim refusal to partake in a few minutes of bantering. I judged you a woman of wit."

"This is not the time nor the place," she said, drawing herself tall. "You've sadly misjudged me if you think I'm susceptible."

He shrugged. "Very well, let's just say that my judgment is faulty, but can you explain something to me? How come you all start out as innocent and full of love as Bea and turn out to be disillusioned and defensive females?"

"I can turn that question right back at you."

He looked down at his hands hanging between his knees as he leaned forward. He sighed, and she wondered what that sigh contained. "You're right, of course," he said finally. He stood, and she felt small and defenseless next to his considerable height. She sensed his restrained power, but felt safe nevertheless. The gentle hands that had delivered Beatrice would never hurt her, but his devilish tongue was another matter altogether.

She had next to no experience with gentlemen like him, and it made her feel uncomfortable. He must see her as a country miss, lacking polish in every area.

Fact is, she had grown up in Sussex with Squire Mansfield and his wife, far from the buzzing metropolis, and from Sussex she'd gone straight to Mr. Rutherford's gloomy home in Somerset. Perhaps the earl was right. She needed some fun and gaiety, but she resented him for telling her that.

"Thank you for delivering the message from my family. I shall go to bed now, and hopefully we can move on tomorrow. I'm forever beholden to you for your hospitality."

He only smiled, his gaze enigmatic. "Good night," he said, and gave her a bow. "I shall never forget the moment I first set eyes on Beatrice, one of the highest points of my life for sure."

She sensed no mockery in his voice, and the memory of the birth warmed her too. "When Beatrice is old enough, I'll tell her all about you—how a knight on a big horse came to deliver her."

"It wasn't a white steed, though, only a quite ordinary dappled gray."

Allegra could not help but laugh at that. "It does somehow take the romance out of the story, don't you think?"

"Only if you let it." With that, he turned on his heel and walked down to the other end of the balcony.

To her surprise, a woman of incredible elegance stepped outside, her eyes flashing at Jack as he moved toward her. She held out her hand to him, but he didn't take it. "I have a birthday present for you, Jack."

Allegra froze as she heard the invitation in the other woman's voice. Had he really brought his lightskirt to Fairleigh as Rose had alluded? It bothered her, but why would it? He had the right to spend his birthday with anyone he liked, and she knew this woman was someone he would like. Embarrassed, Allegra watched her wrap her arms around him as he stood still. Without another glance, Allegra fled into her room.

Four

Jack heard the baby cry several times in the middle of the night and he longed to check on her, but knew that between Allegra and the rest of the womenfolk, Bea was well taken care of. All he wanted to do was hold the baby and rock her in his arms, but the ladies created a wall of solidarity, holding the belief that no man belonged in the nursery. And mayhap they were right, but that didn't diminish his longing.

He'd planned to accompany Minerva to the coast, but she'd begged him to stay another day because she'd succumbed to one of her migraines. What did one more day matter? She would be out of his life for good shortly.

He realized he'd become completely enchanted with the newborn baby. It made no sense that she had such power over him, and Allegra would have laughed at him had he voiced his feelings. Bea had drawn her first breath in his arms, no one else's, and he felt responsible for her well-being.

Bea moving out of his life would be worse than any of his female companions rejecting him. He more or less expected such behavior from them, but Bea was special and so was her mother, something he was reluctant to admit.

Sleepless, he lay in his bed, his hands tucked under his head on the feather pillow. He hadn't given much thought to being a father. He hadn't given much thought to the future. Everything at the estate was running smoothly; the revenue was satisfying; the tenants loyal. He loved Fairleigh, but it was London that had beckoned in the past.

He had for fleeting moments toyed with the idea of marrying, but the notion had passed as soon as it had entered his head. He was tired of matchmaking mamas and their insecure daughters. Since his birthday last year, boredom had been his constant companion, and it surprised him. He'd never suffered from boredom. Had he turned that jaded from his experiences? And had they been so shallow that his life held no substance at all? That thought bothered him no end, and it kept him awake most of the night.

Where had his sense of family honor gone? His father might have kept a mistress or two over the years, but he had never been notorious nor had he ever complained about boredom, as far as Jack could remember. His father had carried the name of Roche with pride and honor. *Not that I haven't,* Jack thought, but he'd never felt that deep responsibility that his name carried, not until now.

Allegra was surprised when a knock sounded on the terrace door just as she was about to climb back into bed.

She was even more surprised to find that unknown woman of utmost elegance on her threshold as Rose answered the knock.

"Good evening," the woman greeted, slightly flushed. "I'm sorry to disturb you, but I wanted to congratulate you on the birth of your daughter." She held out a slim hand toward Allegra. "I'm Minerva Young, a friend of Jack's."

Allegra shook the cool hand automatically and introduced herself. "I take it you're another houseguest?" she inquired.

"You could say that. Jack was supposed to escort me to the coast, where I'm going on a ship to Italy, but our trip is delayed due to the recent events here."

"I didn't know he planned to travel," Allegra said. "And I'm deeply sorry if I waylaid your plans."

Minerva smiled and shook her dark curly head. Her hair had been cut in the latest Grecian style and her simple gray gown trimmed with white lace looked sophisticated in its simplicity. She carried herself with a brittle, slightly nervous air.

"Don't worry. I was taken ill with a migraine anyway, but I feel so much better now. A short delay has not ruined my plans."

She glanced at the sleeping baby in the crib, and Allegra sensed Minerva's longing. "Do you have children?"

Minerva shook her head, her face taking on a pallor. "No . . . but I expect that someday, er, rather soon, I shall face motherhood. I'm not altogether sure it suits me, and it must be terribly cumbersome—"

"You won't regret it," Allegra said to reassure her visitor.

"I am . . . in a delicate condition, and I have some fears. Not monetary, but I'm afraid of pain, and I'd rather not face motherhood alone," she said. All at once she seemed at home and sat down on one of the wing chairs. Shyness did not appear to plague her anymore. Allegra sat across from her in another chair, intrigued now by Minerva's revelations.

"You should not have to face the coming event alone," she said. "Where is your husband?" She already knew that Minerva belonged to another world, but she still deserved respect.

Minerva fluttered her hand in front of her, her cool gray eyes sparkling like diamonds. Allegra could not read the shifting expression on her face, but she sensed deeply hidden secrets, and she didn't want to know too much.

"Oh, I've never been married," Minerva said airily. "Not that I haven't lacked offers, but I'm rather an independent woman."

Allegra thought of Squire Mansfield's wife, the lady who had raised her. Mary Mansfield would have had a severe fit of the vapors at this point in the conversation, or from the fact that the conversation was happening at all, but Allegra had no such qualms. After the adventure of Beatrice's birth, anything else seemed small and unimportant.

"It's the earl's child," Minerva continued, "but he would never wed me. He has made sure I'm taken care of for life, but I'll never carry his name."

Allegra felt a spurt of outrage at such behavior. "If he's a man of honor he will take care of his offspring in a manner that befits the child," she cried. "I shall tell him so myself if I get the opportunity."

Minerva held out her hands as if to ward Allegra off. "Oh no, Heaven forfend that he should be taken to task," she said in outrage. "He will never understand."

"Then he's more of a fool than I thought," Allegra said with vehemence.

"I did not come here to plead my case with you. I lack for nothing. The earl is a most generous man."

"Be that as it may, he needs to stand up and honor his own." Allegra rose, her body aching. "If you don't mind, I'm terribly tired, and tomorrow will be a long day."

Minerva stood as well, her expression apologetic. "I'm so sorry. I never meant to bring up the subject, but I rather surprised myself. All I wanted was a glimpse of the newborn, and I got what I came for." She threw another glance at Beatrice, but Allegra didn't sense any real interest.

Minerva was one who liked herself best. *That is none of my business,* Allegra thought resolutely. She walked toward the door slowly. "Good night, Miss Young."

Minerva hesitated before stepping onto the terrace. "May I ask you a question, Mrs. Rutherford? Your answer is important to me."

"Very well."

"Is the earl the father of your child?"

For a moment, total outrage overcame Allegra, but she quickly calmed herself and shook her head. "No. I was loyal to my husband."

Minerva inclined her head. "Thank you." She left without a backward glance.

The next morning, the earl found himself knocking on the door of the guest room where Allegra and tiny Bea spent their time. Rose, the nervous abigail, opened the door and curtsied when she saw him.

Allegra sat at a table by the window, eating breakfast. She

looked lovely and rested, even in that ominous black mourning gown she'd worn when he first laid eyes on her. He hesitated on the threshold, but she waved him forward.

"I'm having breakfast. I found that I was famished this morning, and so was Beatrice."

"Can I take a look at her?" he pleaded, suddenly feeling reduced to a schoolboy standing in front of the stern schoolmaster. He went over to the small crib—maybe even one that had been his—that the servants had brought from the nursery.

Bea's tiny peaceful face looked rosy and content as she lay among the lace-edged sheets and pillows. Her eyes were open, and he saw that they were deeply blue. She waved her fat arms at him and he couldn't stop himself from gently lifting her out of the crib. Maybe he should have asked for permission, but he wouldn't be able to accept a refusal from Allegra.

The warm sweet-smelling bundle in his arms made his heart melt. All he wanted was to hold her forever and take care of her, but there was no logic in that desire. Only a strange coincidence had brought her into his life.

"She's lovely," he whispered, and found that Allegra had joined him by the crib.

Bea gurgled as if agreeing, and Allegra laughed. "You look silly, my lord. Your eyes are almost crossed and you look as if you're about to fall down any minute in your fear that you would crush her. She's quite hardy you know."

"No . . . I didn't know," he said uncertainly. He handed the baby to her mother. "She has your eyes, and possibly some other traits, though it's too early to tell."

Allegra only looked at him curiously. "All good traits, no doubt," she declared.

He smiled. "Of course."

She gently caressed the baby's soft head. "I hope you had a nice birthday celebration."

He swore silently. She must have noticed Minerva's presence. "I . . . well, as I ran across you on the road, I was escorting a friend to the coast. She's leaving for the Continent in a few days."

"I understand."

A world of understanding lay in those words, and he knew the incident only reaffirmed her impression of him as a rake. The thought bothered him no end, but why would it? He'd never before felt any guilt in his dealings with women.

Before he could reply, a knock sounded on the door.

They both turned to watch an older woman step through.

"Aunt Georgie, at last. You're somewhat late," Jack said, frustrated but also happy to be saved from boggy emotional territory by this worldly and kind woman, his father's younger sister. Lady Georgina looked beautiful with her white hair cut into short fashionable curls and wearing a smart and modish gown. Aunt Georgie always followed the current fashion. He bent to kiss her rouged cheek, and she gave his hands a squeeze.

"I see that you have embroiled yourself in another adventure," she said dryly, her blue eyes twinkling. "I had to hurry down here to save you yet again."

"I can't exactly call it an adventure," he replied. "It was rather an unexpected encounter, one that prompted the use of all of my courage and ingenuity."

"Midwifery isn't a subject you learned at Oxford," Aunt Georgie said, her voice booming. The statement made him slightly uncomfortable, as he didn't want to be reminded of the intimate position he'd found himself in with Allegra only twenty-four hours ago.

"Where is she, then?" Aunt Georgie asked and stepped toward the crib, where Allegra waited.

"Mrs. Allegra Rutherford, Lady Georgina," Jack introduced them, and Aunt Georgie kissed the younger woman's cheek as if they'd known each other for years. His aunt cooed over the baby, and he felt superfluous, yet strangely reluctant to leave. For once he lacked purpose, something he never did. He couldn't remember the last time he'd vacillated over what to do; he always made up his mind and moved forward. He never looked back.

Part of him wanted to linger with the women and the baby, and the other part wanted to run from the room posthaste. He stood uncertainly in the middle of the floor and noticed how the sun lit up Allegra's chestnut hair with gold, almost like a halo around her curls. She looked so beautiful, and the birth of Beatrice had brought a softness to her face that he knew hadn't been there before.

"What's the matter with you, Jack?" his aunt asked. "You look as if you've been struck by lightning."

"Blasted nonsense," he muttered.

"What?" She shooed him toward the door with her hands. "We don't need you, you great looby. Don't you have some accounts to go over? Lands to inspect? I want a nice coze with your young guest, and it's been a while since I had any time with a newly born."

He shook his head in exasperation. "Very well, consider yourself rid of me."

"Good riddance. I shall speak with you later."

"You are going to stay for a few days, aren't you?"

"Don't worry, nevvy," Aunt Georgie said with a laugh. "I'll protect you from these females with my life." With gales of laughter that only riled him, she closed the door on his back.

Unable to settle down to any task, he wandered through Fairleigh. The rooms seemed huge and empty though they were filled with beautiful furniture and elegant statuary and other kinds of artwork. He'd never noticed how large and silent the mansion was, but usually he occupied himself inspecting the grounds or working with the steward in the study.

When he wasn't working, his cronies frequented Fairleigh, as it offered good fishing in nearby streams and riding in beautiful surroundings. Many nights of card games had passed under the roof of Fairleigh, and the occasional social gathering and dinner party, if Aunt Georgie resided here part of the summer. She preferred her own establishment in London, and in the summer she visited friends at various estates.

He went out on the terrace and looked out over the park. The grounds were immaculate, thanks to the dedicated gardeners. The roses bloomed in the formal garden right behind the main building, and some climbed on the sandstone walls. A bumblebee droned past him in pursuit of the next rosebush, and a pair of finches hopped from one branch of the old oak tree to another, singing as they went along.

Peace and quiet reigned. Perhaps too much peace and quiet, he thought. He had yearned for it, but now it only magnified the turmoil inside of him.

As he walked through the house once more, he drew a sigh of relief as he heard the familiar voice of his friend Richard at the front door. He was speaking with Simmons, the butler. With Richard, Viscount Wendon, came Sir James Lake and Robbie McGowan, his two other cronies, who loved nothing better than a good card game. Well, perhaps they liked their opera dancers more, and they highly esteemed their tailors. All three were natty dressers.

Unexpectedly, they had torn themselves away from London. Never had such relief washed through him, even though he'd sought solitude for his birthday.

They slapped him on the back in turn. "We missed you in town these last few days," Richard said in a tone of disapproval. "Not many friends are left; they have all returned to their estates. You went without word though, you old bleater, and right in time for your birthday. You didn't even bother to find out if we had planned something special for you."

"I needed some rest after these last weeks of high jinks and revelry," Jack said with a sigh.

Robbie's blue eyes narrowed. "Don't say you're becoming bored with us."

"Don't say you're becoming an old bore," James added.

Jack laughed. "Never!"

"We came here with the intention of saving you from yourself," Richard said with a wink, "and to celebrate belatedly."

Jack showed them into the library, and then rang for Simmons to bring in a bottle of the finest brandy to toast their reunion. The men settled in wing chairs around the fireplace, and Richard rubbed at an imaginary spot on his elegant coat sleeve.

"We thought that mayhap heartache sent you into the country, Jack," he said.

"Heartache?"

"The lovely if cruel Minerva found herself another protector. The news is all over London by now."

"Everyone is talking," Robbie echoed.

"I know. Minerva never came close to touching my heart. Hers is made of granite, but she held a certain allure when I first clapped eyes on her," Jack said. "I knew her character before I offered to rent her that cottage in St. John's Woods. Grasping and cunning are two other adjectives that come to mind."

Sir James nodded. "Aye, but every gentleman in town desires her, the most sought-after courtesan in town."

"You too?" Jack asked with a grin.

A blush stained Sir James's freckled face. "Be that as it may, she's too expensive for me. You could easily afford her, and I think she was somewhat sweet on you."

"Blast and damn, James, it's done and over with," Jack said. He registered uneasy silence in the room and looked from one friend to another. "What's going on?"

"Evidently there's rumor that you two eloped. She might have found another protector, but 'tis said in town that she's won you back."

Jack had a sinking feeling in his stomach, knowing that Minerva could have spread that rumor just to rile him. "I highly doubt that. She has indicated nothing of that to me. In fact, I'm personally escorting her to Plymouth tomorrow, where she'll travel to Italy with her new beau."

"What? She's here?" Robbie asked incredulously.

Jack nodded. "Upstairs, nursing a headache."

"I wouldn't be surprised if she has truly developed a *tendre* for you, Jack. She looked pale and wan in the park last week; I'd say she was pining away," Richard said, his dark eyes mocking.

"Nonsense. She wouldn't know anything about longings of the heart," Jack said with vehemence. He thought of her glittery smile and sharp eyes and shuddered at the thought that he'd ever been interested in her. Compared to Allegra, whose warm sleepy smile lingered in his memory, almost haunting him all of the night and this morning, Minerva had nothing to offer.

"Minerva is a cold fish," Robbie said as he pushed his fingers through his red curly hair.

"You're well rid of her," Richard said, concern in his eyes. "That is if you truly are."

Simmons brought in the brandy and they saluted each other with generous snifters. It wasn't long before Jack brought out a deck of cards and they seated themselves around a table covered with green baize, cheroots, and brandy at the ready.

"Females are too much trouble," James said. "Always were and always will be."

"Much too complicated," Richard added.

They were deeply into their third card game and their brandy as the door opened and Aunt Georgie stepped inside, not as much as a knock on the door. She threw her arms up in mock outrage. "Gambling in broad daylight, with a newborn in the house, and a grieving widow. I don't know what the world is coming to."

Jack groaned silently and looked heavenward, hoping to gain some strength to deal with his unruly and strong-willed aunt.

"Newborn?" Richard said, his jaw slack. "Minerva?"

The other men held stunned expressions as well.

"Yes . . . well, eh, not Minerva. I helped deliver a baby yesterday morning," Jack said lamely and found that he longed to go upstairs and spend some time gazing at Bea. "A girl."

"This is getting stranger by the minute," Robbie said and put down his cards.

Jack turned to his aunt. "Is there anything you need? I daresay you're completely at home here, and Simmons—"

"I heard voices. I'm a nosy old woman, y'know."

Richard laughed. "Hardly that, Lady Georgina. You're as full of life as ever." He looked at Jack. "Are you telling me, old friend, that you're hiding a newly born upstairs?"

"Not hiding exactly."

"And a widow?" Sir James asked. "This is beyond strange." He inserted a finger under his collar as if it suddenly had grown too tight.

Shooting a look of daggers at his aunt, who'd draped herself in one of the wing chairs and held a glass of brandy, he told the story of Beatrice's birth, leaving out all the delicate details of course.

"That's the outside of enough!" Sir James cried when he'd finished.

Jack took a deep swig from his brandy snifter.

"You have to admire her courage to set out on her trip in the twelfth hour of her pregnancy. All for a wounded brother," Richard said.

"It looked as if he were dying, but we know he had a turn for the better," Jack said, feeling a strange relief at the thought. Just the idea of Allegra haring off with her baby to Bath made a strange sense of loneliness come over him, which was ridiculous.

He didn't even know the woman.

"Widow Rutherford is an exceptional female," Aunt Georgie said. "If a bit unconventional, but I like that."

"It takes one to know one, Lady G.," Richard said. "You have to admire the lady for her dedication to her brother."

"She has not much in the way of family, the poor thing."

"Not much of anything, I'll wager," Robbie said.

"You're wrong on that score," Aunt Georgie said. "She lacks for nothing."

"It's not right to gossip about her," Jack said firmly.

"By Jupiter, do I detect some kind of protective attitude?" Richard said, clearly surprised.

"She is under *my* roof at the moment, and I'm responsible for the comfort of my guests, something I take seriously. You should know, Richard. Have you ever lacked for anything here?"

He shook his head. "No, you're always the perfect host. It's a dashed nuisance really; you're nearly perfect in every aspect."

Jack barked a laugh. "Damned nonsense. I don't know how you conceive your outrageous statements."

Aunt Georgie spoke. "Mrs. Rutherford wants to see you, Jack."

"Now?"

She nodded and glanced at the card table. "I can play your hand."

Jack rolled his eyes and left the room. He found himself eagerly steering his steps toward the upper regions. He'd wanted to spend more time with Allegra and the baby, but he couldn't very well foist himself upon them. As he ran upstairs, two steps at a time, his heart raced. He'd never felt this peculiar when faced with the prospect of speaking to a woman. Normally he was completely in control of his faculties, but now his heart had decided to do a mad jig in his chest.

Allegra sat by the open window, where a breeze fluttered the curtains. She looked serene in her black gown, her hair piled high into a bundle of curls on top of her head, a lacy cap pinned to it for propriety. She smiled at him, and his breath caught in his throat. It seemed to do that a lot lately.

"Yesterday was your birthday, and I wanted to give you something in memory of the day."

"You don't have to do that, Allegra." He stood over her, unable to tear his gaze away from her face. A rosy blush stained her cheeks, and her eyes shone earnest as she handed him a small package wrapped in brown paper.

He unwrapped the present and found a volume of collected poems bound beautifully in leather and gold foil. "Percy Shelley." He gave Allegra an amused glance. "I take it you're a romantic at heart."

"It's poetry I treasure due to its uplifting quality, and the only thing in my possession right now that I would consider a worthy gift under the circumstances."

"Thank you," he said. He took her hand and kissed it, feeling a charge as he touched her soft skin. Without thinking, he pulled her up and into his arms. As if in a trance, he bent his head to kiss her. She fit perfectly into his arms, and he inhaled her sweet fragrance, by now totally intoxicated. Her lips were incredibly soft, and the way she responded, as if melting against him, set his heart on fire. She kissed him back with a passion he hadn't expected.

She came to her senses first, pulling away. Her face glowed pink, and she looked embarrassed. "No need . . . to thank me so profoundly," she whispered. " 'Tis only a slim volume of poetry, after all."

He remembered the book in his hand, and held it up. "One that I shall treasure because it'll always remind me of Beatrice." He glanced toward the crib. "Sleeping, I see."

Allegra nodded, smiling. "Do I detect a hint of disappointment?"

He nodded. "You're very perceptive. "

She sat down, arranging her skirts around her. "I completely understand your fascination. I could stare at her all day without getting tired of the view."

He sat down across from her. "I apologize for taking advantage of you just now. I don't know what came over me."

"I'm not another one of your conquests," she said simply. "I have no interest in dallying, and as I told you before, I don't plan to marry again. Not that it concerns you, but I'm quite set in my mind."

"I never looked upon you as a conquest, Allegra. As far as future marriage, you can't be as close-minded as to think that every gentleman would be anything like your husband."

She looked thoughtful. "You're right, of course. I don't want to be obstinate, but why take risks when life is going well in general?"

"Without risks we grow old before our time. That I know

from personal experience, and some risks are not really challenging."

"You're willing to open yourself up to hurt?"

He thought about it for a moment. "If the gain is greater, I would have to take the risk."

"I'll wager you have left many broken hearts behind, but yours has stayed intact."

He shrugged. "I don't fall in love easily. Most of my . . . ahem, acquaintances, haven't had many expectations. 'Tis a rather delicate subject."

She stared at him frankly. "I'm not a shrinking miss."

"I realize that, but I don't understand why you would have any interest in my adventures."

"I met one of your *adventures* early this morning, and she claimed—"

"I would never have brought her here if it hadn't been for your dire emergency," he said, galled that Minerva had approached Allegra, or maybe it had been the other way around.

"She wanted to know if you'd fathered Beatrice. It amused me to think that she would consider me one your lightskirts—to use an indelicate word that I'm not supposed to be familiar with."

"Vulgarity does not sit easily on your tongue."

"When faced with it, I don't deny its existence," she said tartly. "It matters not what you do. You have not shocked me in the slightest as I could not expect different behavior from you. Nor am I in any way annoyed that Miss Young's presence was foisted upon me. After all, she's a diamond of the first water, as my brother would say. He taught me all the unladylike expressions," she added. "I will however state that I believe you've broken her heart."

He had a heated reply on his tongue, but decided to refrain. He had no reason to get into an argument with Allegra over his erstwhile mistress. He could see no gain in claiming that Minerva had no heart. Females tended to band together, and he had enough with Minerva harping on him for real and imagined behavior on his part.

He said aloud, "What Miss Young resents most is that I would not give her my heart. " *She collects them,* he added silently.

"Would not, or could not?" Allegra asked.

"Both," he said, realizing it was true. He stared at Allegra as if starving, also realizing that in her he'd met someone who could touch his heart. Perhaps it was because of the unusual circumstances under which they'd met, or due to his weakness for Beatrice. He didn't know for sure. All he knew was that he'd never met anyone like Allegra, and that he wanted to stay all day in this room and explore her personality.

"At least you're honest."

"I deal only with honesty. If you lie to yourself and others, you live in a dreamworld. Reality will eventually knock on your door, and then you'll have to pay for those falsehoods. Reality can knock very hard sometimes."

She nodded. "Yes . . . you're right on that score."

"Also, if you're hiding behind walls to protect yourself, reality will eventually break them down. 'Tis only a matter of time."

"You seem to have a great deal of experience in this matter," she said, her voice flat, as if he had touched something she didn't want him to touch.

"I have some, yes. When you avoid situations, life usually finds a way to confront you with them."

She sensed that what he said was true. "I don't know where your observations are leading, my lord, or where this conversation is going. I suppose the walls to which you're alluding are mine?"

"Perhaps," he said, paying attention to every nuance of her expression. He worried he was pushing too hard, but it seemed very important to him that she raised no walls, or at least refrained from building on those that were there.

"It surprises me that you would have any kind of interest in my walls," she said. "Are they presenting a challenge to you?"

He laughed nervously, wondering if she was right. He always liked a challenge, but this was different. "Yes, in a sense, but—"

"At least you're honest about it." She smiled and shook her head. "To be that honest you must be proud of your cavalier attitude toward your conquests."

"That was unfair. You don't know me, Allegra."

"I know your *kind,* and I stay well away from you. It doesn't take a brilliant mind to figure out your true intentions toward unsuspecting females. That you're proud of your behavior is one thing, but you won't be able to add me to your list of triumphs."

Frustrated, he said, "I have no intention whatsoever to join your name to my list. Not that I have one, but I use your crude term."

"You sound angry; I must have touched something within you." She rose and went to stand by the window. "I don't like where this discussion is going. You have been nothing but kind to me, and I don't want to get into an argument about your morals. Your behavior is simply none of my business, and I don't want to leave here with you shouting 'good riddance' after me."

He started laughing. "Of all the ludicrous discussions. I assure you—"

"Leave it alone. Nothing you can say will convince me. Your actions are what speak the loudest, and I'd make my judgment based on those, but there's simply no time left to us. I'm feeling much better and we'll leave first thing in the morning."

"No, you can't."

He saw the one opportunity that he'd ever really had of falling in love fade away. He knew that no kind of pleading or force would help him. The only way he could hope to win her was to show her his burgeoning feelings.

"I think I've fallen in love with you, Allegra."

Five

"You can't be serious, my lord." Allegra looked shocked. "I doubt that you understand the meaning of the word 'love.' "

"If this crazed feeling in my heart is any indication, love has come upon me. For the first time in my life, I might add."

"Really?" Her eyes twinkled with mirth, and her lips twisted upward at the corners. "You expect me to believe this twaddle—from someone like you?"

" 'Pon rep, you're singularly unkind. Here I'm baring my heart, and you make it into a cruel joke on my part."

"You're being excessively foolish. You can't be in love with me; you hardly know me, and I certainly don't know you. Furthermore, I would never put my heart at risk with someone of your reputation, be it true or slanderous. For a fact, I know what's said about you is mostly true."

He stood over her and touched her cheek with one tender finger. "I don't blame you for judging me, or for being cautious, but look into my eyes. Am I sincere or am I lying?"

She paled somewhat, and her smile faded.

"You know I'm speaking the truth," he said triumphantly.

"Be that as it may, I won't have any of this. Please remove yourself and your unwanted attention from me."

"Or else?"

She looked desperately around the room. "Or I'll hit you with the fireplace poker," she said lamely.

"A threat indeed," he said with a laugh and moved closer, "but one that I can't take very seriously." He had stepped so close she had to lean her back against the window to avoid him. He wished he could read her thoughts, but her face was unreadable except for her uneasiness. How could he convince her that his feelings were true? Without hesitation, he cupped her face with his hands and kissed her with all of his heart once more.

Allegra lost all sense of her surroundings just as she had the first time he'd kissed her. Never had anyone touched her with such seductive force and determination. His mouth was both soft and demanding against hers, and she was aware of every nerve ending in her body crying out for his touch. Her skin heated with embarrassment at her wanton reaction, an emotion that switched into anger, as she didn't want to admit the truth about his impact upon her senses. She told herself this could not be happening; not with him; not when she thought she was safe and protected in this house. *Oh, botheration!* She pushed hard against him, but his hold on her did not diminish.

She twisted her mouth away. "Unhand me," she cried.

He laughed softly and rained tiny kisses all over her face, and honestly, they felt wonderful.

"Desist," she pleaded, finding herself breathless, but when he finally removed his hands, she felt bereft.

How could such contradiction exist? She had never felt anything like it. Fear fought with delight, mistrust with daring, within her, and soon an overwhelming confusion had come over her.

"You have taken monstrous advantage of me," she said hoarsely. "No gentleman would assault me in this fashion and then stand there and look like the cat who got into the cream."

He laughed, his face flushed, his eyes sparkling. He looked dangerously handsome, she thought. Much too handsome and untrustworthy. Placing her hand to her heart, she fought her inner battle. He dazzled part of her, the romantic, frivolous part. Her sober side wanted to take him severely to task and make him pay for his misconduct. He, however, didn't seem to struggle with his conscience, or have any doubts about his charm.

"And don't you dare to smile," she continued. "What if Rose gets wind of this? She'll let the whole world know."

He threw a glance at the sleeping maid. "I doubt that she has an inkling of what just occurred."

"Be that as it may, you owe me an apology," she said.

He crossed his arms over his chest. "I apologize for my—according to society's rules—my scandalous behavior, but I can't feel contrite over something I consider wholly right in my heart."

"You're a very peculiar man, my lord. If my legs had more substance, I would make Rose pack my belongings and be on my way within the hour."

"You can't lie to me, Allegra. No matter how much you protest, I know you enjoyed my kiss."

She was not going to give him that, even if he was right. "You're behaving abominably, constantly taking advantage of me with your crude actions. I know I'm in your house, at your mercy, but I expected more respect and decorum from the Earl of Roche."

"Next you're going to say that all gentlemen are cut from the same cloth, and only aiming to take advantage of unsuspecting females."

"You took the words right out of my mouth."

He threw his head back and laughed. "You are entertaining if predictable. If I thought in any way that you were sincerely frightened, I would give you a thousand apologies, but you're a woman of the world."

"That makes no difference. I expect you to behave in a gentlemanly fashion at all times."

He looked uncomfortable momentarily, but it was too late to apologize, she thought. Much too late. She touched her lips absentmindedly, wondering if he could truly see how his kisses affected her—as he claimed.

His face enigmatic, he turned away from her. He picked up

the volume of poems she'd given him and went to stare into the crib. "She's still as beautiful as she was this morning."

Allegra couldn't help but laugh. "It surprises me no end."

"Don't be caustic. You know I'm besotted with her in the worst way." He sounded so serious he touched her heart. If anything, his delight in Beatrice touched Allegra more than his previous declarations of love. Her daughter deserved to have a father who loved her, but it was unlikely that she would ever have one. Allegra didn't want to think about that right now, and Beatrice slept in blissful ignorance.

"I only asked you to join me so that I could give you the book of poems."

He nodded and held it up. "It has not been for naught. I shall treasure it forever."

"And you're prone to exaggeration. Forever is a very long time."

"Well, I couldn't very well say I would only treasure it for *two weeks.*"

She laughed and clapped her hand to her mouth to stem the mirth. "You're rather a trickster, aren't you? A silver-tongued devil."

"I have some Irish blood from my father's side of the family. We have rather a broad streak of luck as well."

"And a way with words."

He shrugged. "I don't write poetry, however much I might wish to do so, especially after I kissed you."

"Of all the gall! You've overstepped all bounds and are proud of it besides."

"I don't do anything haphazardly." He came to stand in front of her, and she stepped back, worried that he would force his attentions upon her once more. "Don't fret," he said, as if reading her thoughts, "I won't touch you again without your permission." He bowed very formally. "I shall behave with the greatest decorum from now on, but I hope you'll remember my kisses and know that's what I want."

"I daresay there won't be any more of those. We're leaving tomorrow."

"I realize there's no persuading you to stay, so I won't even try. I shall be sad to see you go."

She had no response to that.

"I surmise you won't miss me, but I also know you'll never forget me."

She felt another blush rising in her cheeks. The dratted man, she thought. He knew how to throw her off balance, but he was right. How could she ever forget him after what had transpired?

"If I ever see you again at some function in London or elsewhere, you'll be a married and settled man."

"What?"

"Your, well . . . you must know that your mistress . . . well, she informed me that she's increasing. She was eager to see Beatrice and find out more about the childbirth process. I would like to think that you're an honorable man. I expect that you'll make an honest woman of her. After all, you put her in this awkward position, and she deserves respect."

His face lost all color. "This is the first I hear of it. She's leaving the country tonight. Our dealings are finished."

"From what I can see, they aren't. You'd better find her and discuss the matter. With her excellent style and refined manner, I believe she'll be perfect as the Countess of Roche." She motioned toward the door. "Go now."

Obviously annoyed, he left without another word and the air seemed to leave the room with him. She moved slowly to the crib, every limb still aching from the strenuous events of yesterday, but her vigor was coming back by the hour. She no longer had an excuse to stay here, and she could not wait to see her brother.

The following afternoon, the earl watched from the window in the library as Allegra's coach with its repaired wheel pulled away from the front steps at Fairleigh. Life would never be the same again, he thought. He'd said good-bye, and as he'd promised, he'd acted only with stiff decorum. She'd been just as formal, except when she'd turned to go out the front door. The last glimpse had been a conspiratorial smile, an expression that had etched itself in his memory. He knew that neither she nor he would ever forget how they'd met.

A knock sounded on the door, and Minerva stepped inside. "I . . . we . . . I didn't know if you wanted to see me after what I told you yesterday."

He sighed. "I believed you'd found another protector. Besides, it surprises me no end that you didn't tell me about this before."

"I worried about imposing on your goodwill even further, but when I saw Beatrice, I knew that you'd want to know the truth."

"Minerva, I don't ever shirk my duty as you know, but my feelings for you haven't changed, and I've always been very honest about that. A love match this never was and never will be."

"Everyone in your family will be shocked beyond repair when we impart the news," Minerva said, but didn't look very contrite.

"Worse things than marrying a notorious courtesan have happened, but we'll definitely be pariahs among our peers, and the main topic for gossip for months to come. You'll have to get used to that."

She didn't look happy at the thought. Her freedom as a popular "businesswoman" in London would be gone, and she would have to live within the parameters that befitted her new status. The idea of marrying his mistress didn't disturb him as much as the fact that undeniably he didn't love Minerva. As his friends had pointed out, she was cold and calculating, and it was very possible she was carrying someone else's child.

But if it was his, as she claimed, then he couldn't turn his back on it, not after what he'd experienced during Beatrice's birth. He could not abandon an innocent babe, especially not one who would carry his features. If Minerva had decided to have it alone, he had already given her enough funds to live comfortably for the rest of her life, but she wanted more.

"We shall get married by special license as soon as it can be arranged," he said with finality. "Just prepare yourself."

She looked uncomfortable. "I don't know if I'm ready to step into the shoes of a countess."

"Ready or not, I don't hear you protest too heavily," he said with some sarcasm.

She did not reply, and his heart sat leaden in his chest. He had no doubt that this would be a great mistake, but he couldn't back out now.

"The Earl of Roche was your *midwife?*" Reggie asked Allegra, his eyes filled with outrage in his pale and pinched face. "I've never heard such bunkum." He raked a hand through his reddish hair in agitation.

"It's true nevertheless, and despite his reputation, he behaved with outmost decorum at the birth, and I could find no fault with his hospitality." *Except for his behavior toward me personally,* she thought. But she would never tell Reggie about that, partly to protect him from dragging himself off to Fairleigh to demand satisfaction, but also to protect the earl. She didn't know why she needed to protect him.

She sighed deeply. Sometimes she couldn't understand herself at all. Anyway, the interlude at Fairleigh lay in the past, and she saw no reason to dwell on it. It was highly unlikely she would ever run into the earl again. When Reggie grew stronger, she would go back to Shorecliff and live a quiet life while raising Beatrice.

She would never be a man's chattel again.

Just as she had affirmed that, a messenger delivered a delicately filigreed silver rattle to the door at Reggie's house in Bath. Evelyn, his wife, brought in the package to the front parlor, where they were having tea, Reggie stretched out on the sofa, his legs covered with a woven blanket. Allegra opened the note attached to the gift.

Esteemed Allegra, This is a family heirloom that I wish Beatrice to have. She has been very much on my mind, just as you have. Life has been empty since you left. I'll never forget you. I shall do my duty to Minerva, but you're in my heart.

The note had been signed simply "Jack."

Allegra choked back emotion clogging her throat. She would have to send back the rattle, of course.

Evelyn's brown eyes narrowed in her pale face, and she held a look of curiosity, but Allegra knew she would never pry. "I sent word to Jebediah's family that Beatrice had been born." Which was true, she thought, but she left out who had sent the rattle. "I expect we'll hear more once the news of Beatrice's arrival has been spread." She touched the rattle gingerly. "A family heirloom."

"I see," Evelyn said heavily. Her long kindly face held concern. "It looks very costly. A most generous gift, and I've never known anyone in the Rutherford family to be generous."

Allegra stared at her sister-in-law, wondering if Evelyn had ever dared to do anything out of the ordinary. Her mousy brown hair hung in perfect curls around her face, and her starched cap sat primly in place on her head, the lace of her collar touched her chin with utmost respectability. Would she ever banter with a rake behind some potted plant at a ball? Allegra doubted it, but obviously there was no need for flirtations. Reggie and Evelyn were happy with their three children.

"Jebediah was a skinflint," Reggie said firmly. "He probably resented the fact that he would have to provide for you."

"But he did provide, and Beatrice and I shan't suffer the humiliation of living off relatives. I shall have to move out of the main house and into the dowager house, but I don't mind."

"We wouldn't mind having you here, Allegra," Evelyn said kindly. "And little Bea is a blessing."

"Thank you," Allegra said, and took her brother's hand and squeezed it gently. "I would not want to impose. I'm so grateful that your wound is healing nicely, Reggie. I've never been more worried in my life."

Reggie's eyes shone with joy. "You haring across Somerset in your condition to reach my side is a true show of affection."

Allegra squeezed his hand once more and held it to her cheek. "You should never doubt my feelings for the last member of my close family," she said, feeling that clog in her throat again. "You're my only link to our parents."

"And you are mine," he said simply, and then promptly dozed off.

On the following afternoon came another package, this time an empty gold locket and a note of longing from the earl. "If the world was right, the locket should hold miniatures of us together," he wrote. *Well, it won't,* Allegra thought grimly.

Shortly thereafter, Lady Georgina called in, claiming she'd come to Bath to take the waters at the Pump Room. "I couldn't stay here without seeing you again," she said and patted Allegra's arm as they sat alone in the blue parlor, cups of fragrant tea before them on the table. "How's little Beatrice?"

Allegra smiled. "I believe she has grown a lot already. She's such a peaceful child, and a voracious eater."

Lady Georgina leaned forward and whispered, "Jack speaks of her every day with such longing that I believe he's lost his marbles. He *never* speaks in such glowing terms about anything or anybody. I worry about him." Georgie sighed and shook her head in wonder. "I don't know what the world is coming to. Now this encroaching *minx* is trying to get him leg-shackled. I never thought he would fall for such stories and outright traps. I'll eat my hat if Minerva is increasing. *The uncouth creature!*" Georgie looked put out indeed. " 'Tis the outside of enough."

"Well, he allowed such a situation into his life," Allegra gently reminded the older woman. "He's not an innocent, put-upon bystander."

"To think that he brought his *mistress* to Fairleigh. Even as you were in the middle of the birthing process, that hussy was in a bedroom down the hall."

Allegra shrugged. "Don't take on so. What could he do? He was in the process of escorting her to the coast where she supposedly planned to sail away with a new beau. At least that's what the earl said. I have to believe he was telling the truth, and even if he wasn't, Fairleigh belongs to him, and he can do whatever he likes, see anyone he wants to see."

"You young people take things much too loosely. He embarrassed everyone with his behavior, and there's nothing you can say that will change my opinion on that. If he marries the trollop, I for one shall never speak with him again." Georgie's pink silk turban with its white ostrich feather wobbled as she shook her head violently. "Never!"

Allegra couldn't help but smile. "I hope you don't mind me saying so, but you should've trod the boards."

Georgie gave her a haughty glare, but then a twinkle replaced it. "You're shrewd m'dear—a good reader of character. I would've loved nothing better than to have joined the Thespians. My name is my curse."

Allegra replied, "Just as Minerva's name is her curse. No one would blink an eye if she'd joined a theater troupe."

Georgie gave a slow shake of the head. "You're so right. I know you're going to say that you can't hold her birth against her."

"That's true."

"But she uses gentlemen to achieve her own goals in a very calculating sort of way. I never thought my nephew would fall into such a trap. He's not by any means a country yokel who's easily taken in by schemes. In fact, he's rather a smooth character."

Allegra couldn't find anything to say. She dared not broach the subject of the earl. He had been right when he said she would never be able to forget him.

"I wish you were the one he was going to marry, not that strumpet," Georgie said wistfully.

Six

Reggie improved quickly, and Allegra spent two peaceful weeks recovering from the birth and watching Beatrice grow more every day. She had immediately stolen everyone's heart at Reggie's town house in Bath, and there was never any shortage of people who wanted to watch over her.

"Just imagine if we always had that kind of irresistible charm," Evelyn said one day as she rocked Bea to sleep. "The whole world would lie at one's feet."

"You're right on that score," Reggie said, still somewhat pale from his ordeal, but now walking without support. His wound in the side had healed, but pain still overcame him at times. "I will forever be a slave to her every beck and call."

"Heaven forfend," Allegra said. "I don't want her to be hopelessly spoiled."

Reggie put down his newssheet and eyed her fondly. "You can be the ogre of the family and lay down the law to her."

Allegra looked at the rain-streaked windows and the gray sky outside. "That ought to be a father's work, but since she doesn't have one, the duty must fall on your shoulders, Reggie. After all, you are her closest male relative."

Reggie wagged his finger at her. "Don't place the burden upon me," he said with a smile. "You'd better find a decent husband before too long. I shall gladly hand you over to him."

Allegra didn't reply. They had gone over the issue a number of times, and her brother knew very well that she would not easily trade her freedom for the security of a man's name. Yet every day she'd scanned the newssheets for any mention of the Earl of Roche's nuptials to Minerva Young, but there had been none. It was possible they had eloped so as to circumvent the scandal of their wedding, but she sensed strongly that Jack never conducted his business in half measures, no matter what the consequences would be.

She rose and went to stare out the window. A carriage lumbered by, the coachman thoroughly soaked on the box, and the horses glistening with water. The sound of rain against the windowpanes soothed her, but she still suffered a vague longing that had plagued her ever since she left Fairleigh.

She dismissed it as residual emotion from the birth experience, but she kept seeing Jack in her mind's eye much more often than she liked, and the memory of his kisses crept up on her when she least expected it. Why would she even remember? Nothing had really happened. She was sure Jack didn't dwell on the memories, so why should she?

"You grew very quiet upon my mention of the word husband," Reggie said.

"It made me rather pensive, but I have found no one to stir my interest," she lied. "Besides, I still have to be in mourning officially."

"Dashed tedious I daresay." He slowly walked to stand beside her, his face twisting in a small grimace of pain. "I only wish you could find such happiness as I found with Evelyn." He sent an adoring glance to his wife, who returned it.

That longing for Jack flowed through Allegra once more, but she pushed it aside. "I do miss the dinner parties and country dances we had at home before I got married. Those were times of innocence and happiness."

He nodded and directed his stare out the window once more. "The gaiety will return, m'dear. Once your mourning period is over, there's nothing to stop you from joining every kind of social activity."

"Yes . . . I look forward to it." Allegra meant it. She'd always enjoyed dancing and she took pleasure in good food as much as the next person.

"Look, a carriage has stopped by the door," Reggie said, pointing. "I wonder who it is."

Allegra strained to see through the streaks of rain on the windows. "Lady Georgina, no doubt."

"She has taken quite a liking to you, sis."

"Or to Beatrice," Allegra said wryly.

"Or both."

"Or to me. After all, I'm a most charming devil."

Allegra laughed. "That you are, brother mine."

They watched as one of the footmen held an umbrella over Lady Georgina's form as she hurried toward the door. She wore a powder blue cloak with a matching wide-brimmed hat trimmed with feathers and a veil. Allegra heard the distant sound of her chatter, incessant as usual.

Allegra dreaded hearing the latest news about the earl, however trivial. If she were honest with herself, she would admit she worried about hearing that he had wed the "strumpet," as Lady Georgina always called Miss Young. But she also knew it was as inevitable as the sun rising every morning in the east. Not only that, but the two deserved each other.

As Lady Georgina disappeared through the rain-dampened door, Allegra noticed another person exiting the carriage. This was the first time someone else had arrived with the old lady. Her heartbeat escalated as she recognized the Earl of Roche, but at the same time she experienced an enormous reluctance to see him.

Flashes of memories went through her head, and she did not want him to stir up any longings within her as he looked into her eyes. Not only did Minerva Young stand between them, but fears as well, and mistrust. Mostly fears about her own reactions, should he shower her with his charm. Not that he would, of course.

She touched her throat where her breath had caught as she saw him enter. "I should find out if Beatrice has awakened," she choked out, and Reggie stared at her narrowly.

"What's bothering you, sis?"

"Nothing . . . nothing at all."

"You're distracted, and I know why. Lady G. brought someone today, and I suspect it's that ramshackle nephew of hers."

"Who?" Allegra silently cursed her choked voice. Reggie had always been able to read her moods, and it was ridiculous to try to fool him.

He cast his gaze heavenward and heaved a sigh. "Don't be such a ninny, Allegra. I'd say the earl has the power to stir your emotions."

"Nonsense!" She was about to flee out of the room when the door opened and a footman carried in an enormous wrapped package and set it on the floor. After its dramatic entrance came Lady Georgina with the earl in tow.

Allegra blushed as she looked into his eyes. He'd honed in on her immediately. His intense gaze searched hers and she felt as if much too much time had passed since she had last seen him—which was total madness when all was said and done.

"There you are, m'dear," Lady Georgina greeted her, and then cooed over Reggie's progress. "Jack insisted on accompanying me here today, mumbled something about me being in danger of highwaymen. Twaddle, I said, but he has the Hollister stubbornness all the way to his fingertips."

Looking worldly and elegant in a jacket of blue superfine, pale yellow pantaloons, and shiny Hessians, Jack bent over Allegra's hand and placed a warm kiss on her skin. She shivered with delight, but immediately suppressed the feeling and pulled her hand away.

Resenting his presence, she nevertheless had to introduce him to her brother and Evelyn. They greeted him politely enough even if Reggie's voice held some reservation.

"It's always a pleasure to meet any of Lady Georgina's friends and relatives," he said coolly.

The earl's larger-than-life presence filled the front parlor, and Allegra wondered if it made her relatives uncomfortable.

Jack bowed. "I'm honored to meet the man for whom Mrs. Rutherford harbors such great sibling esteem. If it hadn't been for your hardships, I would never have encountered your sister."

Reggie nodded with less reluctance. "The gratitude is all on my side," he said politely. "You aided my sister in a very difficult situation, and for that, I'll be eternally grateful."

"Yes . . . it was a great challenge, but one that I'm thankful for. Mrs. Rutherford showed immense courage and she's very kind."

"Allegra has a heart of gold, and I'm very protective of her."

"Please don't speak of me as if I'm not here," Allegra interrupted. "That chapter is over and done with."

Jack turned to her with a look of tenderness. "I brought Bea a present," he said with obvious delight. "Where is she?"

"Upstairs, sleeping," Allegra replied.

His expression fell. "Oh. I had hoped to see her and give her this." He motioned toward the package, and the footman who had stayed in the room slowly unwrapped a finely carved wooden rocking horse. It had been inlaid with mother-of-pearl and adorned with gold leaf and paint. Allegra gasped at the enormity of the present.

"This is not suitable," she said. "Besides, Bea is only a few weeks old. She would never appreciate the gift. You being here—"

He raised his eyebrows. "But I daresay she would in a few years. Meanwhile, you can appreciate the craftsmanship."

"It's much too extravagant," Allegra protested.

"I said as much myself," Lady Georgina said, "but there's no talking any sense into Jack. When he has his mind set on something, he goes in single-minded pursuit. He won't listen."

"Thank you, Aunt, for divulging my deep, dark character traits," the earl said with a wry smile.

"I think you should thank the earl graciously for his gift," Reggie said simply, and Evelyn nodded. "I for one think the horse is lovely, and 'tis thoughtful of Lord Roche to think of little Beatrice and bring her a present."

"I'll remember her every year," the earl said, his face lighting up again at their approval.

The dratted man had already worked his charm on her relatives, she thought. "That won't be necessary," Allegra said, his statement unnerving her. She viewed the chapter with the earl closed and gone, but here he stood, so eager and pleased with himself. It was highly irregular, and it annoyed her no end.

"I know it's not necessary, but I—and possibly Bea—would find great pleasure in the arrangement."

Allegra gripped his arm and whispered fiercely, "I want to talk to you this instant." She pulled him over to the window where they would have some modicum of privacy.

"I don't know what you're about, but this whole visit is wholly unsuitable, my lord. You're betrothed to another and you come here bearing gifts while your fiancée is languishing God only knows where."

"Minerva is back in London for the time being," he said simply. "I know this is highly against accepted behavior, but then again, I've never worried overly much about convention. I just couldn't stay away."

"I worry about convention, my lord. I'm a mother with responsibilities, and I don't want to be a topic for gossip, and I'm angry that you would put me in the position of such a possibility."

He hesitated for a moment. "I see," he said finally. "But I only thought of Beatrice."

Allegra shook her head. "No, you only thought of yourself."

He looked uncomfortable for a moment, his gaze wandering from her to her family and to his aunt. He heaved a sigh of frustration. "You're right, of course. I only thought of satisfying my own longings."

His close scrutiny of her face made her highly uncomfortable.

"I didn't think of the consequences. I've never had to think of the consequences of my actions because . . ."

"You're the Earl of Roche, someone who is not used to being gainsaid, but you still know the code of etiquette, and I marvel at such arrogance that you would make me embarrassed in front of my family."

He had the temerity to chuckle, and then whispered, "At least I know you're not wholly untouched by my presence."

"You don't regret one second of this," she accused under her breath even though she wanted to rant and rave.

He shook his head. "I do and I don't. I had to see you, and we're in the lap of your family. I only accompanied my aunt on her morning visits, that's all—in the eyes of the world."

"You still don't understand, do you?"

He didn't look the least bit contrite. "What?"

"I meant it when I said I didn't want to see you." She gave him a pleading stare, and wished that her voice had held more conviction, but it mirrored the uncertainty within her. He sensed her ambivalence, but she had to hold firm.

"I beg of you, my lord, to leave me and Beatrice alone."

His gaze fell to the floor, and frustration stood written all over his face. "Very well, I didn't realize how serious you are about this."

"And please remove the rocking horse from these premises. It'll be years before Beatrice can use it, and I don't want to be . . . reminded of, well, you. I can't find a more delicate way of saying it."

"Say no more. I shall remove myself promptly." With a smooth smile that looked somewhat forced, he bowed to her and the rest of the room. "It's been a pleasure," he murmured.

Allegra expected him to ask his aunt to leave, but he only gave an order to a footman by the door and left the room. Within two minutes the servant had rewrapped the horse and carried it outside. Allegra watched from the window as the earl left in the pouring rain on foot, wearing a greatcoat and his beaver hat pressed low over his ears for protection. Her insides twisted as she watched. Why had he returned to stir the emotions she had so successfully stuffed down?

"He's unable to find rest," Lady Georgina said at her elbow.

"I told him this scheme of coming here was unseemly, but would he listen? No. He never does. My nephew has a lot of nerve."

"I think it was the first and the last time he will come here," Allegra said coolly. "His soon-to-be wife would not be pleased to find out that he visited here."

"Pooh! She doesn't care, the hussy. I foresee nothing but misery from that union," Lady Georgina said with a sadness she'd never shown before. "I had hoped for something much better for Jack, but he created this situation and has to live with it. There's nothing I can do."

They both watched him disappear down the street, and Allegra felt a sense of loss, as if a glimpse of paradise had appeared possible for a moment, and then disappeared. It would never come back.

Seven

A year passed, and Allegra shed her mourning garb, happy to don gowns of bright blues and greens, pinks, and yellows. The brighter the better. Every day looked more positive and full of meaning, just as spring emerges from the frost of winter.

As Beatrice took her first halting steps, Allegra felt as if life had completely returned to her after a year of hibernation and reflection. The memories of Jebediah's cruelty had faded, and she was grateful to him for the one great gift that he'd given her—Beatrice.

The servants at Shorecliff supported her wholeheartedly even if a distant male cousin of Jebediah had inherited the estate and had moved in with his large family. Allegra lived happily at the dowager house with Beatrice, Rose, and a handful of faithful retainers who kept her abreast daily with the events at the main house.

I lack for nothing, Allegra thought one day, even if the weeks seemed to flow one into the other without much change except for the weather.

Lady Georgina corresponded faithfully, but she never mentioned Lord Roche, which was just as well. Allegra didn't really want to know the latest gossip about him. Memories of him would emerge when she least expected it. When Beatrice laughed with joy as she ambled across the parlor for the first time, Allegra wished that the earl had been a witness to the miracle.

It would have been nice to share life's wonders with someone besides the servants.

Late in May, one of her neighbors, Squire Hawkins and his wife, Pricilla, invited her to a dinner party. She counted ten guests and knew most of the local gentry, but one gentleman stood out as a peacock among the hens. Not that he wore garish clothes; on the contrary, his coat held the simple elegance of fine tailoring, and his neck cloth fell in perfect snowy folds at his throat.

He bent over her hand and gave her a smooth smile as Pricilla introduced her. A lock of hair fell over his eye and he swept it aside as he assessed Allegra from head to toe.

"Allegra, this is Sir James Lake, one of Lord Hazlewood's nephews. Sir James, meet Mrs. Rutherford."

The elderly Lord Hazlewood owned Penderley, a large estate nearby and Allegra loved to ride along the river that flowed through his property. He often accompanied her, when his crippled back permitted the exercise.

"Mrs. Rutherford? Hmm, that sounds very familiar, but I know I've never met you before," the young man said. "Do I know your husband?"

"If you reside in London, Sir James, it's more than likely that you never met my husband."

His forehead creased into folds of thought. "I know I've heard your name before, but I can't place it, alas."

Allegra smiled and let the issue drop, as she had never met the elegant gentleman. When they went in to dinner she discovered that she'd been seated next to him and wondered if Pricilla was trying some gentle matchmaking. Not that it would work, not with this man, though she could find no fault with him.

The table had been laid with a starched white damask tablecloth, sparkling crystal, and polished silver. An urn centerpiece held an arrangement of pink and red roses with green fronds of ferns, and candlelight softened the guests' features. The aroma of hot beef consommé and fragrant bread filled the air. The wine flowed, and Allegra enjoyed the conversation flying around the table in high, excited voices.

Sir James brought amusing anecdotes from London about

bets and wild phaeton races to Brighton, entertaining the entire table. His delightful conversational skills held everyone spellbound.

"Such dash and daring to race high-perch phaetons," Pricilla said, placing her hand to her heart as if to still its pounding.

"That's true, but other topics are rampant at this time. The most spoken-about recent event happened two days ago, the duel between Lord Roche, who is a personal friend of mine, and Mr. Seth Collins-Young, a hanger-on who claims to have ties to the Barnabys of Everston. He has the reputation of being fiendish with a rapier and a good shot. But so is Lord Roche."

Pricilla gasped and clapped her hand to her mouth. "But duels are illegal, aren't they?"

"They are, but there were so many bets staked on who would win that all of London knew about it. However, the duel itself played out in a different location, decided upon at the last moment so as to foil the authorities."

Allegra had gone cold at the mention of Lord Roche, but what could she expect but another scandal linked to him?

"No one was hurt," Sir James continued. "Collins-Young's hand trembled so much he shot wide, and the earl aimed at the sky."

"Why did they duel?" Squire Hawkins asked. "But keep in mind we have females at the table."

Pricilla snorted in disgust. "The ladies are not as squeamish as you'd like to think, John."

She would be loath to miss any gossip from London, and hung on every word falling from Sir James's lips, Allegra observed.

"It's a tricky situation, and really no secret as all of London knows about it. The earl had planned to marry a Miss Minerva Young, but they kept putting off the nuptials as Miss Young had every kind of excuse to delay the wedding. As I said, the earl is a close friend, so I know many of the details, which I can't divulge here. Anyhow, Miss Young is rather . . . er, well known in London, and the rumors were flying."

How odd, Allegra thought. Minerva would have been eager to wed before it would be obvious the baby she was carrying had been conceived out of wedlock.

"To make a long story short, Miss Young is actually *Mrs.* Collins-Young. Has been since she was eighteen, and no one the wiser about her status. She has been supporting her husband's expensive gambling habits, and he wasn't about to give up any kind of privileges."

"Oooh," Pricilla cooed, all agog.

"The earl took the news with admirable equilibrium; I rather believe he felt relief, but also felt the obligation to keep his word. He had to go through the motions of avenging his wounded pride, though it was Mr. Collins-Young who flew into a pelter while in his cups and challenged the earl to a duel."

"But it doesn't make sense," said Squire Hawkins. "If this Collins-Young fellow lived off of his wife's 'earnings' from the earl he would not want to kill his, er, source of income."

"It's rumored that Mrs. Collins-Young is madly in love with the earl and made up some Banbury story about carrying his . . . well, offspring. Mr. Collins-Young has been seething with jealousy."

All the ladies except Allegra gasped at the indelicacy of the information, but Sir James continued.

"Bear in mind that all this is hearsay, and for all I know 'tis nothing but pure bunkum. You know how rumors tend to get out of hand. For a year, Mrs. Collins-Young has been as willowy at the waist as she always was."

Allegra felt a wave of anger as she thought of how convincing Minerva had imparted this yarn of balderdash to her last year at Fairleigh. All her modesty and distress had been nothing but acting.

"To hear the earl's name mired in rampant scandal is not unusual," Squire Hawkins said.

"That's true but highly unfair," Sir James continued. "The

earl has been nothing but a mind-numbing, upright pillar of the community this last year except for this recent escapade that he did not instigate."

"He made up for lost time," Pricilla said and clapped her hands together as if in awe of the magnitude of the scandal. "All in the face of the authorities."

"Some who laid heavy bets became wealthy overnight no doubt," the squire said.

"As much is true," Sir James said with a laugh.

"The earl has nothing to be proud of surely," Allegra said reproachfully.

Sir James looked at her narrowly as if to judge if she spoke in jest. "Pride was never one of the earl's stumbling blocks."

"Never a boring moment," the squire said with a sigh, as if mourning old, more exciting times.

"Hardly," Sir James said.

"So what came of the duel?" Pricilla asked, still somewhat breathlessly waiting for more scandal to be divulged.

"Everyone involved denied having taken part in any duel when the authorities got wind of the event, and truthfully, the duel was a joke. Mrs. Collins-Young has disappeared from the London scene, but I'm sure she'll resurface shortly, a new wardrobe assembled. She has inspired many of the styles in certain circles, and acquired quite a reputation that will be hard to follow by anyone aspiring to tread in her footsteps."

"Like some of those infamous actresses and actors," Pricilla said innocently.

Allegra wondered if the ladies understood to which kind of footsteps Sir James alluded, and it had been daring of him to bring up the subject, but then again, he belonged to the fast set of the London *ton*.

"Precisely," Sir James continued. "We're all now breathlessly waiting for the next scandal to strike, but this will be remembered as the greatest of the Season."

"No doubt," Allegra said dryly.

Servants carrying a series of steaming and fragrant dishes

containing veal, roast beef, potatoes, and fresh peas interrupted their conversation.

Sir James looked at Allegra searchingly again. "I know you," he whispered in surprised tones. "You're the mystery woman whose daughter Jack delivered last year." When she didn't reply, he continued. "Jack has never been the same since. I don't know what transpired at Fairleigh, but I know it changed him."

"A newborn changed him," Allegra said. "I understand he was looking forward to fatherhood."

Sir James frowned as if weighing the statement. "Yes, but all this nonsense with Mrs. Collins-Young brought an element of seriousness to his life. He was very lucky to escape from a loveless marriage, and God only knows who might have fathered the imagined child. 'Twas all a trap, and Jack's more careful than ever. I believe he's rather jaded with his life and is in no hurry to tie the knot with some conniving miss."

"Not everyone is as calculating as Mrs. Collins-Young."

"I realize that, Mrs. Rutherford. Jack is not one to have his feelings easily engaged, so there's that added difficulty."

"I can understand the caution. Once burned, you shy away from fire."

Sir James nodded. "Have you seen him since last year?"

"No . . . but if you remember, you can tell him that Beatrice now walks and is healthy in every way."

Sir James stared at the plate set before him and the platter of roast beef offered by his elbow. "Your daughter will turn one shortly, and Jack'll be thirty-one. I'd say it's been a long year. I shall speak frankly if I may?"

"Why stop now after the infamous stories you regaled us with earlier," she said with some amusement.

"I feel as if I've lost Jack, and since I have the opportunity tonight, I must ask you if anything transpired during your stay at Fairleigh."

"You're nothing if not forthright."

Sir James nodded. "Shyness is something that never

plagued me. Can you give me any clues to Jack's subsequent despondence?"

"I daresay he dreaded marrying Minerva," she said, avoiding the issue of the earl's ardent kisses. "The delays must've worn him down."

"It was the lies and the dishonesty. Jack plays fair and you can count on his word."

"And there was lost time. He could have concentrated on courting someone else to accomplish his goal of creating a family."

"Could he?" Sir James said, his voice edgy. "As far as I know, he has no interest in courting some young miss." He dabbed at his mouth with his napkin. "I believe, and I think I'm close to the truth when I claim that you said something to him that has haunted him for a year."

"Utter and complete twaddle," she replied, her fork clanking against the plate as her hand shook with nerves.

"Jack never described you as callous or as someone who would hide behind facades."

She eyed him narrowly. "Did Jack send you here tonight?"

Sir James shook his head. "Absolutely not. I'm currently visiting my uncle at Penderley, and this invitation was extended to me. But if you could shed some light, I would be very grateful."

Allegra shook her head. "I have no idea what goes through the earl's mind. If he doesn't confide in you, perhaps you're not supposed to know."

He breathed hard through his nose in frustration. "Very well. I shall tell him that little Beatrice is walking, and that you're well. Then I shall observe his reaction."

"If you feel it necessary, but I suspect the exercise will bore you no end." Allegra wanted to reel the conversation into safer waters, but she could think of nothing else to say.

"Will you join us in London for the little Season?"

Allegra shook her head. "I think not. I see no reason for me to go to London."

"Whyever not? You're still a young woman; you cannot bury yourself forever in the country."

"The country is what I know, and I have no desire—"

"Lady Georgina would invite you in a second if you hinted that you needed somewhere to stay."

"As I said, I have no desire." Allegra uttered the words, knowing they weren't entirely true. She would love to visit the theater and the opera. Then there were the shops in Bond Street and the Burlington Arcade, museums, and exhibits.

"With the right invitations, you'd never be bored, Mrs. Rutherford."

"I'm rarely bored."

He only gave her a quick smile that said he didn't quite believe her, but let it go without argument. The dratted man had too keen a perception, she thought with a ripple of annoyance.

The meal ended with caramelized peaches and cream, and Sir James went on to regale everyone with more stories from London. It was obvious to everyone in the room that *he* was never bored.

A week later she heard from Pricilla that Sir James had gone back to London. "Now that's a nice young gentleman. I had hoped you would strike up a friendship."

"His sights are a lot higher than a country bumpkin like me."

Jack stared into the flames leaping in the grate at his club in London. Like so many previous nights during this cold spring and early summer, he'd lost himself in the dancing orange and gold. Most of the time, his friends left him alone, but tonight Sir James had joined him.

"It's good to see you, James. How are things at Penderley?"

"The same. The visit was rather humdrum except for a few dinner parties to break up the monotony. Some good fishing. And you? What's new since I last saw you?"

"Nothing. I haven't fought any more duels."

"That's a relief, old fellow. I was rather unnerved by that whole episode, but at least you got rid of Minerva."

Jack nodded with a satisfied smile. "In that sense the duel was a great blessing. Truly, the event was long overdue."

"Has she left you alone?"

"Yes. She shan't darken my doorstep again, and I arranged so that Mr. Collins-Young was run out of town as his rather more wellborn relatives found out the nature of his true livelihood."

"Encroaching mushrooms," Sir James said.

Jack wagged his finger. "You're not above subscribing to the services of strumpets, so it's a little too late to be judgmental, and encroaching mushrooms prevail where the ground is fertile."

"I always said Minerva was a heap of trouble."

Jack nodded. "Yes, you did. I give you that, but impending danger never deterred me."

"No, rather spurred you on." Sir James made a grimace and shook his head. He ordered a bottle of claret and two glasses from a passing footman. "I met someone you know."

The earl looked only mildly interested. "Yes?"

"Mrs. Rutherford. That blasted woman who changed your life."

Jack's heartbeat increased and he found that time seemed to have stopped the moment Sir James mentioned Allegra's name. "Really?"

"She said to tell you that young Beatrice is healthy and has taken her first steps."

Jack hung on his every word. "Is that all?"

"Isn't that enough? I met her at some country squire's dinner party, and she seemed reluctant to talk about you."

"That sounds just like her."

"I have no desire to hear why she would show any kind of reluctance. I fear it would be a rather boring story, especially since I can rattle off any number of females who would be more than happy to mention your name, or to talk about you."

"How did she look?"

"She wore some outmoded gown—bright blue I believe. Her hair had no style whatsoever, but I admit the color is glorious, and her eyes are quite striking, a very deep blue. But—a country matron, nothing more. I really don't understand your . . . well, for the lack of a better word, obsession, with her. You speak of her every damned time I see you!" He leaned over and gripped the lapel of Jack's jacket. "It has been a year since you last clapped eyes on her, dash it all. Get past it."

Jack looked into his friend's angry gaze. "I just can't forget her. I wake up every morning thinking of her, and I go to bed every night, no matter how late, or how much wine I have drunk, thinking of her." He paused. "You say she was wearing blue?"

"Yes, a dashing sort of blue, but what does it matter?" Sir James let go of his grip and leaned back in his chair.

"It matters a great deal. She's out of mourning if she's wearing colors."

"Brilliant, old fellow." Heavy sarcasm laced Sir James's voice.

"That means I can approach her, with the approval of society."

"As if you really cared about such things."

"I don't, but she does. She's finally back among the living," he said with a surge of joy that he hadn't felt for an entire year.

"I believe you've lost your wits, Jack. I don't know where my friend went to leave room for this kind of . . . specter. You're but a shadow of yourself."

Jack stared at the footman returning with a tray and a wine bottle, but he really didn't see him. "Not for very long, old friend. I shall rise early and ride into Somerset on the morrow."

His spirits had lifted as never before. He hadn't quite realized how difficult this past year had been. The challenge Minerva had presented had been very difficult, and then there had been the fact that he might be tied to someone he didn't love for the rest of his life. Not only that, but the fact that he had carelessly fathered a child with that woman had confronted him. He'd found out how difficult it had been to face up to his careless behavior. Not only careless, but thoughtless and arrogant as well.

He had lived with no plans except for the next opportunity for revelry. That focus had changed last year, but then the consequences of his careless behavior had overtaken him, and he'd had to deal with them ever since.

Minerva had lied of course, but her lying and stalling had worked in his favor, and now he was eternally grateful for her deception.

He leaned over and clapped his friend on the shoulder. "Do you want to stand up for me at my wedding?"

"What?" Sir James sounded surprised and outraged.

"You heard me. I intend to propose to the woman of my heart, so get yourself ready."

"Now I truly know you're quite queer in the attic, Jack." Sir James looked at him with deep concern and Jack laughed.

"It feels wonderful to have windmills in my head."

Eight

Ponsonby, Allegra's butler, announced a visitor. The sunlight streamed through the windows of the green parlor where Allegra had just chosen a swatch of pale mint green fabric from a pile for new window draperies and was pondering whether to go with gold fringe or an embroidered border down the sides. She needed to consult someone, so when the door opened and she saw the Earl of Roche framed in the doorway in a beam of sunlight, she burst out, "What do you think, gold fringe with this fabric, or an embroidered edge?"

"Gold fringe, of course," he said immediately as he crossed the room with a quick stride. "Gives a much more dramatic effect, don't you think?"

"You may be right."

She totally lost her voice after that as the impact of his presence overcame her. He walked to stand in front of her, his gaze taking in every nuance of her haphazard curls and rose gown. She hadn't dressed for company. She nervously fingered the pearls at her throat. A hot blush rushed to her face.

He looked so handsome and just as she remembered him. Perhaps he had aged a little; she found new lines of maturity around his eyes, and a deeper expression in his eyes, but other than that, he was still the man she remembered, the man who had taken her breath away and never quite given it back to her.

"What are you doing here, my lord?"

"I have come to claim what I lost."

"And what would that be?" she asked and backed away from him.

"My heart."

She couldn't believe she had heard him right, but she didn't dare to ask him again.

He pretended to look under a long tablecloth whose fringe swept the Oriental carpet underfoot. "It may be hiding under here."

"What? You're speaking utter nonsense."

He laughed and looked under the table, then went to peek in a drawer across the room. "No, it's not in here either, and not on that shelf over there." He returned to stand in front of her. "You might deny that you've seen it, but I know you have—late at night when you can't sleep and you examine the truths that won't go away."

"I sleep soundly," she replied, on guard.

"Beatrice wakes you up at times, doesn't she?"

"Yes . . . but that has nothing to do with this conversation."

"But it does, dearest Allegra. When you're alone at night, you remember me vividly. Don't you? When you hold her in your arms, you think back to her birthday, don't you?"

Allegra couldn't deny that. She had thought of the earl almost every day since Beatrice's birth. "I remember you frequently," she admitted reluctantly.

He pushed his hand through his hair as if that would help him clarify what he wanted to say next. She'd never seen him unsure and at a loss for words.

"Did the cat get your tongue?" she teased.

He shook his head. "No, but I don't want to say the wrong things. Conversations can easily derail if not handled correctly."

"I daresay I'm rather easy at conversation—as long as it stays within acceptable perimeters."

He made a gesture of frustration. "That's what I mean! You're sure to find fault with my dialogue, and you're not willing to—"

"I believe you're jumping to conclusions. We haven't even started the discussion, and you're already bogged down in details *about* the conversation we're about to have. How absurd is that?"

He laughed hollowly. "You're right, as always."

"What do you want to discuss? As far as I know, there's nothing—"

"There you go! Do you understand now? You've already cut me off at the knees, and won't even give me a chance to divulge what is on my mind."

"Really?"

Without another word, she sat demurely on a hardback chair and arranged her rose silk gown around her legs. Taking a deep, steadying breath, she looked him straight in the eyes. "Make your delivery, my lord. I shall listen with utmost patience."

"Now you're making a jest out of the situation."

"Get to the point," she cried and flung wide her arms. "After all this nonsense, I'm wholly out of patience with you."

He looked out the window. "Sir James told me you were at some dinner party he attended, and that he regaled everyone with the wild tale of my duel with Mr. Collins-Young."

She nodded. "Appalling, naturally," she teased.

He made a grimace. "It's not the first time I've been the topic of scandal."

"I'm not at all surprised."

The sun slanted across the room, illuminating the gold fob chain across his trim middle. He looked so elegant and attractive, and she could not take her eyes off his face, where his mercurial gaze spoke of the battles within him.

"I had pure intentions of making Minerva my wife. I took full responsibility for my impending fatherhood. However, she kept refusing to allow the family doctor to examine her, and that should've waved a red flag in my mind, but she pleaded extreme fear. Still, I can't remember ever seeing Minerva afraid of anything, and as the Countess of Roche, she would've had everything. Complying with my wishes for her physical welfare would've moved the situation with the nuptials forward."

"I never saw a mention of the banns in the newssheets."

"Because there were none."

"What about the baby?"

"I was excited about having a child of my own, but Minerva took to bed one day, called in her own doctor, and two days later, I was informed that she'd miscarried. I know now it was all a hoax to lure me into marriage, but I never thought she had that depth of duplicity. In the past I'd supported her in luxury."

"She might have desired the title."

He shook his head. "That's the odd part. *She* was the one who kept stalling, and then the truth came out that she was Mrs. Collins-Young. He would've let the truth out if she decided to wed me. He wanted her to remain a courtesan, nothing more. Male pride perhaps. Besides, the marriage would've been illegal, and if I had decided to cut off her allowance, he might've had to curb his expensive habits. She was his 'business venture,' and he always looked at his interest first. As I said to James, it all played out in my favor."

"You do seem to have that magic streak of luck," Allegra said.

"Or as Aunt Georgie always says: I'm a lucky devil, never have to pay for my infernal sins."

"Where's this discussion leading?"

He again had that look of frustration as he gazed at her. "I have to somehow convince you that I'm a changed person. I know it doesn't look that way, but—"

"I see no reason why you'd have to convince me of anything. Your life is yours to do with as you please."

"I know that!" he replied with a hint of disgust. "I have changed. No longer does the old life of gambling and revelry interest me. I most long for a family and to reestablish my roots at Fairleigh."

"Yes?" She perversely enjoyed seeing him squirm.

He looked extremely uncomfortable.

"Now this is when we get to the hub of this conversation,

Allegra. This is where you and Beatrice come into the picture. That is if I can convince you of the importance of my plan."

"To have a plan you must've thought this over at great length."

"I've been thinking for a whole year, and my plan is flawless." His voice gathered in strength as his confidence must have strengthened. "I would like nothing better than to see you and Beatrice happy at Fairleigh. When that's accomplished, I would like us to have children together. You'll lack for nothing."

"What about my freedom? You would always be laying down the law, and that I cannot abide."

He came to stand over her. "I doubt very much that I could ever 'lay down the law' as you put it. You have very much a mind of your own. Are you still afraid that I would turn into another Jebediah Rutherford?" He chuckled. "For one, he was never as handsome as I am, nor did he have the confidence that a marriage can be based on a harmonious give-and-take attitude."

"Words are well and good. You have no problems with words, but I worry about your autocratic heritage. No one gainsays the Earl of Roche—"

"Except maybe his wife."

She grew hot all over, then cold. Now she knew what it was like to stand on the edge of a precipice. Would she have the courage to jump? "I don't know if I like where this conversation is going, my lord."

"Call me Jack. I don't know why you went back to the cold 'my lord' address, but it doesn't suit you." He came to pull her up from the chair. His hands were warm and strong against hers. "I ask you to be my wife, Allegra."

"As in a business arrangement? I carry your children, and you pay for my extravagant gowns?"

He gave that devilish smile. "Something like that. I know you have the courage to try again."

"I won't marry to enter a business arrangement," she said after a tense silence.

His face moved closer and closer. "It can be sealed with a kiss, and what happens after that is between us."

"Sounds very cold, not exactly what a woman wants to hear."

His arms went around her. "Tell me what happened this last year. Did you miss me?"

She nodded. "Yes . . . I hate to admit it, but I did. I moved into this dowager house and I spent time redecorating it and watching Beatrice grow. It was mostly a quiet, reflective time. I've put the past to rest, and I don't hold anger toward Jebediah any longer. He was a bitter, misguided soul, and I happened to come across his path."

"My greatest fear has been that you would not accept my proposal."

"I still haven't accepted it," she said against his mouth. She read every nuance in his deep eyes, the uncertainty, the frustration, the longing.

"Not accept because of me, but because of your desire to keep your freedom."

She nodded, inhaling his male fragrance and becoming more intoxicated by the second.

"But let me assure you, Allegra, sometimes a good marriage is a venue for more freedom as you can rest in the knowledge that your endeavors are supported by a husband—namely me." He paused, anxiously scanning her face. "Just put me out of my misery, will you."

"Yes . . . where is your pistol?" she whispered, her lips gently touching his.

"I have a lewd reply on my tongue, but I refuse to answer your question. Just answer mine."

"You left out the most important ingredient to this partnership," she said, her hands moving into his wavy hair.

For a moment he looked confused. "I love you, Allegra. I'm so lost in love with you, that I don't know how to express myself," he murmured.

"I expect to hear you express yourself for the rest of our life together," she said.

"Does that mean you're accepting my proposal?"

He stood there breathless, waiting, and in that moment she knew he loved her, and that she loved him back just as much. Jumping off a cliff didn't seem so hard after all.

"With all my heart. I love you, Jack, more than I can say. I have loved you since that moment when you laid Beatrice in my arms for the first time."

He closed his eyes as if a great pain had eased. "Thank you, my love. You won't regret this decision."

"I know. So when are we getting married?"

"How about tomorrow?" he said with a laugh.

She shook her head. "No . . . this time I want to make it right. We'll do it on your birthday. Beatrice's birthday gift will be a father, and yours, well, you'll gain a daughter and a wife. That's probably more than you deserve, but seeing as you're an exceptionally lucky individual . . ."

He chuckled. "You have the answer—as always."

"Of course, but that goes without saying."

He sealed their bargain with a passionate kiss that sent her world spinning, and she didn't mind it in the slightest.

THE MUDDLED MATCHMAKERS

Victoria Hinshaw

One

The coffee room at Boodle's Club in St. James's Street was almost silent. From time to time someone coughed or rattled the pages of a newspaper, but few noises diverted Sir Malcolm Seymour from his gloomy thoughts. He glared at the pinpoint of ruby light reflected from the fire in his glass of claret. If he swirled the wine, the light danced and shimmered. If he held it motionless, the jewel tone lay quiet, glowing and frozen.

Dawn, his daughter, was like that point of light, quiet and unmoving, when she needed to be stirred up, spun into the lively, shimmering young woman she had once been. She was the best of daughters, devoted to her little son, loyal to the memory of the husband with whom she had shared only a few weeks before he went off to the war and met his death. Above all she was kind and attentive to her mother, a lady whose health complaints were as acute as they were numerous.

Nonetheless, Dawn's life should not be so circumscribed. It was neither fair nor reasonable for a lovely young girl, a mere twenty-four years of age, to do nothing but cosset her mother and fret about her fatherless son. She should be out in society, enjoying the company of friends, living again and perhaps even finding another husband.

"'Evening, Malcolm."

Sir Malcolm started out of his trance and squinted up at Alastair Grayson, the Earl of Carey. "Carey, 'evening."

"May I join you?"

"By all means."

"I could use a glass of that claret." The earl motioned to a waiter, gave his order, and settled into an armchair. "The club is quiet tonight. I suppose everyone is off at another of those extravaganzas Prinny has conjured up to celebrate the victory. I myself have had my fill of bread and circuses."

"As have I." Sir Malcolm swirled his claret and watched the sparkling ruby radiance spin in his glass. "My concerns of late have been more of a domestic nature. I confess I am not in much of a mood to celebrate, however gratified I am at our dominance over Napoleon."

"Your concerns, then, are much the same as my own. I, too, am relieved at the conclusion of the war, but I cannot shed my worries about my son."

"About your eldest?"

"Yes. Hugh is . . . not like himself anymore. Withdrawn, Almost four years have passed since his wife's death. If anything, he is more despondent now than he was at first."

Sir Malcolm searched his memory while Carey accepted the glass and took a sip. Unless he was quite mistaken, the young Lady Grayson, Hugh's wife, had died in childbirth. "I am sorry to be so absentminded, but I do not recall if the child . . ."

"Oh, my granddaughter is quite healthy and growing rapidly. Hugh dotes on her, as do I. He has diverted all his energies onto the estate, studying new varieties of plants brought from foreign soils. He spends a great deal of his time poring over arcane publications about the latest discoveries of exotic botanical species." The earl shook his head sadly. "I spent a year or so mourning after my Martha died, but I found the gumption to move on with my life. And I was well over forty at the time. Hugh is twenty-six. He ought to find another wife, get back into public life."

Sir Malcolm straightened up and tossed down the last of his wine. His mind whirled with an outlandish thought. Would Carey be game? "Alastair, what do you know of matchmaking?"

"Matchmaking? A constant pastime of the ladies, but certainly not an activity for males."

"To put it bluntly, you have no lady and my lady is nearly an invalid. Other than you and me, who could undertake the assignment? Now let me tell you all about my daughter Dawn."

"Mother, you have no need to worry about a thing. Father has seen to all the arrangements." Dawn Neville adjusted the soft cashmere shawl around Lady Seymour's shoulders.

"I am certain to suffer a chill this near the sea." Lady Seymour sighed and glanced toward the windows overlooking the esplanade, drawing the shawl across her chest. "Should we not have heavier draperies hung?"

"Perhaps. I will ask Mrs. Stamper this afternoon." *Poor Mother, always on the verge of the dismals, worn to a nubbin by worry.*

"Whatever possessed your father to bring us to Weymouth?"

"The poor old King found many healthful attributes here. He believed the sea air did him a world of good."

"Then why do they not bring him to Weymouth now?"

"I believe all his doctors are at Windsor. Papa had only your health in mind when he made these arrangements. He said he was very fortunate to find this house."

"Mama!" a small voice squealed from the passage.

Dawn opened the door to find her four-year-old son Teddy rubbing his eyes, his lower lip trembling, on the verge of tears.

"Here, darling, do not cry." Dawn scooped up the child and hugged him close, her precious boy.

His nursemaid hurried toward them. "I am sorry, ma'am. He woke in a strange bed and would na' be comforted."

"That's all right, Rosie. I will bring him back to you later."

Rosie dropped a brief curtsy and took herself away.

Dawn kissed her son's rumpled curls. "We are all here at the seaside, darling. Say good afternoon to Grandmother."

"G'aft'n," Teddy mumbled, still half asleep. He laid his head against Dawn's shoulder and closed his eyes.

"He will be back asleep in just a moment." She sat near her mother's chaise and leaned back with a smile, slightly rocking Teddy from side to side.

Lady Seymour reached over to caress his hair. "He is growing so fast."

"I hope there will be other children nearby. He is too often alone."

Her father stepped through the doorway. "I happen to know there is a little girl in the house next door. She is the granddaughter of an old friend of mine, the Earl of Carey."

Lady Seymour arched her brows in surprise. "Lord Carey? How very nice for you, Malcolm. I hope I shall have the pleasure of seeing him."

"Yes, that is what I was about to tell you, my dear. He is coming to dinner this very evening."

Dawn watched her mother's face change from pleasure to chagrin in an instant.

Sir Malcolm paid no attention to his wife's expression. "I have already spoken to Mrs. Kendall in the kitchen and I am assured she is quite up to the task of preparing a meal for the five of us."

"Five?" Dawn ceased her rocking and shifted the sleeping Teddy in her arms.

"Yes. Alastair's son and heir, Lord Grayson, is here with his daughter."

"But we have only arrived this morning," Lady Seymour said.

"They arrived several hours after we did. As I understand it, they have yet to engage household help, not having had Dawn's foresight to engage the servants by post."

Lady Seymour passed her hand across her brow. "But I am not sure I am up to the . . ."

"My dear, I am sure that Lord Carey would understand if you are too fatigued to join us, though he would be sadly disappointed. I trust you will try your best."

Dawn stood and spoke softly over Teddy's head. "You rest now, Mother. I will see that all the arrangements are to your standards, as soon as I put Teddy back to bed."

"Why yes, dear, that would be most helpful. And have Tyson see that my lilac gown is presentable, if you please."

Dawn gave Sir Malcolm a quick smile. "Of course."

Together father and daughter backed out of Lady Seymour's bedchamber, softly closing the door.

Hugh Grayson marked the page in his botanical journal and placed it on the table beside his chair. From his second floor bedchamber he could look out over the broad bay, its smooth waters dotted with boats of all sizes from rowboats to triple-masted frigates and East Indiamen. No one could fail to be moved by the beauty of the scene, though Hugh wondered what in the devil he was doing here. His father had insisted he spend the next six weeks in Weymouth.

Hugh's queries as to why Lord Carey wanted to visit the seaside met with the ordinary reasons, for the air, for the sea bathing, to benefit Emmy, but nothing specific. He hoped his father did not suffer some illness, a recurrence of his gout, or some new aches and pains. So far, it did not seem his father was seriously ailing; indeed he was in the best of spirits, had even accepted an invitation to dine this evening at the adjacent house where one of his old friends resided.

Hugh would rather have tried one of the town's old inns, renowned for their antiquity. That would have to wait for another night.

He glanced again at his book, wishing the meal would be informal and his return would be early. Perhaps he would be able to slip away while his father and the neighbor chatted over their port.

In Emmy's room, he paused to place a kiss on the sleeping child's forehead. Her tiny hand curled beside her button nose, her fair lashes lay long upon her pink cheek. She was the very picture of girlish beauty, and as always, he felt the ache of love, of his parental responsibility and his desire to protect her from all danger and disappointment. She was so precious and so fragile. . . .

He turned away, his throat thick with emotion. In a moment, he coughed, driving away the sting, then spoke to the nurse. "We will be at the house next door. Send Harold if you need us."

Harold, his father's valet, Emmy's nurse, and Lamb, their coachman, were the only three servants who had accompanied them to Weymouth. Tomorrow he would have the agency send over a few candidates for the posts of cook, housekeeper, and footman, enough to keep the household operating efficiently.

Hugh met his father in the foyer and followed him down the steps and a few feet along the paving stones to a brick house almost identical to their own.

In the drawing room, Sir Malcolm welcomed them with a wide grin. "Alastair, wonderful to see you again. And, Hugh, it has been many years since I last saw you. May I make you known to my wife and my daughter, Mrs. Neville?"

As he uttered the requisite niceties, Hugh had to stop himself from staring at the pretty young woman who curtsied before him. He could not recall when he had been so instantly taken with a lovely countenance and such sparkling blue eyes. Her mother, wrapped in a thick shawl and holding a handkerchief to her chest, nodded a greeting.

He settled in a chair and listened to the conversation among the two elder gentlemen and Lady Seymour. She recited a long list of ailments and her respondents offered a variety of theories on the salubrious effects of the water and air at the seaside. This was sure to be a long evening.

He dared not let his glance wander to Mrs. Neville. If she happened to meet his gaze, he would have to speak to her, and no subject came to mind beyond the nature of the Weymouth climate. He tried to assume a pleasant expression, a look of rapt attention to the empty discourse across the room. He had never been any good at social conversation and usually tried to avoid situations in which it was required. Such as this very moment.

"Would you not agree, Hugh?" Lord Carey's voice startled him.

"You are always the best judge, Father." He dared not confess he had not grasped a word in the last few moments. Apparently his answer sufficed, for the talk continued. Soon dinner was announced and they rose from their chairs. Lord Carey offered his arm to Lady Seymour and followed Sir Malcolm out of the room. That left Hugh no choice but to offer his escort to Mrs. Neville.

He bowed to her, keeping his gaze averted. Yet, from the corner of his eye he could not miss her half smile as she lay her hand on his arm, still saying nothing. Hugh wished he could hear her voice again. A quarter hour ago, when she greeted his father, her tone was soft and melodious. Since then she had not spoken.

Sir Malcolm directed them to seats and immediately launched into an account of his daughter's resourceful selection of a cook for their summer residence. "She had the aspirants send a few examples of their receipts, and clearly this Mrs. Kendall had the superior choices. Clever idea, eh?"

Lord Carey nodded. "Yes, indeed I would say so. What do you say, Hugh? Should we not try the same system?"

Hugh was about to agree when Mrs. Neville spoke.

"Perhaps, Lord Carey, you should wait to make that decision until you have sampled the dishes we serve tonight. There is some distance between the list of ingredients on a sheet of paper and the tenderness of a joint or the delicacy of a butter sauce."

Hugh forgot his determination to avoid looking at her. She leaned forward, blue eyes twinkling and eyebrows arched mischievously. Her tone was as lighthearted as her words, and her full lips curved in a luscious grin. His fingertips tingled with the urge to applaud.

His father chuckled. "How right you are, Mrs. Neville. But

from the delicious fragrances already in the air, I would say that your system must have worked to perfection."

The footman, as if given a theatrical cue to enter the stage, offered a steaming platter of oysters and clams to Lord Carey.

Throughout the two removes, Hugh felt more and more at ease. He said little but kept his attention on the conversation, most of which centered on the food and its excellence.

Mrs. Neville offered only a few comments from time to time, delivered in her quiet yet musical voice. Hugh observed her, usually quite indirectly. This was one evening when he was grateful for his good peripheral vision, for he could hardly restrain himself from staring at her.

He felt excessively guilty for his fascination with the lady. More than three years had passed since his wife's death, a time in which he had voluntarily isolated himself from the company of ladies like Mrs. Neville, attractive and lively young women who might tempt him to forget his Beatrice and her suffering. Yet here she was, fortunately married to someone else, but nearby for their entire summer sojourn in Weymouth. Perhaps it was time for him to learn how to conduct himself in social situations again. He had to learn how to talk with ladies without tearing himself apart with guilt.

So comforted, he gave a little smile in her direction. Her eyes met his for an instant before she looked down shyly. Her chestnut hair was dressed simply, pulled away from her face and tied with ribbons matching the light blue of her gown. Her cheeks were pink, marked by tiny dimples on either side of her exquisite mouth. Something about those lips made him drag his glance away and fidget with his napkin.

Grateful to find a diversion, Hugh helped himself to a ripe pear from the fruit bowl and concentrated on trimming away its stem. He cut off a chunk, put it in his mouth, and chewed slowly, savoring its fresh sweetness and letting the succulent juice trickle down his throat.

He gave a tiny sigh of pleasure, quickly catching himself and glancing around the table. His father and the Seymours had not noticed. But Mrs. Neville was watching him, that little mischievous smile alive on her face. He felt himself redden with embarrassment.

"They are particularly delicious, are they not?" She spoke softly, only to him. "I could barely resist gobbling up the entire basket this afternoon."

He swallowed and picked up another slice. "Where does your cook find them? I should like to know who grows such excellent specimens."

"Mrs. Kendall tells me she has her secret sources. I suspect she may be more forthcoming after she feels secure in her position. After all, we only arrived this morning."

"Perhaps I should pay her a visit later. She might have a recommendation for the position in our house."

"Ah," she said, "you must promise not to try to lure her away. I am already quite taken with her abilities."

"Perhaps she has a twin sister."

Sir Malcolm turned his attention to Hugh. "Who has a twin sister?"

"I was just saying I wish your Mrs. Kendall had a twin sister to cook for us."

"Yes, I wager you do." Sir Malcolm gave a hearty laugh.

Lord Carey leaned toward Lady Seymour. "I suspect you will have many guests eager to be invited to your table this Season."

Lady Seymour waved a hand in the air. "La, I pray I shall be well enough to entertain now and then. Of course, Lord Carey, you and Lord Grayson are always welcome at our table whether I am up to joining you or not. Sir Malcolm and Dawn will be glad of your company anytime."

"Why, I thank you," Lord Carey said. "If tonight's repast is any indication, we shall avail ourselves of your hospitality frequently."

"And now, I beg leave to retire for the evening. It has been a most fatiguing day." Lady Seymour stood, as did Mrs. Neville.

Hugh rose with the others and bowed his good evening and thanks. He was sorry to see Mrs. Neville follow her mother from the room. Just as he was beginning to feel more comfortable near her, she was gone.

The men sat again and the footman brought a bottle of port. The conversation between his father and Sir Malcolm turned to the news from the Vienna meetings on the peace settlements. Arrangements were being made for the Little Corporal, as they called Napoleon in some circles, to be exiled to Elba, where he could occupy himself with ruling a tiny island instead of most of the continent of Europe.

Hugh let his gaze linger on the fruit bowl. He had not studied the varieties of pear trees that grew in England. Perhaps one of the books he brought along had a section on fruits that would tell him more. He would have to see what information he could find from the cook as well. His thoughts drifted back to Mrs. Neville watching him savor the pear. Her eyes were . . .

". . . to lose so many young men. Dawn's husband had been gone only a few months when he was killed . . ."

What the blazes? Dawn Neville is a widow!

Dawn tiptoed out of Teddy's room, pleased he was sleeping soundly. Her mother was settled for the night, too, all the potions and drafts dutifully measured out and consumed, the draperies adjusted and readjusted, the oil lamp positioned and repositioned, the bedclothes arranged and rearranged. At last, with a familiar sigh of self-pitying tribulation, Lady Seymour had whispered good night.

Dawn closed the door of her bedchamber behind her, threw herself on the bed, and tore the ribbons from her hair. What she wanted to do was cry, weep away her frustration, so carefully masked for the last few hours. Instead she flopped over on her stomach and sank her face into her pillow. How could Father have humiliated her like that? She would never have believed he would do such a deceitful thing as to take a house next door to Lord Grayson, then dangle her before him like a prize sow at market day.

She slammed her fist into the feathers and wiped away a tear. When her father had whispered in her ear that Lord Grayson was a widower, just as they were all making their introductions, she had been tempted to excuse herself entirely. She wished she could hide away and never reveal the depths of her mortification. But something, some sense of daughterly duty, some aversion to impropriety, kept her in her place.

This was so unlike her father. Completely out of the ordinary. Never before had Sir Malcolm hinted he would interfere in her life. Oh, once or twice, or perhaps three times he had suggested she might eventually look for a second husband.

She would never marry again. Her only aim in life was to raise her son without interference. She had seen how a new husband could be envious of his wife's children. Peg's new husband sent her little son off to board with the vicar several parishes away. Peg never got to see him. Or Maria, also a widow from Peter's regiment. Her new husband wanted his own son and though he was never cruel to Maria's fatherless child, he definitely treated him as an outsider in his family.

Though people always told her little Teddy needed a father, she knew better. She had heard even worse stories than Maria's and Peg's. Now her father had installed the family right on top of an eligible widower like Lord Grayson. Dawn gave the pillow a final thump, then clutched it to her chest. It was so odious, so awkward, so obvious.

But had it been obvious to Lord Grayson? The man hardly gave her a second glance except when they spoke about the pear. He had not acted like a man on the lookout for a second wife. It was his father who had carried on most of the conversation. Perhaps Grayson was just as much a dupe in this situation as she was.

Dawn fluffed the pillow, set it in place, and smoothed the cover. She had to admit that Lord Grayson was quite attractive, in a distant sort of manner. Most of the time at the table, his thoughts must have been far, far away. His dark hair lay in casual waves, his brown eyes set deep under generous brows. The wide forehead, the chiseled features, all were handsome in a very classic way. Peter's face had been more boyish, with golden hair and light blue eyes. In height Peter had been about the same, just less than six feet, but Lord Grayson had a more muscular build.

She reached for the miniature of Peter she kept by her bed. It was rather a poor likeness, a hasty job by a second-rate artist, but it was all she had. She often tried to recall every detail of his face, and sometimes she thought she remembered his looks exactly. Other times, she admitted reluctantly, the particulars were blurred.

Her tears fell faster now, altered from vexation to sorrow and regret. Theirs had been a short courtship and an even shorter marriage. In all, they had known each other only seven weeks, though in their youthful exuberance, they promised each other everything, adoration, passion, and joy. But he would never come back. No matter how much she had prayed the announcement of Peter's death had been an error, she knew from the letters she received from his fellow officers that he had died in Spain.

She shivered and blew her nose. A self-indulgent tantrum would not change the situation. Her father was pushing her at Lord Grayson, and the target was either oblivious to the fact or completely uninterested. Whichever it was, she must spend the summer here, some of the time in his company. Her father would never consent to take them home, and her resistance would only provoke his most obstinate reaction. Sir Malcolm's good nature was well known, almost as ubiquitous as his stubbornness.

She curled herself around the long-suffering pillow. Lord Grayson seemed unaware of her father's intentions and anything but eager to know her. As the heir to the earldom, no doubt he would look to the highest circles of the *ton* if he needed a second wife. She had never even had a London Season, having married Peter before her mother had convinced any of their relatives to take on her presentation.

Which made her father's reckless aim even more humiliating to her. When they realized Sir Malcolm's purpose, perhaps Lord Grayson and his father would simply flee Weymouth and solve her problem in one fell swoop.

That optimistic thought sustained her as she prepared for bed. But when she drifted off to sleep, her dreams were disturbingly dominated by the dark eyes, wavy hair, and broad shoulders of her newest acquaintance.

Two

"My valet managed to brew up a pot of coffee, and Emmy's nurse fried us some bread, but I must say whatever you have with you smells delicious." Lord Carey ushered Sir Malcolm into his dining room at midmorning.

"You have your choice of currant buns or Mrs. Kendall's egg muffins, a tasty delicacy that is new to me." Sir Malcolm set a heaping plate on the table and swept aside its covering napkin.

"Thank you." Lord Carey took a muffin and bit into it. "Yes, very tasty indeed." He poured a cup of coffee for Sir Malcolm. "Hugh has gone to the agency to engage a cook. Your Mrs. Kendall gave him a recommendation."

"Did he speak of last evening?" Sir Malcolm asked.

"Not a word. Other than praise for the cook."

"Then I take it he was not immediately enchanted by Dawn."

Lord Carey chewed slowly before swallowing. "Considering Hugh's recent behavior, I should say his silence might be a better sign than if he mentioned her at all."

"You mean he would not want you to know if he was attracted to her?"

"Exactly."

Sir Malcolm helped himself to a currant bun. "That may be Dawn's reaction as well, keeping her own counsel. So what do we do next?"

"I suppose we need to keep them together as much as possible."

"Yes, together. Certainly they need to become acquainted, learn a little about each other." Lord Carey tented his fingers and stared at them for a moment.

"Once Hugh returns, perhaps we should take a stroll on the esplanade, meet each other in front of the houses and fall in together as if by chance."

"Excellent idea, Mal. When we are about ready, I will send over my valet with the message, and we will meet right outside in a quarter of an hour."

"So be it."

"But, Father, I have promised to read Mother another chapter." Dawn folded a letter and set it aside.

"Nonsense. Why stay inside when the sun is shining? You have not seen anything of the famous Weymouth sands and the bathing machines."

"That can wait until I have tended to Mother. I have promised Teddy a walk on the beach this afternoon. Surely there is no need to go now."

Sir Malcolm shook his head. "Are you not curious about the town? I welcome your company to have a look around. We are only a short distance from Gloucester Lodge, where the royal family stays. Teddy will not care about that, but surely you would enjoy seeing it."

He was curiously insistent, Dawn thought. Suspiciously so. "We will be here for two months, Father. I will have many opportunities to walk the streets of the town."

Dawn reached for the book, but Sir Malcolm stayed her hand. "Humor your old father, my dear, and take a stroll with me this morning. The weather is fine and who knows when a storm might blow in?"

She wiped an instant frown away. Even though she was certain what he intended, how could she refuse? "Let me tell Mother I shall read to her later, and I will get my bonnet and parasol."

Her tasks accomplished, Dawn preceded her father onto

the esplanade, a wide pavement that followed the curve of the beach. She was not even slightly surprised when they met Lord Carey and his son.

"Why, Alastair, out for an amble, eh?" Sir Malcolm's voice was excessively hearty.

Her father, the old fox, must have seen the two men and grasped the chance to drag her along and thrust her in poor Lord Grayson's face again. A wave of embarrassment warmed her cheeks. Now she was trapped again in the company of a man who had no interest in her whatsoever, and who was barely amiable.

"Seemed like just the thing for such a lovely day." Lord Carey's tone was equally exaggerated.

Dawn began to suspect that her father might not be alone in this escapade. She dipped a shallow curtsy to father and son. Lord Grayson bowed in return but kept his eyes lowered. His face showed no reaction to the fathers' charade, as serious and impassive as it had been most of last evening. Something about his countenance, she realized, had a tinge of sadness. The rather poignant look in his eyes made her want to bring him a smile. *Nonsense, don't be a goose.*

Sir Malcolm and Lord Carey fell into step together, moving in the direction of the harbor. Dawn followed along and Lord Grayson had no choice but to walk along beside her. She felt uncomfortable remembering those dreams she had had last night, but how could he know? The silence seemed to stretch unbearably.

At last she could stand it no longer. "Were you able to engage a cook, Lord Grayson?"

He turned toward her almost as if startled to find her there. "Ah, I believe so. Yes, your Mrs. Kendall gave me a recommendation, so I went to the agency this morning and they will endeavor to send her to us tomorrow."

"I hope Mrs. Kendall's help will prove valuable."

"I am certain it will."

Before Dawn could think of another subject for conversation, Lord Carey turned back to them. "Hugh, take a look at that little sloop coming into the harbor."

"A handsome yacht." Lord Grayson squinted into the sun.

Dawn shaded her eyes and gazed at the brilliant water of the bay. She knew nothing about boats, but she assumed they were speaking of the one heading toward them under the power of just one little sail in front of the mast.

"Exactly the same as your uncle's, is it not?" Lord Carey leaned against the railing where the river met the bay and peered at the boat. "It is not his, just one very like it."

There at the end of the esplanade, at the mouth of the river, they took in a dramatic change from the quiet of the beach. Upriver, the harbor was packed with vessels of all sizes beneath a forest of masts. They heard the shouts of the men as they loaded or unloaded, mixed with the creaking of the cranes as cargo swung off the decks. The docks were lined with barrels, crates, and bales, the cobbled streets crowded with horses, wagons, and carts. It could not have been more different than the scene directly before their houses, the comparative serenity of the golden sand rimming the sweep of the bay glittering under the sunny blue sky.

"There is a good deal more to Weymouth than I imagined." Dawn spoke to no one in particular.

Lord Grayson nodded and drew her attention. "Do you enjoy yachting, Mrs. Neville?"

"I'm afraid I have never been in a boat, other than a tiny rowboat on the lake. Perhaps I shall have the opportunity to go sailing while we are here."

"Capital idea," Sir Malcolm said. "Sailing. We all should go. Part of the attraction of the seashore."

Dawn could have bitten her tongue. Now Lord Grayson would think she was anxious to spend more time in his company. She tried to shrug away her attraction to his melancholy manner. He was a youthful, strong-looking man, a truly handsome man, but she must not let herself get carried away by his good looks and air of tragic detachment.

Lord Carey suggested they head back past their houses and

walk farther east along the esplanade, which followed the curve of the beach for more than a mile.

Lord Grayson gave her a little half smile as they turned to aim their steps in the opposite direction. Be careful, she warned herself. There was something very appealing about a man who carried a secret sorrow, a riddle which drew her empathy and compassion. She wanted to reach out to him, help him surmount his sadness. But those tendencies were dangerous, very dangerous. Dawn was reminded of the first feelings she had had for Peter, concern for his imminent departure to fight in the war. Not exactly the same but close enough to give her a sense of unease.

She gazed out at the sand beyond the walkway. A few people walked near the edge of the water and small children cavorted in the shallows. Teddy would love to play there later. Clusters of tall bathing machines stood on the beach, awkward-looking on their high wheels. Aha, she thought, at last a proper subject for conversation.

"Lord Grayson, do you plan to try a bathing machine and take a plunge in the seawater?"

"Bathing in seawater? Is that not for those who are ailing? I have no complaints."

"I believe the effects of dipping in the water are considered to be beneficial for everyone. I admit to curiosity about it myself."

"Then you shall give it a try? Now that you mention it, I suppose I should not miss out either."

"Do you swim, Lord Grayson?"

"Not for some time, I am afraid. As a boy we used to splash around in the river near our house and I remember a few races across the pond." Lord Grayson paused, as if lost in memories. After a few more steps along the pavement, he nodded his head and smiled at her. "Yes, after due consideration, I believe I would say I swim, Mrs. Neville. And do you know how to swim?"

She lowered her voice to a conspiratorial near-whisper. "My father never knew, but yes. Many years ago I was taught by some friends. We would sneak away from those watching us and spend a stolen hour at the lake. I always had a hard time explaining why my shifts were wet and dirty." The last words slipped out before she realized the intimacy of the image. She felt her cheeks turn pink.

But Lord Grayson did not seem to notice. "Those were happy days. We captured frogs and chased the ducks and had contests to see who could throw stones the farthest."

"Oh, yes. Some of the girls pretended to be squeamish about the frogs, but I loved their bulgy eyes and funny croaks."

Again silence prevailed. Dawn watched the children playing on the beach, splashing in the water and piling up mounds of sand. Even from this distance she could hear their happy shouts. "Tell me about your daughter."

"Ah, Emmy is a pretty child, very sweet. And your son?"

"I am taking my little Teddy over there to the sand this afternoon. I think he will enjoy it, just as those children do. Will you take Emmy?"

"I doubt her nurse will allow her so near the water."

Dawn squashed her instant reaction and nipped off her reply. A nurse should not be allowed to dictate a child's activity. But then, she had never seen little Emmy, so what right did she have to comment? Rosie, Teddy's nurse, was often more concerned about him dirtying his clothes than anything else.

Sir Malcolm brought them to a stop near the statue of the King. "Alastair has a fine suggestion for us, my dear. He proposes we all take our evening repast at the Old Ship's Inn this evening. I fear your mother was sadly fagged by last night and would not be able to come down again this evening. What do you say?"

Dawn shook her head. "I should stay with Mother and Teddy. You go ahead with Lord Carey and Lord Grayson."

"Nonsense. Your mother will be abed even before we leave the house. So will Teddy. And do not tell me Mrs. Kendall will object. She can use the afternoon to reorganize the kitchen, a necessity she told me of this morning."

"Then it is decided," Lord Carey said. "I will send to reserve a private dining parlor for us at eight."

Dawn started to renew her objection, then kept her words unspoken. Father was correct, Teddy would be tired from his afternoon on the beach and Mother would be groggy from her drops. And the thought of dining in the old inn was quite agreeable.

She looked at Lord Grayson, whose gaze seemed focused on some distant object. He was not paying any attention to the conversation. His thoughts were again far, far away. The tiny crease in his forehead made her want to reach up and soothe it away.

What are you thinking, Dawn, you addlepated ninny?

When they stepped inside the Old Ship's Inn, Hugh had to stifle a broad grin. The aroma of cigar smoke and the yeasty tang of ale . . . the clink of glasses, hearty voices, and bursts of laughter . . . the low-beamed ceiling and the light flickering on the yellowed wall . . . he had not been in such a place for many years. Memories of his youth flooded forth, when the older fellows had snuck him into the village tavern near their estate to initiate him into the masculine pastimes of tossing dice on a rugged plank table and downing a pewter mug full of bitters. The first time they took his blunt and left him thoroughly jug-bitten. From then on, he learned their ways and occasionally, over many a bracer, even beat them at their own games. These were memories he had not recalled for a long time, and he found himself nostalgic for those days. Before his marriage. Before Beatrice's death.

Hugh left his carefree youth behind when he fell in love with a tiny ethereal waif, all sweetness and golden ringlets. He burned for her, and she adored him in return. Within a year of their wedding, she was dead, lost giving life to their child. He ached with guilt—guilt he still felt every day.

He followed his father and sat where directed in the private dining parlor, paneled in dark wood and fragrant with the delectable smell of roasting beef. He propped his elbow on the table and rested his cheek on his palm, wishing he could wipe away his memories and concentrate on the upcoming meal. But it was futile.

After Beatrice died, he had withdrawn from everything, his friends, his partners in the hunting box near Melton Mowbray. He stopped going up to London for any purpose and stayed alone for hours in his apartments in the great mansion at the family estate. Yet he could not endure nothingness; his mind had craved exercise. One day he read of some new species of tree brought to England from abroad. He sent for a catalog and joined a botanic society as a corresponding member, isolated from company but allowing his interests to grow in new directions. Eventually he hired a man to oversee the hothouses he built and the gardens he developed. Two things brought him satisfaction—his plants and his daughter, but seeing Emmy grow also fueled his continuing guilt over Beatrice's death.

Hugh pulled his wandering thoughts back to the ale set before him. The others were already drinking. He looked at Mrs. Neville and saluted her with his tankard. It was offensively buffle-headed to ignore her.

Mrs. Neville was an attractive widow, exactly the kind his family thought he should find. But he did not want another wife. Even considering the possibility made his remorse return.

"Very tasty ale, would you not say, Lord Grayson?" Mrs. Neville had no idea of the dark turn to his thoughts. Her smile was friendly, unencumbered by disturbing memories and thorny concerns for his future.

He tried hard to return the lightness of her tone. "I find the local brews worth sampling almost everyplace I go."

Hugh was pleased to see her nod, equally pleased that the necessity for further conversation was diminished with the arrival of their dinners.

The inn's proprietor joined them after their roast round of beef, buttered crabs, and fresh scallops dressed with lemons, herbs, and peppercorns. Only a bit of encouragement convinced him to share some of the legends of the town, tales of the smugglers, the ships that went to fight the Spanish Armada, the gruesome entry of the plague, carried on ships' rats. He spoke of the two sides of the river on opposite sides in the Civil War, the roundheads bombarding the King's men, the monarchists torching the parliamentarians' ships in the harbor.

Sir Malcolm's eyes glowed with pleasure. "And what of the smugglers, the brotherhood of flaskers and slippery free traders, where did they work?"

"Indeed they were all over, anyplace they could find a landing spot along the coast."

"But they came here from time to time, to the Old Ship's Inn?" Lord Carey asked.

"So they say, in the old days."

"But no longer, I presume?"

"My lord, I'd be bamming you if I said that ever' man who darkens my door is as honest as yerself."

"Well said."

The proprietor launched into another lengthy tale of long ago. Sir Malcolm and Lord Carey hung on his every word.

Hugh looked at Mrs. Neville. She listened no more closely than he did. He leaned nearer and spoke in a whisper. "Tell me about your afternoon at the water's edge. Did your son enjoy the sand?"

"Teddy was delighted." Her eyes were alight as she spoke softly. "At first he was quick to draw back from the water, but his curiosity got the best of him and he insisted on wading out until the water washed over his feet. He squealed and danced in the shallows. Perhaps your daughter would like to join us someday."

"Perhaps." Hugh thought it unlikely the nurse would approve.

Lord Carey stood.

"Hugh, will you please sit with Mrs. Neville while Mal and I have a cigar with our host in the taproom? He has some fine brandy for us. We will send some in for you to try."

Hugh stood as well. "Of course, Father."

When they were gone, Hugh resumed his seat, cleared his throat, and drummed his fingers on the table. It seemed highly improper for his father and hers to leave them alone together, even if they were only a short distance away.

Mrs. Neville wore a smile and gently shook her head when his gaze met hers. "They are not very subtle, are they?"

"Subtle?" He did not catch her meaning.

"Leaving us alone like this."

"I wonder at the propriety of it."

"I suspect that is precisely their purpose, to push us into a closer acquaintance."

"To push us?" Hugh did not follow her thinking.

"Do you think we came to be in houses side by side merely by chance? Our dinner last evening, our stroll this morning, our presence here at the Old Ship's Inn—all are far from coincidental."

"You mean my father planned this?"

She gave a little shrug. "At first I thought the whole caper was my father's idea, but I saw today in our supposedly chance meeting and in your father's suggestion to dine here, that it must be a plan they hatched together. My father was aided and abetted by the willing participation of yours."

At once the situation became clear to Hugh. How had he not seen it before? All the reasons the earl had presented for their sojourn in Weymouth were ruses. He rubbed his hand across his brow. "I believe you are correct. My father has often said he wished I would get out more. He believes I spend far too much time on the estate but I have seen no need to seek out the society of others."

"My father has expressed much the same opinion about me. I suspect they concocted a plan to place us in proximity and assumed we would form an attachment."

Unaccountably Hugh broke into a grin. "I am quite

amazed. The thought of the high-and-mighty Earl of Carey arranging a secret rendezvous for his son . . ."

Hugh's grin grew into a rumble of laughter. "Now that you have awakened me, I can see the whole plan very clearly indeed."

"You find it ridiculous?"

"I cannot think of a more unlikely man to undertake the role of matchmaker than my father. Yet, I have no doubt it is a cooperative venture. Do you think Lady Seymour is in on it?"

"I do not think Mother is aware of the plot. She is devoted to Father, to Teddy, and to me, but her concerns center almost exclusively on herself and her megrims. No, she would not be part of the plan."

Hugh looked into Mrs. Neville's face and tried to smother his smile. She looked more offended than amused. "I hope my laughter has not given you the wrong impression. I was imagining our fathers mapping out their strategy like Wellington mapping out his battle plan."

He was rewarded by her smile. "Yes, the image is comical. I would never have thought it of my father either. He has never tried such a thing in the past."

"Nor has the earl. It is most unusual."

"I must say at the outset, I have no intention of marrying again. Ever. You need not worry that I will fall in with their scheme."

"Ah, I see." Hugh shifted in his seat, lifted his empty tankard, and inspected its depths. Whatever could he say to her unforeseen declaration?

"What do you think we should do?" she asked. "I would like to think they have only our best interests in mind."

"I, too, hope their motives are entirely charitable. I suppose we could simply tell them we know of their plan and we will not succumb to their machinations."

Her smile took on a wry twist. "I wonder if outright opposition would not be futile, not to mention counterproductive. My father is a fair man, but stubborn. If I were to resist his plan, even if I were to reveal I have discovered his aim in bringing us to Weymouth, I fear he would dig in his heels and become absolutely unmovable. I am embarrassed to be the one who finds herself a piece of merchandise to be offered up to you. I almost told him how humiliating I found it to be dangled before you like a plum for the picking but I worry about his reaction."

"Mrs. Neville. I certainly do not consider you as any sort of merchandise. No, indeed." He pondered the situation for a few moments. Her smiling image as they talked about the pear flickered in his head, and he had to force himself back to the issue at hand. "You are right about them being stubborn. Like Sir Malcolm, my father is unlikely to give up easily once he has set his goal. Neither of them will be easily discouraged. They will only try harder, with more energy."

"I have somewhat resigned myself to assuming a thick-headed demeanor, as though I could not see through his efforts."

He tried to stop grinning. "Sorry, I suppose it is not really funny to be hoodwinked. The amusing part is to think of the conspiracy and how they see it."

"They could be the subjects of a Gillray cartoon."

He nodded. "Yes, they certainly could. I agree with you that we should not reveal our knowledge to our fathers, at least not yet. We will see what else they come up with and we will talk again."

"I predict we will have no shortage of opportunities for conversation." She gave a little laugh.

Hugh joined her laughter and reached over to pat her hand.

The door opened to Lord Carey and Sir Malcolm, each carrying two glasses of brandy. Hugh snatched his hand away from hers.

The earl spoke in a jovial tone. "We decided to bring these in to you. They say it is the finest from Cognac and aged carefully right here in the cellars."

Sir Malcolm gave a snort of glee. "No one knows how it

arrived down there, but they are happy to have it for special occasions."

An hour later, Hugh stretched out his long legs and rotated his ankles. His newest boots needed a bit more breaking in.

He pulled the lamp closer and picked up his book. Earlier he had marked a passage dealing with the cultivation of pear trees. Sir Malcolm's cook had promised to give him directions to the farm that grew the fine specimens she prized so highly.

Perhaps someday he would invite Mrs. Neville to accompany him to inspect the orchards. That would give their fathers a surge of satisfaction. Maybe they would lessen their attentions if he and Mrs. Neville spent time together on their own initiative.

For a moment he let himself consider Mrs. Neville's situation. Everyone said young and attractive widows were on the lookout for a husband, especially those who had a child. Of course, those were the same "everyones" who said all widowers with children were searching for a second wife to care for their offspring. That was most certainly not him.

The very last thing he wanted was to be married again. Mrs. Neville certainly had made clear her lack of interest in marriage. If she meant it.

In the years since he had lost Beatrice, he had rarely endured the company of females other than his nieces and his servants. He had forgotten how to behave, how to talk to a lady. Until he came to Weymouth, his life had been quiet and calm. He had his work; he had his daughter.

Emmy was growing very fast, almost beyond his capacity to understand. Poor little thing had never known her mother. Every time he looked at Emmy, he saw his wife's bright blue eyes, refreshing his guilt every day.

Emmaline. He worried about every little chill, every breeze; he feared she would be as fragile as his Beatrice had been. Dare he take her to the sandy beach to play as the Neville child had done? He simply did not know.

One thing was certain. His father had pulled the wool over his eyes. He could not help smiling again, even as he sat alone. Who would ever believe the Earl of Carey, a man renowned for his political insight and diplomatic acumen, would have come to the little seaside town of Weymouth to trap his son into acquiring a new wife?

He closed the book he had never begun to read. Though he would deny it vociferously, Hugh found the thought of spending more time with Mrs. Neville a pleasant prospect. And thoroughly alarming.

Three

"Good morning, Alastair. And it is a good morning indeed." Sir Malcolm settled himself on a bench in Stewart's Coffee House. "Is the brew tolerable?"

"Quite fine, my friend. Smells freshly roasted and ground, just the way Boodle's does it in London." Lord Carey took a sip and nodded. "Very close."

"Then I shall find it satisfying. Ah yes, and satisfied is what I feel after last evening. Did you see Hugh's hand on Dawn's when we came back into the room?"

"He was already moving away when I got there, but I could tell from his awkward look he had been up to something. Touching hands, you say?" Lord Carey wore a buoyant smile.

"That is all I saw. But I must say this is progress."

"So are we finished? Have we accomplished the match?"

Sir Malcolm shook his head. "I do not know if they will carry on themselves. I suppose we should continue to plan some activities. Dawn is trying the bathing machine this morning and then promised to take Teddy to play on the sand." He took a list from his waistcoat pocket. "I have compiled an inventory of local attractions we might visit. I suggest we begin with a drive to the village of Abbotsbury this afternoon."

Before Dawn set out that morning, her father had recounted his guidebook's story of King George's first experience with sea bathing. A brass band, hidden in a nearby bathing machine, waited for him to step into the water. At the exact moment, the band began to blare "God Save the King." Dawn wondered if the fanfare startled him as much as the shock of the cold water reputedly did.

A row of bathing machines stood near the water. The closer Dawn came, the more ridiculous the machines looked, like large wooden sheds on four huge wheels, as awkward as a Gypsy wagon trying to be a smart gig or a hearse pretending to be a curricle. In fact that was precisely what they looked like, huge funeral wagons. The horses dozed in the sun, in no hurry to draw the machines out into the water.

A robust female stood before the stairs up into a bathing machine, hands on hips and smiling broadly. "Here, missy," she called. "Ye kin take a plunge with Jenny. Best dipper in all Weymouth, if 'ee do say such meself. Many times dipped the old girls from the Lodge, too. No better 'n me herebouts."

Jenny's machine was decorated with a colorful sign that read "God Save the King," a little faded from the sun.

"This is my first time in the sea." Dawn admitted her lack of expertise before the dipper found out for herself.

"Then I tell ye what we do. While ye git inside and take off yer clothes, the mare pulls the machine into the water till it's purty deep, right up to the top step. Then ye come down the steps and into the sea. I hold ye so ye don't sink. 'Stand?"

Dawn nodded. "Yes, I do."

"When ye done, ye get back in, dry off, and put yer clothes back on. I bring the mare around to this end and we pull the whole thing back up to the beach. If ye don't have a bathing dress, there's some in there. Ready?"

Dawn nodded and climbed the steps. Inside the briny smell was stronger, but it was clean, though rather dark after the brightness of the sun. When her eyes adjusted, she followed Jenny's directions and draped herself in the voluminous cotton gown, tying the drawstring top in a double loop. The machine rocked and lurched along, bumping to a stop after a few minutes.

Jenny opened the door and beckoned to Dawn. "C'mon,

missy, don't be shy. It like to feel cold at first but I'll hold ye, won't let ye go."

The water now reached the highest step.

"All at once, now." Jenny pushed her a little and Dawn jumped forward and dropped into the sea. The chilly water took her breath away for an instant. She was grateful for Jenny's strong hands holding her, for the gown was heavy and drew her downward as it swirled around her legs.

"Don't thrash. Hold still. Let yerself feel the water."

As she grew accustomed to the temperature and sculled her hands a little, Dawn found the effect brisk and bracing. She was suspended in the water, her legs moving freely, the gown swirling around her in the currents created by her movements. She remembered how much she loved to swim in the pond as a child. How had she ever forgotten? How had she ever let herself be laced into a corset, her legs encased in stockings and her feet in tight shoes?

"Now don't ye go off, missy."

Jenny kept hold of the billowing skirt as Dawn rolled over on her back and looked up at the cloudless azure sky.

"Wonderful. I think I can keep myself up now, Jenny."

"I be watchin' every moment." Jenny let go and Dawn arched her back and lay back on the water, her hair swirling around her head. She felt invigorated and relaxed at the same time, floating free, yet protected.

She let her mind wander back to the previous evening, when she had told Lord Grayson of their fathers' scheming. Thinking about the look on his face when the truth struck him made her grin. He had not suspected what his father was up to.

His laughter had surprised her. He had previously seemed so sober, so melancholy. But when he realized how his father had duped him, his expression had leaped from the hint of a frown to a grin, though he said he seldom indulged in hilarity.

Lord Grayson was particularly appealing when he smiled. Handsome and charming, perhaps a man she could care for . . .

Dawn pinched herself and burst out of her reverie. What was she thinking?

At the conclusion of the session, she climbed back up the steps and into the machine. The wet and weighty gown pulled on her shoulders, dripping and heavy. She picked at the knot, but it was soaked and pulled tight. Jenny followed her into the tiny room.

"Here now, I have towels for ye to dry off. Get that wet thing off before ye get too cold."

She brushed Dawn's hands out of the way and efficiently unknotted the drawstring, pushed the garment off Dawn's shoulders and let it drop to the floor. Dawn wrapped herself in a large towel and Jenny wrapped another around her head to absorb the water in her hair.

"Now I get that mare rehitched." Jenny left Dawn to her dressing.

At first, Dawn shivered a little, but as she dried she felt energized, glad to have the warmth of her clothes, but elated to have bathed in the sea. She dried her hair as best she could with the towel, then pulled a comb through her long tresses. She was hardly aware of the movement of the machine until it drew to a halt on the beach.

When Jenny opened the door to let Dawn step down onto the sand, she blinked at the brightness.

"Thank you, Jenny. I will be back soon."

"Yer welcome, missy. Ye took to it real good."

"Oh, Mrs. Neville, your hair is all wet." Rosie was waiting on the hard-packed sand.

Dawn nodded. "I think we should go home and rinse it with clear water. It will be crusty with salt if I just dry it."

"You must go lie down now," Jenny said. "A bit o' bed rest, sleep if you can."

After the prescribed half hour of rest, Dawn was full of energy for her excursion to the strand with Teddy. Rosie followed along behind them with the basket and rugs and Teddy skipped and bounced in his eagerness to reach the sand. Dawn smiled fondly at the little fellow, whose pristine white shirt would soon be smeared with sand and saltwater.

Last evening, Dawn had neglected to mention that she, too,

had removed her stockings and held up her skirts to wade beside her son in the sea that morning. She wondered what Lord Grayson would think of such an improper act. Yet she noticed many other adults as well as the children on the sands had removed their footwear.

They spread the rugs near the waterline on sand recently smoothed by the outgoing tide. Teddy immediately unbuckled his shoes and danced into the shallow water. The sunlight was strong and Dawn tied her straw bonnet tightly beneath her chin, then wasted little time in joining her son's barefoot gambol. The breeze seemed as clean and fresh as a sunbeam.

For a moment she lost herself in the wash of the wavelets over the sensitive arches of her feet, wiggling her toes into the squishy sand. The coolness contrasted with the warmth of the dry sand where her feet slid down deep. Lord Grayson, always dressed in perfect turnout, would probably never take off his boots and stockings. What a wonderful experience he was missing.

Teddy collected handfuls of captivating objects, tiny shells and a few round pebbles, as smooth as glass. He found a white feather, a piece of narrow rope unraveled on either side of a knot. Several sticks bleached to near white by the sun and rubbed almost as smooth as the stones. A piece of cork from a fishing net float painted blue on one side.

Dawn sat down on the rug and spread the damp hem of her skirt to dry. Her thoughts drifted back to Lord Grayson and how nice he looked when he laughed. What did her father think would happen, that they would develop a romantic attachment for each other just because they lived side by side? That seemed like a flimsy basis for affection.

Yet she had to admit she found Lord Grayson quite attractive. If she had been looking for a husband, which she most assuredly was not, would he not be an ideal prospect? She gave herself a little internal slap. *Where do these ridiculous notions come from? You have no excuse to lose yourself in idle dreaming about romance, when Teddy's welfare is your only important concern.*

"It is time, Mrs. Neville." Rosie spoke from her rug placed well back from the water.

"Thank you. Come, Teddy, we must go home." For a moment Dawn wished she could stay here rather than jaunt off to some obscure village. But upsetting her father was impossible.

For the second day in a row, the tears welled into Teddy's eyes at the prospect of leaving the pile of sand he imaginatively called his castle.

"My darling, tomorrow we will build another one. And we will dig a moat." He sniffled as she brushed the sand off his feet and hers, and put on their stockings and shoes. Rosie shook the rugs and they headed for the house, Teddy lagging behind with a sulky look.

When they almost reached their doorstep, Lord Grayson called out a hello. Holding his daughter's hand, he walked toward them from the direction of the harbor, looking every bit the London Corinthian. Dawn felt as disheveled as a scullery maid who had just scoured a dozen grimy pots.

Emmy's face was flushed and frowning, probably from the warmth of her apparel. The little girl was decidedly overdressed, clad in a knitted jacket over her dress and a large brimmed bonnet. She looked hot and fussy and gave Teddy a withering frown, full of envy.

Teddy held out a pearly pink shell.

"Are you giving that to Miss Grayson, Teddy?"

He nodded.

Emmy stared at the shell as if it might bite. Very slowly she reached out and took it from Teddy, who buried his face in Dawn's skirt.

She turned it over in her fingers. "Look, Papa, how pretty."

"What do you say to Teddy, Emmaline?" Lord Grayson dropped to one knee beside his daughter.

"Thank you, Teddy."

"Was it not generous of Teddy to share his shells?"

Emmy nodded.

Dawn ruffled Teddy's curls. "You are a true gentleman."

He looked up at her with wide eyes. "I know," he said with honesty.

Dawn noticed Lord Grayson stifle his grin as he stood. "I will see you shortly," she said, feeling a stab of alarm that he might not come along.

He bowed. "I am looking forward to our excursion, Mrs. Neville."

"So am I." Dawn swallowed her unnecessary apprehension, took Teddy's hand, and went into the house. She found she anticipated their trip to Abbotsbury with pleasure after all. Apparently her insubordinate thoughts had strayed into forbidden territory, and she must now wipe out every trace of her silly and inappropriate imagination.

As they rode in the carriage toward Abbotsbury, Sir Malcolm read aloud sections of a guidebook he had purchased. "Stone cottages, built of rubble from the ruins of the ancient abbey, present a picturesque portrait of traditional English life. Once a stronghold of Saxon pirates and Viking invaders, the village began to prosper after the establishment of the abbey in the eleventh century . . ."

Hugh sat beside Mrs. Neville, any lingering doubts of his father's intentions banished from his mind. At the beginning of the journey, he had offered his front-facing seat in the open barouche to his father, then to Sir Malcolm, but they claimed to prefer the rear-facing seats, surely a fib in his father's case. Lord Carey had often remarked about the queasiness he experienced while sitting backward in a moving vehicle. Mrs. Neville had correctly analyzed the circumstances before he had the slightest suspicion. The entire situation made him feel a foolish gudgeon.

The barouche clattered along, and Sir Malcolm ran through a list of hamlets they would pass.

Hugh listened, but found more interest in viewing Mrs. Neville than the countryside. In her blue dress, she almost matched the color of Weymouth Bay. A cluster of daisies was tucked into the ribbon on her straw bonnet. She could not have looked more delectable if she tried.

The deuce! Here he was back at the argument he'd been carrying on with himself all last night and this morning. If they were going to pretend a mild attraction to placate their fathers, how should he proceed? He found Dawn Neville very pretty, amazingly easy to talk to. Three days into their stay and already he found her company appealing. And threatening to his efforts to observe his promises to himself.

Bosh and nonsense, he told himself. He was no longer in the market for any kind of love. Definitely not! Though if he were, she was very tempting. He tried to resume his attention to Sir Malcolm's commentary.

"The swannery was established in the fourteenth century . . ." Sir Malcolm held the book steady as the carriage lurched over the uneven road.

After the huge Tithe Barn came into view, the carriage soon rumbled onto a cobbled street. They passed thatched cottages that looked precisely as Sir Malcolm's book described them. Once they reached the Ilchester Arms, obviously a centuries-old coaching inn, Hugh helped Mrs. Neville step down from the carriage. She shook out her skirt and favored him with a slight smile. He offered her his arm and escorted her to a parlor inside.

While Lord Carey arranged for refreshments, Sir Malcolm settled in his chair and opened his book to read on.

Hugh quickly intervened. "I understand you partook of sea bathing this very morning, Mrs. Neville."

He did not miss the speaking glance exchanged by Sir Malcolm and his father.

She nodded. "I found the immersion quite pleasant, even exhilarating. I intend to go again, very soon. And I recommend the experience to all of you."

Hugh looked at his father. "What do you say? Are you willing?"

Lord Carey grimaced. "I wish I could say it has an appeal to me. But I can think only of the coldness of the water."

"Sir Malcolm?"

Dawn's father looked back and forth between Dawn and Hugh. "If you wish my companionship, I might be tempted."

Dawn patted his arm. "Father, I am sure you would enjoy it. At least once."

Their conversation was interrupted by the arrival of a man bearing glasses of ale and a pot of tea for Mrs. Neville.

Three-quarters of an hour later, after he read out loud another few paragraphs about the attractions of the village, Sir Malcolm suggested that Hugh accompany Dawn to St. Catherine's Chapel. "I doubt that Alastair and I are up to the climb. That hill sounds formidable. But you young people will find it rewarding, if only for the view, or so this scribe says."

Hugh finished his glass of ale. "I should like to try the ascent, if you are willing, Mrs. Neville."

Dawn nodded slightly and rose from her chair.

"I trust you two will finish that account of Abbotsbury's charms so that we can explore the village upon our return from the chapel."

Sir Malcolm agreed. "Capital. Alastair, shall we lay out a route to walk before we drive to the Swannery?"

Once outside, Hugh offered his arm to Mrs. Neville and with a smile she placed her hand in the crook of his elbow. They started off down the flagged stone pavement. Like him, she wore solid boots suitable for climbing.

"I see you are prepared for rough territory."

"Oh, yes, I wear my sturdiest boots if I think there is any opportunity for surveying some ruins or walking cross-country. I can rarely resist exploring."

They turned into Chapel Lane and started up the slope, soon leaving the cottages behind. The sun was dulled by a thin layer of clouds and a light breeze blew off the sea.

Hugh shortened his stride to match Mrs. Neville's. "I have given our fathers' scheme some thought."

"And your conclusion?"

"I agree with your view. Defiance would bring out their

natural obstinacy. If we pretend to play along, things will be much more tranquil."

"We can expect many outings such as today's."

"Indeed, they will contrive to bring us together frequently."

"And then send us off alone." She grinned and shook her head. "Just like this."

"And we will go willingly, just like this. They have The Scheme and we have our Counterscheme."

"That makes us sound as devious as our fathers."

He squeezed her hand. "Ah yes, deceit versus deceit."

They rounded a curve in the lane and saw the chapel far ahead, outlined against the sky.

Hugh stole a glance at Mrs. Neville. "You said you were reluctant to wed again, Mrs. Neville. Why is that? I am sorry to pry, but I am curious."

"You may think all widows are eager to find new husbands, but, I assure you, I am not one of those. Several of my friends married a second time, and things did not turn out as they expected."

"How so?"

"One of my friends had two children from her first marriage. After she wed for a second time, her husband sent the children away to school against her wishes. She saw them only a few times a year."

"Did she not object?"

"Perhaps not strenuously enough."

"That seems like unusually harsh behavior."

"Perhaps. Another friend had her daughter banished to the care of a governess who allowed the husband's older children to torment her."

"How could such a thing happen?" Surely these stories were exaggerated. Hugh could not imagine any man who cared for his wife being so callous.

"Her only recourse was to leave her daughter in the care of her grandmother."

"That might have been best for the child."

"But Lily's husband was so angry he did not allow her to visit home more than one hour a week."

"Abominable. I hope those are unusual cases."

Dawn shrugged. "No matter what, I will not allow such a thing to happen to me and to Teddy."

"Of course you would not allow it." Just the thought of his Emmy being mistreated made Hugh angry. No wonder Mrs. Neville was so cautious. He wished he could say something to ease her concerns.

The closer they came, the higher the hill looked. The well-worn path led them up the lower stretch in easy stages. When the climbing became steeper, Dawn let go of his arm and lifted her skirt to keep from stumbling.

She kept her eyes on the path. "I have often thought that the apparel we wear has a great deal to do with the hobbling of women's abilities. I can only hope we will never again succumb to the tyranny of gowns like our mothers and grandmothers wore."

"So you would be a fashion rebel?"

"Perhaps, though I enjoy a pretty dress much as the next woman. What I dislike most is the restriction of my movements."

"They say that women choose their raiment for the effect it might have on gentlemen."

"Then it is a wonder women wear anything at all."

He felt his jaw drop in surprise, then broke into laughter.

"I yield to your deductive ability, Mrs. Neville."

"Thank you. I suppose that few societal or commercial accomplishments would be achieved, however. At least until people became bored by constant proximity."

"You are quite the philosopher."

They continued on, clambering over some stony spots on the path.

"Will you allow your daughter to come with Teddy and me to the water's edge, Lord Grayson?"

"I am afraid she is much too fragile to endure so much wind. Do you not fear Teddy taking a cold?"

"He seems to thrive on being outdoors as much as possible. I truly believe that fresh air is good for children. For all of us, as a matter of fact."

"Emmy's nurse is very careful to dress her warmly."

"It is not my place to contradict your methods, but when I saw Emmy this morning, I thought she looked much too warm. Her face was flushed and she seemed distressed and ill at ease."

"I regret I have so little ability to foresee her needs. I am sure I rely on the nurse much too often."

She stepped around a craggy outcropping of rock and lifted herself up three rough steps. "I know little about raising children myself, other than to follow the example of my own parents, who gave me constant love and a bit of indulgence to my fancies. I believe children require the same things we all need—affection, companionship, and a very light hand when it comes to establishing rules or exacting punishment for violating them."

"Well said. But how does one accommodate a frail constitution?"

"If I might be so bold, Lord Grayson, Emmy looks like a strong child to me. You said her mother was tiny and delicate. Emmy seems to me to resemble you and your, ah, robust constitution." Her cheeks grew pinker either from the exertion or because she was embarrassed to call attention to his body, he knew not which. Whatever the cause, Hugh found her stunning and wished he could take her in his arms.

At last they reached the peak of the hill and stopped to catch their breaths. More than anything he wanted to feel her lips on his. He looked away quickly and scanned the horizon. In one direction lay the lagoon, the narrow strip of land called Chesil Beach, and the sweep of the sea beyond. In the opposite direction rolling hills led to a high ridge, an ancient route traveled by Celts, Romans, Saxons, and Normans. Every wave of new invaders had used the ridgeway, Sir Malcolm had read.

He allowed his gaze to return to Mrs. Neville.

She laid her hand on her chest and stared at the prospect. Hugh admired the sparkle in her eyes, the high color on her cheeks, the wind whipping her hair. She was all that was desirable in a woman. He cared little for the sweep of the sea before them or the rolling hills behind. The sight of her parted lips, the curve of her cheek, the arch of her throat, filled his eyes, his heart.

Hugh stepped to her side and took her hand.

She turned her head and smiled at him. "A magnificent view."

"Yes, magnificent." Hugh gazed at her, surprised his words had come out gravelly. He should not be thinking of kissing this delightful woman, but nothing else seemed right at this time and in this place.

He pulled her to him, slowly the last few inches, giving her time to retreat if she wished. Lightly he brushed her mouth with his. "Magnificent."

He had taken her by surprise, but in a moment her stiffness eased and she leaned into his next kiss. He tangled his fingers in her blowing hair and slid his other arm around her waist, holding her tightly.

When at last he released her, she sighed, then gave a little laugh. "Do you think our fathers can see this far? Are they toasting the success of The Scheme?"

Hugh paused, at a loss to explain himself. *Grayson, you nodcock, grab any reasonable excuse for your rashness!* "They may be toasting their success to . . . ah, their ability to get us alone together."

"Yes." She busied herself with the ties of her bonnet. "I suppose they are pleased with themselves. I guessed you were just . . . I thought you were . . . pretending?"

"Ah, yes, precisely. Pretending." *Nothing is further from the truth. Deception had nothing to do with my kiss, unless it is self-deception. . . .*

Was her smile a bit thinner now? Could he see a tiny frown mar her expression?

She turned to the building behind her. "I believe Father

said King Henry's men spared St. Catherine's when they destroyed the abbey because it served as a landmark for sailors."

Hugh drew a deep breath. He would have to be very careful not to repeat his wayward behavior. Perhaps it was not wise to follow their planned counterscheme. For he was certain he would be tempted to kiss her again.

Her hand enfolded in his arm felt so very right; his arms around her were a perfect fit. Her soft yet fervent response to his kiss had been too wonderful. All his good intentions blew away, his promises nothing more than ephemeral wisps of wind.

Four

Lord Carey stood at the edge of the esplanade, holding a spyglass to his eye and peering out at the sunny bay. "I cannot quite make out which of those boats is the one Hugh hired."

"Dawn is wearing a straw bonnet with a blue ribbon. Can you see her?" Sir Malcolm asked.

"Confound it, they bob up and down and it is hard to stay focused on any one of them. Do you want to have a try?"

Sir Malcolm grabbed the telescope and squinted. "There must be a hundred boats out there. This is a small one, you say?"

"Yes, a sailing skiff, with a mainsail and a jib."

Sir Malcolm shook his head and handed the glass back to Lord Carey. "I am afraid I would not have made much of a naval man."

"Nor I. Hugh has always enjoyed sailing with my brother and his cousins, but I prefer dry land."

"Dawn seems to have taken to the water, both bathing in it and skimming the surface."

Lord Carey closed the spyglass. "Yes. I have noticed how the two of them manage to get away from us now and then."

"They danced again at the assembly night before last. How long do you think it might take for Hugh to come up to scratch."

"He is damnably closemouthed. I dare not ask him."

"Nor can I ask Dawn." Sir Malcolm smacked his lips together. "I don't know, Alastair. In our day it seemed three weeks was long enough to fix an interest, would you not say so?"

"Indeed. All we can do is push them gently. If we come right out and show our cards, I imagine one or both of them would bolt. Then all our efforts would be in vain."

"God forbid. This matchmaking business is exhausting. I need a drink."

Hugh beckoned to Mrs. Neville to join him at the back of their box in the Theatre Royal. In the deep shadows he thought they might talk instead of spending another hour on a lamentably poor performance of a decidedly mediocre play.

Mrs. Neville, her silk skirt rustling, slid into the chair beside him, against the back wall. "I hope I did not wake Lord Carey."

Hugh looked at his father, whose regular deep breaths and chin drooping on his chest evidenced his judgment on the presentation. Sir Malcolm's head, too, had fallen to one side and rested against the drapery as he slumbered. "Both of them are employing their skills as theatrical critics."

Her voice was soft, barely above a whisper. "I quite agree with their evaluation. If it weren't for the farce yet to come, the theater would have emptied long ago."

"So it would. May I compliment you on your lovely gown?" She wore a simple dress of pale blue. He could not turn his gaze away from her low-cut neckline.

She fluttered her fan and looked away. "This is mother's favorite, and I was so hoping she would join us this evening."

"She is feeling poorly again?" He was relieved she turned the topic to something safe. If they began talking about themselves, he feared he would ignore his internal caution not to kiss her once more.

"Much better, actually. I suppose she is saving herself for the breakfast tomorrow."

"Then she is going out more?" In trying not to stare at her décolletage, he focused on the tiny strip of bare skin between the top of her glove and her sleeve. Just room enough for his lips to caress.

"Since she found the Vapour Baths, I believe she is improving. She is quite enjoying Weymouth, not that she will ever admit it. Mother adores all the gossip. Several ladies of her acquaintance call on Tuesdays and Fridays."

"Were these ladies she knew before?" He longed to roll down her long glove and tickle the inside of her elbow with his tongue.

"She has known Lady von Riche and Mrs. White for a long time. Mrs. Linden is the newest of the group."

"You must be very pleased she has found amiable associations here." One by one, as he freed her fingers from the glove, he would sample each one, just as he would taste a sweetmeat. But sweetmeats would never be so delicious.

"Yes, I can spend more time with Teddy and leave on our fathers' jaunts every afternoon with a clear conscience."

"You may have noticed I took your advice about Emmy's apparel. I told Nurse to dress her no more warmly than she herself dresses." When Mrs. Neville nodded, the diamonds in her ears sparkled in a ray of light, and his thoughts moved to how tenderly he would nibble at her ear.

"I think she will be a happier child if she is not overheated. But you have not brought her to the sand yet?"

"Emmy longs to look for shells, but I am reluctant to expose her to the sun and wind. Nurse says Emmy will develop freckles and coarsen her skin." And from her ear, he would let his lips drift across her cheek to her lovely mouth.

The smattering of applause that marked the conclusion of the play was loud enough to rouse Lord Carey and Sir Malcolm. Hugh and Mrs. Neville quickly moved back to their chairs at the front of the box.

"Ah," said Lord Carey, joining in the lukewarm clapping, "just the kind of theatrics I most admire. Entirely soporific."

Sir Malcolm blinked and rubbed his neck. "Better than a sleeping draft."

To Hugh, the advantage of having Mrs. Neville sitting in

the brighter light was that he could feast his eyes on her more easily. He glanced away. Once more, he had let his imagination run amuck. Once more, he had let his yearnings rule his reason. Once more he had let his desire challenge his resolve.

"Good afternoon, Mrs. Neville." Emmy executed a slightly shaky curtsy. She preceded Hugh into the drawing room, where Mrs. Neville rose to meet them.

Dawn took Emmy's hand. "Very nice, dearest. Try not to let your knee touch the floor."

Emmy dipped down again, and Dawn held her steady.

"Good afternoon, Mrs. Neville."

"Even better. Once more, very slowly, with your eyes on mine. Do not look down."

Emmy attempted the curtsy for the third time. "Good afternoon, Mrs. Neville."

Dawn drew the child into her arms. "I am proud of you, Emmy. You will be the most graceful young lady in London when your time comes."

Hugh watched the two of them with a full heart and a catch in his throat. They were just like mother and daughter, Dawn so patient and gentle, Emmy so respectful and compliant. This was the third time he and Emmy had come to take tea with Mrs. Neville. He was not sure where Teddy went during these little sessions, but he was grateful Dawn reserved her time just for Emmy. Since he had not succumbed to his daughter's entreaties to play in the sand, this gave her something special to do in which Teddy was not included.

Dawn curtsied deeply to him. "Good afternoon, Lord Grayson."

He bowed low. "Good afternoon, Mrs. Neville. Thank you for inviting Emmy and me." He was determined not to allow his thoughts to rove as they had a few nights ago at the theater.

Emmy looked from Mrs. Neville to him and back, her big blue eyes wide, her golden curls dancing.

"Now we may all sit and enjoy our tea. First I will be seated as the eldest lady present, then you, Emmy. And finally, the gentleman. Each of us observes the courtly conventions of behavior, and we can have a cheerful conversation. I understand you will accompany us to Dorchester tomorrow, Miss Grayson."

Hugh could tell Emmy was trying hard not to wiggle or to snatch one of the jelly tarts from the tray before Mrs. Neville.

"Yes. I so want to see the town." Emmy twisted her dress around her hand.

Mrs. Neville leaned over and whispered, "Be careful of your lovely lace trimming, my dear."

Emmy smoothed out the wrinkles, and accepted the teacup Mrs. Neville handed her. Hugh watched, ready to leap to the rescue if it began to tip.

Carefully, Emmy set it on the table beside her. She would be a stunner someday, he thought. Whatever would he do when he had to outfit her for routs or cope with a cocky young sprig come to call?

He caught Mrs. Neville's eye and smiled. She had never mentioned his kisses, never mentioned the afternoon at the chapel. Just for a moment he let himself think about how beautiful she looked . . . No! He was slipping his traces again.

Concentrate on her practical advice. . . . Last week, when he saw shelf after shelf of lovely dolls in a Dorchester toy shop, he wanted to buy one for Emmy. He had consulted Dawn, and she had suggested they bring the children to town, which was a very short carriage ride from Weymouth. Then Emmy could make her own choice.

Mrs. Neville admitted she almost bought one for herself, so beautiful were the faces on the German china dolls. Teddy, she was certain, would pick a sailing boat, one he could tow through the water with a string.

He had a sudden vision of Mrs. Neville holding one of the dolls in her arms . . . no, it was an infant, her infant. And the look she gave it was worthy of Leonardo or Raphael at their very best.

Hugh's teacup rattled on its saucer and he narrowly

avoided upsetting it. He had to stop this infernal daydreaming. While his daughter was getting such fine guidance in becoming a lady, this was not the time to stain his breeches or crack a cup. He intended to be just as good a pattern for Emmy as the exemplary Mrs. Neville.

Dawn stared at the pages of her novel but did not see the words. Instead she saw Lord Grayson, the warm smile he wore more often lately, his velvety dark eyes. Did they soften when he looked at her . . . or was she merely wishing . . .

Why, Dawn, what is the matter with you, dreaming about Hugh? Here was a rare moment of solitude when her mother, father, and son were all napping, and she was mired in fretting about her ambiguous views. No matter how often she reminded herself of the sad consequences of her friends' marriages, she could not help believing Hugh Grayson would be a different kind of husband. A thoughtful and considerate man. A man who respected her views on a variety of subjects. A man in whose arms she would love to lie.

She held the book a little closer, ruminating on memories of the many afternoons they had spent together. Especially the lovely kiss, the only one, weeks ago. Since then they had been alone many times, pushed into one circumstance after another by The Scheme and Counterscheme. But Hugh had not tried to kiss her again. . . .

She put the book aside and rested her head on the back of the chair. The weeks had passed quickly. She could hardly believe it was approaching the end of August. Lady Seymour had condescended to come downstairs at least a few times a week, received visitors, and even ventured a few steps along the esplanade. She had made several friends when she went to the Vapour Baths, ladies who apparently enjoyed their detailed exchanges about aches, pains, megrims, putrid throats, and catarrhs.

Teddy was as brown as a walnut from their daily visits to the beach. He reveled in his moments of glory, building, decorating, and destroying castles. His collection of beach objects grew daily; she and Rosie removed the most odiferous items each night after he was asleep.

On several sunny afternoons, Lord Grayson had hired a small sailing skiff, only large enough for two or three persons. He had taken her out to sail around the bay, once with Teddy, who longed to go again. Lord Grayson was fond of Teddy, and he was all that was amiable to her parents.

In the evening she and her father often dined with Lord Grayson and his father, sometimes with Lady Seymour in attendance. They often made up a table of whist if they did not go to the theater or the Assembly Rooms.

Yes, she and Lord Grayson were successfully carrying out their Counterscheme. Both of the fathers mistakenly thought the *tendre* between them was progressing. But the possible affection, she thought, was one-sided. Other than that one little kiss, Lord Grayson had shown no evidence of falling in love.

He was unfailingly polite and gallant, but often distant. For this she ought to be grateful, she supposed, for she still honored her pledge to make Teddy's welfare the primary focus of her life. No matter how much Lord Grayson seemed unlike those husbands who banished their stepchildren, could one ever be certain what might happen in the future?

Of course she did not love Hugh, Lord Grayson. How could she when he did not return her feelings?

Did she even know what love was? A few weeks of passion with Peter? Looking back, she thought it had been little more than infatuation. She seemed so much older now, so much more knowledgeable about the world and about how to get along with people.

Lord Grayson was simply a man not interested in finding a wife. At least, he was not interested in her as a prospect. He was very attractive, very eligible, a baron, heir to his father's titles and estates. Certainly other women must have tried to breach his defenses. He seemed to regard her as a friend, and as a partner in their project to foil their fathers' efforts. But he had never spoken about marriage or his feelings about finding a new wife.

Good, she told herself. *That makes us entirely the same, no interest in marrying again. None at all. Now, if she could make herself believe that lie . . .*

Dawn wandered through the bountiful garden just outside the Weymouth town limits. Tall stalks of Brussels sprouts and leafy rows of heavily laden beans were carefully tied to wire supports. At the edge of the garden, lovely multihued flowers nodded in a faint breeze. Mrs. Kendall assured her that Mr. Taylor grew the very finest fruits and vegetables in his spacious orchard and garden, and from the looks of the neat ranks of plants, Dawn was convinced their cook was correct.

She and Lord Grayson had arrived half an hour ago in his handsome curricle drawn by a fine pair of bays. Mr. Taylor and Lord Grayson had immediately gone to the brick wall where a dozen carefully espaliered pear trees grew. Though she was interested in the techniques that ensured the abundant production of the fruit, the explanation soon grew too specialized. Maximum sun and warmth she understood. Protection from blight and insects she appreciated. She even grasped the need for proper soil conditions and cross-pollination. But when they discussed the merits of double grafting and seasonal pruning, she gave up on the discussion.

She watched how animated Hugh became as he talked to Mr. Taylor about the pear trees. Oh how she wished he felt the same when he was with her.

Ninny! In truth, unless she sprouted leaves and grew roots, Lord Grayson would never look at her with the glow his eyes held now.

She tried to banish such thoughts from her head. She was not interested in him as anything more than a friend. Nothing more than that.

She stared at a row of feathery carrot tops. The beauty of the garden with its softly buzzing bees and delightful scents belied the hours of arduous labor it must have required. Until she came to know Lord Grayson, she'd had no idea how interesting the plants were, how many new varieties came from abroad, how carefully they were cultivated.

"Mrs. Neville." Lord Grayson signaled to her from the other side of the garden and she returned his wave.

When she reached his side, he was beaming.

"Mr. Taylor has agreed to give me some cuttings to graft on my root stock. And I have agreed to bring him some of my latest pepper plants from the tropics."

"I am glad to see our visit has been worthwhile."

"Indeed, I am most pleased."

Dawn dropped a little curtsy to Mr. Taylor as they made their good-byes. "You have a fine garden, the richest I have ever seen."

"Thank 'ee, miss."

Lord Grayson wore a wide grin as he drove his pair toward Weymouth. "It was worth having the team sent here, even if this is the only day I use them."

"Why did you send for them?"

"Do you want the honest answer, or the reason I gave my father?"

Dawn tightened the bow holding her bonnet. "I always advocate honesty."

"Except when it comes to The Counterscheme?"

"Oh, my, I hope we are not being dishonest."

"Merely dissembling, I would say. I told my father I was concerned that the horses would not get their proper exercise."

"And that was not true?"

"A half-truth. I want the team and curricle to explore the countryside."

"Then you are tired of our adventures in the barouche?"

"I believe Sir Malcolm is running out of pages in his guidebook. But in truth, I thought you and I might do some exploring without our fathers. You said you enjoyed exploring."

"Oh, I see." She felt a peculiar quickening of her heartbeat.

He swung the team into a narrow lane leading to a grove of

trees. "But today I thought we simply might stop and enjoy some of Mr. Taylor's ripe fruit before we go back to town."

He brought the curricle to a halt in the shade, climbed down, tied the team, and assisted her to the ground. They spread a blanket near an ancient oak.

Dawn seated herself and closed her parasol. "How did you know about this place?" She fairly trembled at the thought of being so isolated, so quiet, so far from company.

"I asked Mr. Taylor if he knew of a spot where we could sit and enjoy his produce. He said he sometimes brought his boys here to climb this tree."

Dawn looked up into the branches. It would have been an excellent exploit, but she dared not ruin her white gown.

Lord Grayson chuckled. "I know what you are thinking. Perhaps we should come back when we are wearing old clothes."

"I would like that very much." Dawn took the pear and bit into it.

"Ambrosia, I believe." Lord Grayson's eyes closed as he tasted the fruit.

For a few moments, they savored their pears in silence.

"I need to build a south-facing wall of dark-colored brick to maximize protection and warmth." He seemed to be thinking aloud. "It will take at least three years to bring newly grafted trees into partial production."

"In the life of this old oak, that is a mere moment." She took the last bite and chewed slowly, her gaze fixed on the low hanging limbs.

He lifted her hand and brought it to his lips, whether to kiss her fingers or lick the juice, she did not know. What she did know was that her heart jumped inside her and she suddenly felt as light as one of the leaves that drifted to the ground beside them. When his mouth found hers, she could taste the pears in his kisses, deliciously sweet, impossibly stirring.

She wished he would continue his caresses for the rest of the afternoon. Until dark. Until . . .

Five

Lord Carey pursed his lips and stared at the flickering candles in the Card Room chandelier. "Hugh drove Dawn to a farm yesterday. Did she say anything about the visit?"

Sir Malcolm blew a cloud of smoke toward the ceiling. "Said the orchard had fine pears. Talked about some vegetables. Said nothing about Hugh. Don't know what possesses those two."

"If they were up to anything corky, she would not tell you, would she?"

"S'pose not."

"I suspect he had his team sent in order to get her away from us. He said his team needed exercise. Though the stable boys at Caringhurst take them out every day. Do you suppose he is bored with our company?" He gave a bark of laughter.

"If I were that young jackanapes, I would use that curricle to whisk Dawn off, all right, but not to some fruit farm." Sir Malcolm heaved a great sigh. "It don't matter. He needn't put up with us much longer. I have almost finished my list of sights."

"We'd better dredge up some new idea. We have several weeks left in Weymouth before I need to get home to tend to the harvest."

"As do I. I say, Alastair, what we need is for that curricle to break down and strand them."

Lord Carey thumped his fist on the table, causing several players to look up from their hands and shush him. "True! But how do we arrange it?"

* * *

Dawn lifted Teddy out of the sailing skiff and into Rosie's arms. "What do you say to Lord Grayson?"

"Thank you for taking me in your boat, Lord Grayson."

"You are most welcome, Teddy. It is my pleasure."

Dawn watched Rosie lead her son away and waved as they reached the turn.

Lord Grayson coiled the mainsheet. "Are you ready to cast off, Mrs. Neville?"

"Yes. I am most eager to see the Isle of Portland." She shoved the skiff away from the dock and sat back as the sails filled and Lord Grayson steered into the harbor. They had to tack once to clear the breakwater, then breezed into Weymouth Bay.

A perfect day, Dawn thought. The late afternoon sun glinted off the ripples as they headed for the Isle of Portland, across several miles of open water. Dawn leaned back in the boat and turned her face upward, glorying in the warmth of the sun and the cool of the breezes. What a pity it was so dreadful for the complexion. But just for a few moments, she would let herself bask in nature's gifts.

She wished she had the courage to ask Lord Grayson what meaning she should assign to those kisses yesterday. After their return home, they spent the evening sitting beside one another in the most proper way imaginable at the performance of a string orchestra. Neither of them referred to the afternoon in any way, beyond extolling the garden's botanical superiority.

A man's kiss was often a prelude to further intimacy. Or so she had been told. But she and Lord Grayson were united in their opposition to The Scheme. So why did he wish to kiss her?

"Your son is a clever little fellow."

She readjusted her bonnet and tucked her hair back. "Do you think I would disagree? I find him exceedingly intelligent, as I am sure all mothers see their children."

"Do you have a tutor for him?"

"Not yet. I have taught him a few of his numbers, and he is able to read simple texts."

"You are an admirable mother as well as an instructor."

"Thank you." Dawn could not help thinking again that Lord Grayson would never be one of those men who would send a stepchild to the attics in the sole care of an unsympathetic governess. But what idle speculation. They had agreed to their Counterscheme as an escape from their fathers' plans, not as a step on the way to the altar.

He trimmed the sails. "I enjoy children who are curious and questioning."

"You spend more time with Emmy than most fathers do."

"She, too, is a bright child. But . . ." His voice faded.

"But you are still unwilling to let her come with us to play in the sand?"

He heaved a deep sigh. "I may be overprotective, but I worry about her. Emmaline was very angry Teddy could go sailing this afternoon and she could not."

"You know what my thoughts are on that subject."

"Yes. I am trying to allow her more leeway, but it is not easy."

At least he thought about the possibility. Perhaps eventually he would give in.

They sailed closer and closer to the cliffs until the cold, stark walls of stone loomed above them. Their boat seemed very tiny compared to the great mass of limestone that formed the Isle of Portland. She looked up at its enormous height in awe, then back at the town and the beach, so very small in the distance.

"There is one little cove here someplace where we might land later. On the map, it is near the ruins of Rufus Castle."

"I brought a basket with some chicken, some bread, some pears."

He laughed. "I, too, brought food and a bottle of wine." They sailed along the base of the cliff, staying away from the rocks and watching the birds that nested in tiny caves on the face of the cliff.

"How do they find the little ledges and slits in the stone?" Dawn pondered the question as she squinted up at the side of the cliff. "Is it just my imagination or can I hear some baby birds calling from their nests."

"I can not see any, but I somehow feel sure they are there."

"Father read me several passages from his guidebook. There are many quarries on the Isle from which they cut great blocks of limestone. St. Paul's Cathedral in London is built of Portland stone."

He nodded. "Now that you mention it, I do believe I once heard that. I read in the local newspaper that the stone is esteemed far and wide. They mentioned a shipment leaving last week, bound for Italy."

They lingered in the shadow of the cliffs, pointing the skiff into the wind and letting the sails luff and watching the water swirl around the craggy rocks at the base. She could spend hours here, in companionable silence.

Both turned to watch a distant pair of fishing boats sail round the point, coming in from the sea at sundown to head for Weymouth harbor. They were only a bit larger than the skiff in which Dawn and Hugh sailed, running low in the water as if well loaded.

"Looks like they have been successful. Plenty of fish in the market." Dawn decided to go there herself and choose their dinner.

"Looks like they are racing. Watch the fellow in blue."

Even from quite a long distance away, she could see him crouching at the tiller. He waved at his companion and she could imagine hearing his shout of challenge. The other boat seemed to have a fresher wind and gained on the first. The racers fairly flew over the water while their own boat bobbed in the lee of the Isle.

Flocks of birds circled and flew back toward the cliff. Dawn watched the birds disappear into the rock, apparently returning to their invisible nests. "It looks like they are flying headfirst into the stone, one after another."

Suddenly the sky darkened. She looked up to see a huge black cloud covering the sun. At the same moment, a gust of wind shook the boat and whipped the sail back and forth with ferocity.

"Hold on, Mrs. Neville. I fear I have not been watching the sky. Looks like a storm is blowing up."

Instead of sun-tipped wavelets on deep blue, the water turned to an angry gray, the waves deepening and rocking the little boat. Dawn had to grip tightly to keep her seat.

As Hugh hauled in the sail from its wild swinging, a gust caught it and sent them careening to the side, almost tipping into the water. In moments, it was dark as night.

Lord Grayson's face was tense as he eased the sheet and let the little boat swing off the wind, only to have another gust swirl around them from behind.

The velocity grew and the blasts whistled ominously in the rigging. She began to feel truly nervous.

"What can I do to help?" Dawn had to shout over the scream of the wind.

"Just hold on. I'm going to head straight for the harbor."

But once they got away from the Isle and into the open bay, the ever-increasing wind howled and tossed the boat like a toy. The rain slashed at them, sharp as needles. With every wave the boat rose high and crashed downward into the trough before the next high ridge of water.

Dawn's bonnet had blown away without her even realizing it was gone. She was soaked in minutes and she clung desperately to the side of the deck. Her pulse raced and her breath came in short gasps.

Lord Grayson's voice was tense. "Dawn, sit down on the bottom of the boat and hold on. Take the tiller and try to hold her as steady as you can. I am going to reef the sail."

Steady? Dawn wanted to laugh out loud. As they topped another huge wave and plunged downward, she had no idea what "steady" could mean. They were being tossed about like the pieces of cork Teddy threw into the surf.

Through the darkness and pouring rain, she tried to make out Lord Grayson's efforts with the sail. They rose up and crashed down again and again, and she was unable to tell the rain from the flying spray of the sea. If he were swept away, she would have no idea what to do.

The wind howled and whipped at the billowing sail. He shouted something as he grasped the spar and struggled with the canvas. The sail came a third of the way down the mast.

It seemed like an hour passed before he finished and took the tiller from her.

He leaned close and spoke into her ear again. "I made the sail smaller. We need it to keep the boat upright, but the less area of surface, the better. Are you very frightened?"

"I cannot see where we are heading."

"Nor can I. The wind will carry us eastward and, I hope, eventually to shore. All we can do now is hold on and stay aboard. If we should tip over, we must stay with the skiff."

Dawn knew her swimming skills in a placid lake long ago meant next to nothing in this wicked sea. Heart pounding, she clutched the deck. She was confident Lord Grayson could handle the boat, if only she could hang on.

Oh, Teddy, my darling boy. Will I ever see you again?

Six

Sir Malcolm was drenched though the walk from his house to Lord Carey's had taken only two or three minutes.

He removed his cloak and draped it over a bench. "Don't care much for the looks of that wind. Are Hugh and Dawn here?"

Lord Carey wore a worried frown. "I was hoping you had come over to tell me they were at your place."

"Then, they must have gotten caught at the dock and are waiting out the storm."

"Yes, that must be where they are."

Both men paused and looked at each other with concern in their eyes.

"We both are thinking the same thing. That storm blew up out of nowhere." Lord Carey led the way to his drawing room.

"We had better organize a search."

"I have a very bad feeling about this."

Dawn's fingers cramped from her death grip on the gunnels, her sopping wet hair plastered against her face. After hours of paralyzing fear, could she feel the wind decreasing? She prayed it was not a trick of the storm.

The boat lessened its pitching enough that she felt safe in letting go with one hand to push her hair out of her eyes. In the inky blackness, the sea still tossed them, yet the wind's ferocity diminished little by little. The boat did not plunge from one trough into another with the same speed.

When she turned to look at Lord Grayson, she could barely see his dim outline. "Is it letting up?" She still had to shout to be heard.

"So it seems. Are you all right?"

"Yes. I think so." At the moment, Dawn felt too numb to assess her bruises or stiff joints. "Do you have any idea where we are?"

"We have been carried far eastward. I hope we will be able to see well enough to keep from hitting any rocks before we reach the shore."

"You have managed to steer the skiff through this storm, Hugh. I have every confidence you can land it too."

"I hope your faith is not misplaced. I regret I let my attention get distracted from the weather changes. A sailor always has to keep one eye on the sky."

"I did not notice the clouds either. We were busy watching the birds."

Even during this little exchange they could let their voices return to a more normal level, so fast was the storm abating.

She felt as though the whole night must have passed, but it could not have been more than a few hours since the rains came. Their sunset cruise had become a midnight adventure. Her father and mother would be frantic. And Lord Carey.

Lord Grayson seemed to guess her thoughts. "I am sure our fathers will launch a search party the minute the storm is over."

"Until it is light again, I doubt anyone can do much except worry." She shivered in her wet clothing. How she longed for Jenny's towels, about a dozen of them, to share with Hugh.

In another few moments, a half moon appeared, sliding out from behind the storm clouds. The heavy waves continued but when they finally spotted the shore, Lord Grayson was able to trim the sail and approach a narrow beach beneath a high chalk cliff.

The closer they came, the more the shore seemed entirely deserted. No fires or lanterns burned through the darkness. Dawn strained to find an identifiable landmark.

Lord Grayson brought the skiff about and sailed in closer. "We blew for miles. I do not recognize anything."

"Nor do I. Is it better to continue to sail or go in and beach the skiff?" Dawn could not help shivering.

"I think we need to go ashore. We are both soaked through and the breeze is cold. It looks like there is a strip of sand along the cliff."

"Oh, I hope so."

"I cannot tell if there are any underwater rocks ahead."

Dawn held her breath as they eased toward the shore.

"Can you let down the sail now?" Lord Grayson asked.

"I shall try." On aching legs, Dawn crawled to the mast, unwrapped the line from around the hook, and slowly lowered the sail.

Lord Grayson took off his saturated boots and his wet jacket. "I am going to go overboard and pull us in."

"What can I do?"

"Not a thing now. Hang on when we go through the breakers."

She gritted her teeth when he jumped over the side. If he disappeared . . .

"It is shallow enough to stand here," he said, going to the bow of the skiff and pulling it slowly toward the sand.

When the bottom scraped, Dawn hiked up her dripping skirt and climbed out into the shallows. Together they hauled the skiff higher, to the dry sand.

Lord Grayson gave a sigh of relief. "Looks like the tide does not reach this far. We should be safe here."

"Yes. Safe."

He took her in his arms and hugged her tight. Dawn closed her eyes and reveled in the feel of her feet on the unmoving ground, of his arms around her. For a moment or two, she did not feel the weight of her dripping skirt around her limbs or the chill of her rain-soaked hair. She felt only thankfulness to be back on land and in the peace of his embrace.

When at last he let her go, Lord Grayson peered down the beach. "I wonder if there are any cottages around here."

"Is there a way to climb the bluff?"

"I will look around."

Dawn strained to see him against the cliff, but a cloud had drifted over the moon and she lost sight of him. She turned back to the boat and lifted her bundle from the place she had wedged it under the deck. The oiled cloth was wet, but appeared to have protected the contents.

She felt like shouting in glee when she found the chicken and bread none the worse for their bumpy ride.

In a few moments, Lord Grayson returned. "I do not see a way we could climb up. But I found a few pieces of dry wood we might ignite if my tinderbox is not wet."

"The food is all right, so we shall not starve before we are rescued."

They headed to the shelter at the base of the cliff, where the overhang had saved a few feet of grass and sand from the rain. Dawn took off her soaking boots and tried to wring out her skirt. Her mouth felt parched, her face crusted with a layer of salt.

Lord Grayson's tinderbox was dry enough to ignite a few tufts of grass and some twigs, which he fanned into a small fire. Dawn sought more dry wood and placed it near the fire.

In the firelight she could see Lord Grayson frown and shake his head. "We could be within a quarter mile of someone's cottage, but there is no way we could know. Or even walk far enough to look. Our boots are ruined."

Dawn shrugged. "So we should sit down near the fire and eat the chicken." She spread out the oilcloth, turning the wet side to the sand. She groaned as she lowered herself to the ground. Not only had she begun to feel her bruises, but the wet fabric of her dress clung to her like a coating of ice, clammy against her legs and arms, even her torso.

"There is a bottle of claret in the bottom of the boat."

He returned in a moment with the bottle and a sharp stone, pounded the cork into the bottle and handed it to Dawn. "The wine has been sadly shaken up, but it is better than nothing."

She put the bottle to her lips and tipped it up until her

mouth filled with wine. Never had a liquid tasted better. She handed the bottle to Lord Grayson and, famished, bit into a piece of chicken.

When they had finished most of the meat and half the bread, Dawn wrapped the remainder in a tight bundle again. "We will need this in the morning."

Lord Grayson nodded. "Yes. I suppose we will. Are you warm enough?"

"I feel the heat of the fire, but my dress is wet and cold."

"If you remove it, I will hang it on some sticks and we can dry it in a shorter time."

She considered this for only a moment before she slipped it over her head and handed the sodden mass to Lord Grayson. She hoped her chemise and petticoat were covering enough in this dim light.

He suspended her dress, his shirt and jacket on twisted branches of driftwood, close enough to catch the heat of the flames.

Dawn undid her hair and ran her fingers through it, fluffing out the strands. Where it had been tightly wound, it was only partially soaked. She tried to avert her eyes from the sight of a bare-chested Lord Grayson, but it was difficult. The light might be faint, but she could not help noticing his broad shoulders and how his wet hair reflected the fire. She wished he would wrap his arms around her again.

He sat down beside her. "I want you to know how sorry I am that you were submitted to such a frightening experience."

She rearranged her petticoat. "You handled the boat with great skill."

"Nonsense. The first skill a sailor needs is the sense to watch and judge the weather. I should have seen that storm coming and gone ashore long before it arrived. Or at least we should have followed those fishing boats. Once the wind came up, we had no hope of finding that cove. That we have been swept here is entirely my fault."

"Now it is my turn to say nonsense. I did not see the sky

darkening either. I believe it blew up so quickly we never would have made it in."

His forehead was furrowed and his eyes deep in shadow. "I should not have taken such a small boat out so very far. I apologize."

"The ones who deserve our apologies are my parents and your father. Certainly they are fearing the worst right now."

"Right. They will have a few more hours of worry, too. I have no idea what time it is. I left my timepiece behind."

"In the midst of the storm, I thought time stood still. But I am sure it was only a few hours."

He nodded. "I suppose it is no more than midnight. Quite a few hours until the sun begins to rise. I fear your reputation will be ruined."

"Pooh. As far as anyone in Weymouth is concerned I am entirely a nobody. I have no status to lose here."

"What about Lady Pearl? When she hears about our misadventure, she will luxuriate in describing it to all her correspondents. The story will spread. I can just see her writing, 'So very unfortunate they had to spend the entire night marooned on a beach. Alone. One wonders what the poor things did to keep warm.' "

Dawn giggled. She knew exactly what people would think. "Easy answer. They built a fire."

She went to her skirt and rearranged its folds, shivering a little in her damp petticoat.

"You *are* cold," he said. "I wish I had something to wrap around your shoulders."

"Your coat and shirt are as wet as my things."

"I do not suppose you would like to sit closer to me?"

"And make the gossips correct in their assumptions? Why not?"

She moved nearer, barely touching but able to feel the warmth of his body. He put his arm around her and pulled her tight against his side. His flesh was warm, and she felt a spreading glow deep within, a glow that had nothing to do with the fire.

"Dawn, I endangered your life in that boat . . ."

"It is equally true that you saved my life in that boat."

He gave a rueful smile. "It is a strange man who puts a friend in danger so that he can rescue her. And when I think of Teddy . . ."

She closed her eyes and leaned her head on his shoulder. "I think I am too tired to argue this point."

"So am I."

For several minutes they sat without saying anything, staring into the fire, listening to the wash of the waves a few yards away.

After a while, he left and collected a few more sticks of wood to add to the fire. He adjusted his shirt and her dress, turning the dampest places toward the fire.

When he sat down again, he sounded very tired. "Things are getting drier."

"I am very glad. We would not want our fathers to find us unclothed."

"Indeed not."

He stretched out and pulled her down next to him. "Mrs. Neville, there is a bit of the sun's warmth left in the sand."

She whispered into the dark, "Would you not prefer to call me Dawn?"

"A lovely name."

She snuggled against him and pressed her cheek to his skin. "My mother wished to name me Aurora, but father thought that sounded pretentious."

"I prefer Dawn, one perfect syllable. Just like Hugh, as I hope you will continue to address me."

"I did not think you noticed." With her ear to his chest, she heard the beat of his heart.

"I noticed and I liked it very much." He moved his arm around her and caressed her hair. "Dawn, can you tell me about your husband?"

She sighed, for a moment unwilling to cast back into her memories when the present was so very pleasing. "Poor Peter. My father did not want me to marry him. But I defied him.

We married in haste and had so short a time together. We were very foolish young hotheads who should have obeyed our parents. But then I would never have had Teddy."

"So you married before you even had a Season in London?"

"Yes. Sometimes I wonder if he had come home, if we would have stayed in love. I should not give voice to those doubts, I suppose. I adored Peter, but I knew he liked to gamble and think up wild pranks with his fellow lieutenants."

"You lost him before your love had a chance to mature, just the way I lost Beatrice."

"I believe that love can grow, but ours never had the opportunity. What was she like?"

"Very young and beautiful. An angel. When she died, I blamed myself."

"And dedicated your life to mourning her?"

"When you put it so bluntly, it sounds foolish, the actions of a melodramatic child."

He touched her cheek and she turned toward him, her eyes staring up into his.

With a little moan, he pressed his lips against her forehead.

He spoke again, his voice so soft she had to listen carefully. "I wanted children. She was so very young . . ."

Deep down in her heart she felt the pain in his tone. "Hugh, Beatrice did what all women long to do. You cannot blame yourself. Living with such guilt is hardly living at all. Beatrice would not have wanted you to suffer too."

He knew she was correct. His guilt was a crutch to keep him from facing life again. But he could not find the words to tell her.

Exhaustion silenced their conversation for long periods of time. Dozing, talking, an occasional kiss, tending the fire. Slowly the night wore on.

When, at last, the sky began to lighten, Hugh stared into the flickering flames. He had never opened his heart to anyone as he had to Dawn. Perhaps it was because they had shared such a terrifying experience. Perhaps because he trusted her with his very soul. Or because he had been lonely too long.

When it was light enough, he scanned the sea. The waters were calm and a light breeze blew. No sign of last night's turbulence remained.

Their clothes were dry though stiff with salt. Hugh handed Dawn her gown and averted his eyes while she dressed. He put on his shirt, shook out his coat, and tossed it into the boat.

"Are you up to sailing back? I think we can easily launch the boat from the beach."

Dawn looked at him in surprise. "But you will get all wet again."

He shrugged. "These clothes are hopelessly ruined, so it makes no difference if they get soaked again."

"Then by all means, let us get back to Weymouth as soon as we can."

They had sailed a considerable distance toward the west when they saw two boats headed their way. Hugh felt certain the rescue parties were aboard.

Seven

Lord Carey folded his handkerchief and placed it in his pocket. "Thank heavens they are safe."

Sir Malcolm still had a tremble in his voice. "When we talked about that curricle breaking down, I never considered what could happen."

"Nor did I. But at least they are safe now and sleeping. I presume Hugh will do the honorable thing. From what he said, he is eager to make Dawn his wife."

"He said that outright or in so many words?" Sir Malcolm's voice now had an edge to it.

"Ah, I would say it was in so many words, if you know what I mean."

"Not good enough, Alastair, not good enough by half. M' wife has palpitations and spasms. She cannot speak without a fit of hysterics."

"Do not worry. Hugh will do the honorable thing."

"If he don't, I have a horse pistol around someplace."

Dawn reclined on a couch, her book forgotten, as she fretted about Hugh. He had disappeared yesterday, just hours after they returned from their night on the beach. If Lord Carey knew where his son had gone, he did not say. Dawn was well aware of her father's opinion that Hugh should marry her posthaste. Had he fled to escape those marriage plans?

Lady Seymour had been entirely overwrought and collapsed with agony over Dawn's disappearance. Upon her return, she'd recited long descriptions of her agony, her travail, her panicky spasms, excruciatingly painful in their abundance. Dawn, almost falling over in her exhaustion, simply excused herself and walked out well before her mother was finished. She had fallen into bed without even a bath and slept almost all day.

She tried to resume her usual life this morning, but she had little appetite for it. And less as the day wore on. She heaved a sigh, opened her novel, and looked for the place she had left off.

Before she found it, her father knocked on the door. "Are you awake?"

"Come in, Father."

"My dear, we are all gratified at your safe return from the storm. Lord Carey and I have discussed the situation and we agree you and Hugh must be married without delay."

"What do you mean?"

"Exactly that, my dear. Certainly you are not surprised. You two not only endured a harrowing adventure, you were alone all night together. We should announce the betrothal immediately."

"This is what Hugh wants?"

"He is a man of honor and propriety. He would not see you ruined."

"Ruined? I could have been drowned and you worry about my social reputation? How very silly, Father. I will not marry Lord Grayson unless he wishes to have me because he loves me, not because he pities me."

"You have no idea . . ."

"Yes, I have exactly the idea. I have grown to care for Hugh, that I admit. Your plan worked in that regard, Father."

"Hummpfff. What plan?"

"The time has come to confess. We saw through your efforts with Lord Carey long ago. You two have been playing matchmaker."

"I would not put it exactly that way, Dawn."

"Why not? You cannot deny it. But that is not the point. I

may have developed a very soft spot in my heart for Hugh, but I am not sure he feels the same way."

"His father says Hugh will marry you."

"That is not good enough. I will not fall in with a plan to bamboozle him into marrying me. How very lowering, Father. I am offended. Anyway, he has left Weymouth. What does that say about his eagerness to make me his wife?"

"I believe he has gone on business."

"Perhaps. But if he was so anxious for a betrothal, would you not think he might discuss the matter with me before he went?"

Sir Malcolm rubbed his chin. "Hard to tell what his schedule might involve."

"Oh, Father, how could you be so silly?"

"I do not think he is the kind of man to go back on an obligation."

"Obligation! That is the very last straw. I refuse to be an obligation. Why would I want to be the wife of a man who is forced by an accident into marrying me? The very notion is insulting, ridiculous, and impossible."

"Now you look here, Dawn. No daughter of mine will spend the night with a man and not marry him. No, indeed."

"As you well know, we were much too frightened, too wet, and too cold for anything untoward to have happened. And no one but you, Mother, and Lord Carey know of the incident. And those fishermen. They are hardly likely to spread gossip at tea parties with Lady Pearl."

"You have heard me."

Suddenly Dawn laughed. "Father, this is really quite amusing. The only other time we had a strong disagreement, I wanted to get married and you tried to stop me."

Sir Malcolm gave a snort of laughter. "And I was bested that time too. My dear, I am ready for my dinner and through with arguing. We shall see what the next few days bring."

Dawn preceded her father into the dining room, where the table was set for two, Lady Seymour being too overwrought to come down. Dawn may have won this battle, but what a

Pyrrhic victory it was. When her heart said she could make Hugh love her someday, why did her head make her hesitate?

Hugh rolled over in his bed and stared at the ceiling. It was light outside though he had no idea of the time, morning or afternoon, or how long he had slept. His body was a mass of aches and bruises. He had managed only a few hours of sleep in Weymouth after the ordeal on the boat; then after a short conversation with his father, he had ridden home to Caringhurst, straight through, stopping only to change his horse and eat one meal. Every muscle cried out at its misuse. But it was his brain that troubled him even more.

His heart told him he loved Dawn Neville. His body told him he wanted her. His brain told him he had challenged the guiding principle of his life for the last four years. He had pledged to himself to honor Beatrice's memory forever. He was thoroughly confused.

What Dawn had told him about her marriage made sense to him. She loved Peter and loved the memory of their time together. She was a realist; Peter would never come back, never be part of her life and her child's life. She was a practical woman; she had Teddy to raise.

Was it time for him to be realistic and practical? Was it time to reinterpret his pledge to the memory of Beatrice? Dawn said he should not live with guilt. Weighed down by guilt, he lived only half a life.

Dawn would be a wonderful mother to Emmy. And he would do his best to be a good father to Teddy.

Hugh gingerly rolled out of bed and called for his bath. "Hot and steaming," he told the footman.

"Yes, my lord." Barton hurried off, trying hard to make up the deficiency in the operation of the house when the butler was not in residence.

When he was soaking in the hot water, he tried once more to sort out his thoughts. Like Peter Neville, his Beatrice would never return. Like Peter and Dawn's, the love he and

Beatrice had shared would never change, frozen always as it had been in those few months.

Dawn had argued that Beatrice would be very unhappy if she thought Hugh was so grief-stricken and isolated that he could not go on, could never again know happiness or satisfaction or love. "Think if the situation were reversed," she had explained. "Would you have wanted Beatrice to mourn you for the rest of her lifetime or would you have wanted her to find happiness again, to give your child a happy life? You would not have wanted her to become a recluse, hidden away from society."

He was not entirely convinced, but then he had been thinking in a completely different mode for nearly four years.

"More hot water, my lord." Barton came into the room with two brimming cans.

"Thank you, it has grown a bit too cool."

He stood to let Barton pour the hot water into the tub. Sitting again, he leaned back and sank to his chin in the newly warmed water, feeling the heat penetrate each of his sore muscles.

He was caught in a dilemma of his own making. First, he had made some foolish vows when Beatrice died. In the passion of his grief, he had vowed to mourn her for the rest of his life, to honor their love by giving up all interest in other women. It was an oath he had never revealed to anyone. Now, after four years, he was ready to begin a new life.

At last he climbed out of the water, dried off, and dressed, knotting his cravat in a simple bow. As the twilight grew into night, he walked to the church and sat in the graveyard near Beatrice's marker. How simple it had seemed when she died. When her life ended, his had, too.

He propped his elbows on his knees and his chin on his hands. He should not have left Weymouth without telling Dawn he would return. She would wonder what was wrong.

He stared at the gravestone, ran his hand over the carving of Beatrice's name. But it was Dawn's face he saw, Dawn holding Emmy in her arms and hugging her. Dawn who said she had confidence in him even at the height of the storm. Dawn whose lips he could almost feel on his, whose fingers he wanted to entwine in his. It was Dawn who lived in his heart.

As he sat in the gathering darkness, he saw his life moving forward. He had pear tree cuttings to plant. He had a daughter to raise. He had a woman to love.

He looked again at Beatrice's grave. He would never stop loving her, just as Dawn would never stop loving Peter Neville. But his future was with Emmy and with Dawn and Teddy.

He strode back to the house. "Barton, I am famished. Would you have them send up whatever they can find in the larder? And break out a bottle of Father's best burgundy, if you please. Bring a glass for yourself and join me in a toast."

"A toast, milord?"

"I am getting married, Barton." He could not stop the grin that spread across his face.

Barton's face crinkled in a wide smile. "Indeed, milord. Very good indeed."

Dawn sat on the beach rug, her dress already wet around the hem, her feet bare. Teddy piled up the sand into an ever-growing castle. He was adorable, completely lost in his imaginary world, oblivious to her heartache.

She pushed a lock of hair off her forehead with the back of her sandy hand. Her bonnet kept slipping down her back. It was warm here in the sun, even though she had long ago removed her shoes and stockings. She felt her hair coming unpinned in the breeze. Her dress, the old one she had turned over entirely to beachwear, was wrinkled, damp and limp. But Teddy was thrilled with his fort decorated with rows of pearly shell shards. He placed a stick at the top with a scrap of string serving as a flag.

She scooped up a handful of wet sand to shore up a drying wall that threatened to slip down into the moat.

"Dawn. Teddy." Hugh's voice sounded from a distance.

Teddy hopped to his feet, the fort forgotten in an instant.

Dawn watched him approach, walking just beyond the reach of the wavelets, holding Emmy's hand. The thump of her heart increased with his every step. In all her worry about the future, she had forgotten how very handsome he was.

She stood.

He grabbed her in a big hug and picked up Teddy, too, oblivious of their wet clothes and sandy hands.

"I brought Emmy to the water. She has been wanting to come for weeks." He spoke to Dawn, his gaze capturing hers. The children chattered at him but his eyes never wavered. He knelt down and set Emmy and Teddy down. "I am back to stay, Dawn."

She nodded, her throat unaccountably thick and tears welling into her eyes.

He turned to the fort. "Now what is this, a new defense against the enemy?"

Dawn did not say a word while Teddy told them of the strength and power of the mighty walls. By the time he finished, Hugh's fine gray breeches and white lawn shirt were wet and wrinkled, the high polish of his Hessians scuffed with sand.

"This may seem a rather unromantic setting, my dear, but I cannot suppress my question another moment. Is there room in your affections for Emmy and me? Will you consent to becoming my wife?"

Dawn's heart leaped, but she needed to be sure. "I want to know if this is truly what you want, Hugh, not the result of The Scheme by our fathers or your honorable attempt to salvage my reputation."

"I love you, Dawn. My motivation is just that simple. And I solemnly promise never to slight Teddy, for I love him as if he were my own."

"Then I accept. I have fallen in love with you. Just as our fathers wanted when they brought us together, we fell into their snare."

Hugh looked at the children searching the sand for more shells. He set the basket and rug down on the sand and took Dawn in his arms. His kiss was the sweetest she had ever known.

On the terrace, Lord Carey lowered the spyglass and handed it to Sir Malcolm. "Take a look. They are kissing, over and over again."

Sir Malcolm squinted into the glass and let out a bark of laughter. "Alastair, I would say that you and I excel at this matchmaking business. We could rival some of those old ladies at Almack's any day."

Lord Carey poked his elbow into Sir Malcolm's ribs. "Yes, I agree. But if you go to Almack's, you go alone!"

"Heaven forbid! I am finished with woman's work."

Chuckling in satisfaction, they retired to the library for a glass of port.

A FATHER'S LOVE

Donna Simpson

One

"I think it is hideous that Mr. Martindale is trying to foist that child off on polite society instead of decently placing him with some family that can be paid to decently take care of it in their own home." Mrs. Greavely, the acknowledged village gossip, spoke emphatically, her jowls waggling as a string of spittle flew and hit the candelabra.

Lady Theresa counted the times the woman used "decently" in her speech and added it to the five hundred and thirty-four times she had used it previously through the long years of their acquaintance. The total was now five hundred and thirty-six. She also made a note to herself to have the cleaning staff pay special attention to the spit-daubed candelabra.

Miss Tratt stared, her gooseberry eyes wide with disapproval. "The poor creature is all about in the head, it's true, but why does that mean he must be sent away from his family?"

Lady Theresa would have been impressed by the spinster's compassion had she not believed that the woman was only taking the hitherto unknown Mr. Martindale's side—that mysterious gentleman who had just rented Meadowlark Mansion two miles distant from the village of St. Mark-on-Locke—because Mrs. Greavely had come down against him. Miss Tratt had a long-standing grievance with Mrs. Greavely, and always took whatever side was opposed to her.

The three ladies, among whom at thirty-one Lady Theresa was the youngest by a couple of decades at least, sat in a parlor of the "big" house, as the villagers called Lady Theresa's home, a lovely old mansion set in the Somersetshire countryside. No one called it Galatea's Garden House, the awkward if picturesque name her mother had many years before tried to make stick.

"What is wrong with the child?" Lady Theresa asked, frowning down at the piece of needlework she was doing, a tapestry that would eventually be framed and raffled at the harvest festival in September. It was supposed to be a lovely little conceit on the house name, a depiction of Galatea hiding in the willows, but it was not working out. She was a competent needlewoman, but this may have been a bit ambitious for her abilities. It looked lopsided.

Mrs. Greavely leaned forward over her own needlework, a surprisingly lush silk-embroidered seascape, expertly rendered, and said, "He is demented, of course. He makes odd noises, doesn't talk at all otherwise, and he has his own odd . . . well, for want of a better word, "nurseman," a strong-armed fellow who looks like he used to be a seaman, to keep the idiot. Who knows what the boy is capable of! We could all be murdered in our beds!"

There was a bloodthirsty gleam in the woman's eyes. Miss Tratt looked like she wanted to ask for more details, but her enmity with the other woman prevented her.

Theresa tossed aside her work. "I think we have done enough for one day, haven't we, ladies?" Disgusted and unsettled by the ghoulish Mrs. Greavely, she wanted to be alone for a while.

Disconcerted but obedient to the foremost lady in the village, the two women trotted off in separate directions.

It was a gorgeous June day, but Theresa restlessly roamed the house, the long dark halls, and the ancient chapel, the small turret rooms and the new wing, now three hundred years old and only "new" in appellation.

What was wrong with her? She had no patience anymore, and could not bear the tittle-tattle of gossip, nor the small-minded backbiting inevitable in a closed village society. In past years, she had been able to balance the spiteful venom of the few against the genuine goodness of most of the citizens of St. Mark-on-Locke.

From an upstairs window she spied her papa coming back from the horse stables and descended the stairs, accosting him in the hallway and twining her long arms around his rotund waist, leaning her head on his shoulder. He patted her arm, made uneasy, she could tell, by her outpouring of affection.

"What is it, poppet? The old biddies got you down again? I saw them leave, or I wouldn't have come in yet."

"It's not them. I'm bored and restless."

"You're always like that when we come back from the London Season, all that gaiety, balls, and so forth. Takes a while to settle into the village routine, my dear."

"It's not just that, Papa." A sudden daring scheme entered her head. "Would it be horribly impolite if I were to call on the new resident of Meadowlark Mansion before you do?"

"Yes, though I needn't have answered, for you know the answer as well as I; a lady must never call first on a stranger, before her father or husband or brother, etcetera. So I must assume that was a rhetorical question and you mean to be guided by your own wishes anyway, as you usually do."

She straightened up as they walked into the great hall. Lighter of heart, she headed to the stairs leading to the family chambers in the west turret, throwing one mischievous glance over her shoulder. "How well you know me, Father. I do like to stir things up, don't I? It is why no one wants to marry me despite my many charms."

"Now you are talking nonsense."

A half hour later Lady Theresa Barclay, daughter of the Earl of Leighton and preeminent lady of St. Mark, as the village was affectionately shortened to, mounted her gig with the aid of a strong groom and, placing her capacious basket on the seat beside her, clicked at the gray mare. Down the long, twisting avenue from the mansion and through the high, wrought-iron gates, and then out onto the rutted country lane, she guided her rig expertly. It was past St. Barnabas Day but not quite Midsummer Day, and summer, though days away in truth, was verdant upon the countryside.

The day was sunny, perfect for a drive between the high green hedgerows. Swallows swooped and dipped in the shade. Beyond the hedgerows the heavy perfume of clover, driving the bees to distraction, hung over the grassy fields. A willow warbler trilled a warning to his brood as Theresa drove the gig past, and robins chattered uneasily.

At first she took it all in, but after a while became lost in thought. In the normal course of the drive she would stop many times to gather self-heal and great burnet, or to see if the wild roses had begun to bloom yet. Coming home from London after the Season was always thus, getting back in touch with nature and her home county of Somersetshire after the hustle and bustle and tumult of London. Usually she felt a little at odds for a while, for she loved London, with all of its distractions and entertainment. But she had, for only the second time, not enjoyed London this spring, and she was still puzzling out why. The previous time was because she had been jilted; the pain and humiliation had made that year a black memory to her.

But this year had just seemed flat and boring, though she met the same people and did the same things. Perhaps that was the problem. Her whole life had become predictable.

It was time to disturb the surface and see what happened.

She approached Meadowlark Mansion with some trepidation. How did one go about breaching polite behavior without alienating people?

As it happened, she really didn't need to worry about that.

The Honorable Mr. James Martindale was mired in muck, his second-best boots cleaving to the mud; anytime he tried to move, he got sucked in deeper. How had this happened? He was raised on the land and ought to be familiar with its pitfalls, but he had never tried farming before. The third son of an impoverished viscount, he had made his fortune in the city, in the trade so despised by his peers. Now, with a comfortable fortune, he had rented Meadowlark Manor with a view to buying it if it suited him and his family.

He was trying to think of a way to get out of the muck without losing his boots when he heard the high, keening wail that meant trouble, and then Angelica's screams started.

Wasting no more time, he abandoned his boots, waded out of the mud as quickly as possible—not that quick, since he was five feet from the edge of the boggy quagmire—and ran. He stumbled, his stockings sliding down from the weight of the odorous muck and he half hopped, half ran, shedding them as he went and praying that nothing too terrible was going on. That was the problem. The screams could mean nothing or something dire; there was never a way to tell ahead of time.

But one thing was for sure, Bobby Turner was going to be sacked. This was the third time in as many weeks the screams had erupted.

He circled the stable and started up the long path to the mansion, but halted abruptly, his mucky feet soggily coated with grit from the track.

Jacob, squealing like a banshee, was under the arm of a determined-looking young woman who was marching, with her wriggling burden, across the grass toward the house. Angelica, leaping and flailing her arms, screamed at the lady, while she, in turn, shouted back in his daughter's face with equal vehemence.

"What in God's name is going on here?" he yelled, striding forward, forgetting what a sorry sight he made as he approached the melee. "Angelica, shut up. Jacob, it is all right, young fellow, and, whoever *you* are," he said to the woman, "let go of my son!"

"Oh," she said, letting Jacob slide down to his feet. "Do you not care then that he was about to step into the stew pond fully dressed, hatted, coated, and wearing boots?"

Two

"What do you mean?" he exclaimed. "Angelica, what is she talking about?"

The girl sullenly scuffed one foot over the other and glowered at her brother. "Jacob wouldn't listen to me," she said. "I told him he couldn't, but he was going to walk right in. He saw a fish, I think."

James put one hand over his heart and closed his eyes, muttering a prayer of gratitude. "Where is Mr. Turner?" he bellowed, when he again opened his eyes. He then gazed in consternation at the elegant young woman in front of him. "I must beg your pardon, but since I haven't the foggiest notion who you are . . . and yet it appears I must be grateful to you."

She put out her hand. "I am the Earl of Leighton's daughter, Theresa Barclay. I am committing the unpardonable social sin of calling before a proper introduction, but in light of circumstances, I do believe you will forgive me."

Dazed, he took her hand and shook it. Her tone was so matter-of-fact she might be speaking of the offer of a receipt for pickled quince rather than just saving his son from almost certain death. He turned from the young woman and knelt by Jacob, who was staring with fixed attention at a spot on the ground.

"Jacob," he said gently, forcing his son to look directly into his eyes. "You must remember to obey Angelica when Mr. Turner isn't about." As usual, he had no idea if he was being understood, though he had suspected for some time that Jacob understood far more than he was given credit for. "Where is Mr. Turner?" he asked Angelica.

"Cook insisted that he was to mend the clothesline in the laundry yard."

"But I specifically told her never to take him away from his duties with Jacob!"

"But she says that you don't understand a thing, and that household duties won't wait, and anyway Jacob is perfectly able to mind without some great lout of a fellow watching over him."

James sighed and shrugged, glancing up at the lady who stood, politely, hands folded in front of her. He saw her gig in the lane, and stood, saying, "We won't keep you, Lady Theresa, if you're on your way somewhere?"

"I was on my way here, so it does not signify how I arrive at the house. If you'll have your groom drive my gig to the stable and care for my horse, I'll walk up to the house with you, as I'm sure you need someone to mind Jacob while you, uh . . . " She looked down at his muddy bare feet and legs and colored delicately, averting her gaze. "While you wash up."

Lord preserve him from a managing female, he thought. But she was right.

The house was as lovely as she remembered, Theresa noticed as she was guided to a parlor by Angelica, but sadly in need of a good clean. There was dust on the lintels and picture frames, and the windows were smudgy. Jacob pressed his nose to the window, kneeling on a chair and gazing out on the sloping front terrace down to the stew pond.

Theresa took a deep breath and examined Angelica. Other than the sullen expression, the girl was quite pretty. If only she did not grimace so. "Are you happy, Miss Martindale?"

The girl blinked once and glared. "What?"

"Do not say 'what'; say 'I beg your pardon?' "

Jacob turned and sat on the upholstered chair and watched them.

"You have no right to tell me how to speak."

"That is absolutely correct," Theresa said, lowering herself onto a hard, upright chair and folding her gloved hands on her lap.

The girl waited, but Theresa had nothing to add.

"Aren't you going to tell me that I ought to listen anyway, just because you're a grown-up lady?"

"No." Theresa maintained her position, her gaze unwavering.

Silence.

"Then why should I do what you say?"

"Because politeness is self-serving."

"What?"

"Is your hearing impaired?"

"No. I meant, what do you mean?"

"Then that's what you should say." Theresa glanced around the room and smiled at Jacob. He was solemn and unblinking.

"What do you mean that politeness is self-serving? Shouldn't one be polite just because society says one must?"

"If you like. But also, being polite will serve you better in the long run. When you're polite people like you, and then they'll do things for you and give you things." The ladies of the village would be horrified if they could hear her feeding this impressionable girl such dangerous philosophy. However, it got the child's attention.

Angelica blinked, opened her mouth to say something, and then shut it again.

"I didn't know Mr. Martindale had a daughter as well as a son," Theresa said.

"I may as well not exist," Angelica grumbled, throwing herself into another chair. "It's only Jacob that is important."

Theresa turned her gaze from admiring the room. If she were mistress she would change only the color, from blue to yellow, to take advantage of the glorious sunshine that flooded it. She stared at Angelica. "Do you really think that or do you say it because you are pouting and feeling sorry for yourself?"

"You're very rude!"

"So are you." She smiled brightly. "There, isn't that nice? We have something in common."

"I'm not rude, I'm a child."

"How old are you?"

"Twelve."

"That's practically grown up! Certainly old enough to know how to be courteous. Haven't you been to school?"

"No, I had a governess, but she left because she wanted to go back to London. She didn't like it here."

"I often feel that way, but then when I'm in London I'm convinced that only home will do."

Angelica stared at her. Jacob slipped off his chair and came to stand at her knee. His gaze was unblinking still, but now his eyes were focused and alert. He reached out and touched her bonnet, which had a small bird perched on the brim. He began to pull it off, but Theresa put up one hand and gently said, "No, Jacob. You may not pull it off."

"He can't understand you," Angelica said.

"Oh? Can he hear me?" Theresa looked directly into Jacob's eyes. "Can you hear me, Master Martindale?"

"Nobody's sure. He . . . he was like this when he was born. My mama died giving birth to him."

Theresa wondered if the girl was saying that trying to shock her, for no one in polite society should have spoken of such things; but no, Theresa did not think the intent was to shock. Angelica had a hurt look in her blue eyes.

"Do you remember your mother?" Theresa was aware that Jacob had gotten even closer, his eyes fixed on her face. He touched her cheek once and then slipped away from her, wandering the room, touching things and humming, it sounded like.

"Just as a smell, or a feeling." The girl blinked and frowned, fighting back a tear that was threatening to trickle from her left eye. She sniffed. "I was only four when . . . when it happened. Governess said Mama was too old and that she had no business marrying a young man like my father and having children. It wasn't natural and she was being punished for trying to move up the . . . the 'social ladder' improperly."

Theresa felt a slow anger burn. She would have to make sure that governess never came back, poisoning a child's mind against her poor dead mother that way! "That is incorrect and your governess was a very ignorant woman."

"Ah, here you all are," Mr. Martindale said, striding into the room. He rubbed his hands together and clapped them once. "Shall we have some tea, and maybe some biscuits? Lady Theresa, would you do us the honor of taking a late tea with us? I know it isn't the done thing to eat this time of day, nor to take tea with company, but I'm so very grateful to you for rescuing Jacob, and I'm also famished. Where *is* Jacob?"

Theresa said, "He's behind the large blue sofa trying to pretend that he has escaped us."

Angelica's eyes widened and she raced around the sofa and dragged him out by his shirt collar. "How did you know that? I didn't notice him hiding there."

"If you have ever hunted a chiffchaff in a copse of alders," Theresa said, "you would know that one keeps one's eyes and wits sharp if one is to see where their nests are. I have excellent vision and hearing. A boy is a great deal larger than a chiffchaff." She was disconcerted to see Mr. Martindale trying to suppress a smile. What was there to smile over?

"Shall we have tea in the summerhouse?" he said. "I've just had it cleaned out; it should be lovely this time of day. Cooler."

"Certainly," Theresa said, standing. "I will follow you, sir."

What an odd young lady she was, James thought, watching her demonstrating to Angelica the proper way to pour tea. In his few conversations with local people, before they learned of Jacob's problems and began to shun him, he had heard that she was a spinster and over thirty. She had lovely skin, clear gray eyes, and a regal manner, but no one would mistake her for a dewy twenty-year-old. And she was not pretty, more handsome, getting perilously close to plain, and unmarried with a good reputation. He would have to be careful.

Dora, a maidservant, brought a covered tray out to the summerhouse, and laid it down on the rustic table, curtsied, and took the cover off to reveal sandwiches: tongue and cress and goose liver paté. There were also some delicate petits fours and seed cake.

James stared at the tray. He hadn't ordered this, nor had he had any idea they even had such delicacies in the house. It wasn't that he couldn't afford it; he could afford whatever they wanted, for he had made his fortune and was very well off indeed. But where had it come from?

"Lady Theresa, you seem to have brought good fortune with you, for I have never had such a lovely repast."

"On our way out she snuck into the kitchen and told Cook that you worked very hard and deserved a proper luncheon and that if she didn't provide it she ought to be ashamed," Angelica said, calmly taking a tongue sandwich and biting into it with relish.

A *very* managing female. And one looking for a husband? She was calmly handing Jacob a cress sandwich and telling him where cress came from and how to gather it. The boy appeared to be listening, though he opened the sandwich and picked out the green herb and ate it first, and then the bread and butter. Lady Theresa seemed not the slightest perturbed.

"So, have you managed to browbeat my nurseman, Bobby Turner yet?" he asked wryly, taking a paté sandwich and finding it very good. "Where on earth did Cook get this marvelous paté? And why haven't we had this before?" he mumbled, chewing.

"I brought the tongue, paté, and cress. The tongue is from the village butcher—if you bully him adequately, he will have Mrs. Butcher cook it to perfection for you—the paté my own cook makes, and the cress I gathered myself."

He swallowed. She was watching him with a measuring look as he ate, and he just knew she was measuring him for a wedding suit. The unmitigated gall, he thought, trying to work up some anger toward her. She was ordering his life already, and he barely knew her. The anger was being stifled by his mouth watering over the wonderful taste of the paté. He hadn't realized how hungry he was.

Angelica, her gaze flicking back and forth between her father and their guest, said, "Papa, Lady Theresa says she can show us where to get the cress."

"Hmm. How did you manage to intimidate my cook into compliance in such a short time?"

"I'm an excellent manager of staff," she said, with a challenging tilt to her head.

"I'm a good manager myself, Lady Theresa," he said. "I have successfully built my business into one of the best cloth manufacturers in England. My mills now produce cloth for military garments, flags, upholstery, drapery fabric . . ."

"I haven't disparaged your own abilities, sir, by claiming my own." She said that with a lift to her eyebrows. "I'm sure you are a very good manager . . . of your manufactory."

It went without saying that his vaunted abilities had not stopped his son from almost tumbling into the stew pond. He huffed a bit into his collar, but Jacob was watching him—still eating cress but watching his father, too—and so he couldn't retort as he would like to.

"I intend to engage a housekeeper. The last one left a week ago. She was not suitable anyway." She had quit over a dispute with the cook, in truth, but he hadn't liked her. She had a mean spirit and said despicable things about Jacob when she thought he could not hear.

"So you have, in three weeks, lost a governess and a housekeeper. Female staff are troublesome to you."

"Females of all sort are troublesome to me," he said, and then regretted his rash words almost immediately, despite their honesty. He had been plagued, in London, with the attentions of numerous ladies looking for husbands. That his newly minted fortune came from trade didn't wholly exclude him, since, as the younger son of a viscount, he had aristocratic ties to counter the ugly business in which he was engaged.

He was about to frame a reply to delicately say as much, but she surprised him by standing.

"Mr. Martindale, would you consent to allowing your daughter to come for a ride about the countryside with me? I'm on my way to visit a gentleman who has broken his leg and lives alone. I am taking him some of the same tongue we have been enjoying, and I would very much like Miss Martindale's company."

"I suppose . . . if Angelica would like to go, but I doubt if she would."

"I would like to go, Papa. May I?"

He shrugged. "I shall order your gig, my lady."

Three

Her abrupt departure was motivated by nothing less than Mr. Martindale's transparency. In her gig, ribbons firmly in her hands, Theresa glanced over at the girl beside her.

"Your father thinks I'm after him to marry," she said, clicking at her mare.

The girl giggled. "Do you think so? How big-headed of him."

"I suppose he has been approached by his share of ladies with matrimony in mind," Theresa said grimly. "I just don't happen to be one of them."

"Why not?"

"I don't wish to marry."

"Ever?"

The country lane narrowed, and a cart drawn by two heavy, plodding draft horses trundled down the middle. Theresa pulled to the left and waited for it to pass.

"One should never say never," she said. "That's like saying that you never intend to die. I suppose there is a certain inevitability about some things. Someday, perhaps when I am old, I may want companionship. Until then . . ." She glanced away.

With unnerving perspicacity, Angelica said, "Did a gentleman disappoint you?"

Ruefully, Theresa glanced sideways at the girl. That was an episode in her past to which no one who knew her referred. "I suppose I cannot draw back now from the rather informal conversation we engage in."

"At least you talk to me," she said glumly. "Papa only ever shouts or warns or commands. 'Angelica, watch out for Jacob.' 'Angelica, I told you to mind your brother.' It is fatiguing."

Theresa shouted out loud with laughter and her horse snorted in sympathy and danced a little. She settled the mare down and said, "The way you said that was so very much like a London belle. 'It is fatiguing.' You will do very well with the languid air so many ladies must cultivate."

"What is it like? London and the Season," Angelica said, eyes shining.

"London?" She was not unhappy that the subject of her disappointment at the hands of a gentleman had been dropped, and so she gladly engaged in conversation about the London Season, a topic she well knew. "London during the Season is the most fascinating place I would *never* want to live. There's so much to do and see, and there is no better place to shop. I must show you some watered silk I brought back with me this Season. It is exquisite!"

Angelica sighed happily. "I would love above all things to see it. May I come to your house?"

"Of course. We'll ask your father when I return you. But first, on to Mr. Gudge's home. Poor old curmudgeon; he broke his leg some time ago, so you mustn't mind his bad temper." She clicked, and her mare smartened her pace.

They spent the rest of their afternoon talking about London. Angelica was a sharp and avid listener, and the day passed quickly. Theresa couldn't remember when she had enjoyed her charity visits so very much.

". . . and I would like two pounds of the tongue sent to Meadowlark Mansion," Theresa said the next morning to Butcher. "If Mrs. Butcher would be so kind as to prepare it the way she does for me, I would be much obliged."

No one stared to see such an eminent lady in the butcher's shop, for everyone had known Lady Theresa since long before her hair was put up, and everyone knew that she never left anything that was important to her to anyone else to do. And food rated high on her list of important things. Even while her mother was alive—and that lady had only died five years before—Lady Theresa had had the handling of all the household duties, for Lady Leighton had been an ethereal beauty with not one whit of common sense. Her husband and daughter adored her for that, and protected her from any unpleasantness such as having to tell Cook what to make for dinner. And so Theresa had grown up as a "managing woman."

When the village ladies waiting for her to finish her order with Butcher heard the destination of the two pounds of tongue, there was general dismay, a feeling that hung in the air like an odor of which no one would speak. Theresa frowned at the sly side glances Mrs. Greavely traded with Dame Alice, wife of a local knight.

Theresa had always been fond of Dame Alice, and so was surprised to see her in agreement with Mrs. Greavely on any front. She had thought better of the woman than that. As Theresa left the butcher shop, the two women followed, and the bolder of the two, Mrs. Greavely, accosted her.

"Lady Theresa, are we to understand you have not only been to that house, but are now taking over the management of it?"

Pausing only momentarily, Theresa answered, "Not at all." She began to walk again, sparing a glance up at the sodden skies. A distant rumble of thunder rolled across the heavens and she quickened her pace, only to find the two women accompanying her.

Dame Alice, trotting with them like a fat cob after racehorses, said between puffs of breath, "I'm sure Mr. Martindale is very nice, but that son of his . . . there's a reason God made him like that. Evil somewhere in that family!"

Theresa stopped abruptly and swiveled to look at the two women. "Is that what this is all about? Some superstitious nonsense about that poor boy? I'm ashamed of you both!"

Dame Alice looked away nervously, but Mrs. Greavely bridled and said, "Lady Theresa, there are things in this world that we don't understand. There's a reason no decent family keeps their idiots. It is unlucky and against God. And Mrs. Hurst says the boy soured milk just by looking at it! She also said that . . ."

Theresa felt her face redden. Thunder rumbled ominously. "Mrs. Hurst—may I assume she was the recently dismissed housekeeper for Mr. Martindale?—is an ignorant old besom! Jacob is a dear, sweet child who . . ."

Mrs. Greavely thrust her face close to Theresa's. "Lady Theresa, mark my words, that boy is cursed. And so is the whole family because that man has not the sense to put his boy decently away somewhere with someone to look after him. And it is the girl who will suffer for it. I hear she is wild and incorrigible already. Mrs. Hurst says she has an unnatural affinity for the stable boys. Was seen talking to them, just as bold as may be. No good will come of it, mark my words. And we do not want that kind of folk buying Meadowlark!"

So this was the kind of filth that was being spewed about the Martindales. And the poor man just wanted somewhere to "decently" raise his children! And Angelica! What chance would she have if she was labeled early as a wanton? It was despicable, and Theresa was just about to open her mouth to say as much when the heavens opened and sheets of rain lashed down, driven by a sudden wind. She said a hasty farewell and raced on to the drapers.

She had much to think of and much more to plan. This contemptible meanness in her village couldn't go unchallenged, but she must tread carefully and summon every bit of knowledge of village ways to her aid. She would not let Jacob and Angelica suffer. In that moment Mr. Martindale's handsome smile rose to mind. He would make a valuable addition to their village social circle if he decided to buy Meadowlark mansion, and she must see that he had every reason to stay.

For the children's sake.

Four

James Martindale sat, head in his hands, thinking that perhaps he ought to move back to London and forget his plan of becoming a country gentleman. What was he doing, after all? He had just had to sack another servant, one of the grooms, for saying that Jacob gave a mare the evil eye and caused it to miscarry its foal. It was not that country folk were more ignorant than town folk—he had heard his share of rude comments from those in his town household, and from supposedly more enlightened people, too—but in London he had weeded out the empty-headed among his staff.

However, only a few of his London people had come with him, and a country house required a larger staff. How was he ever to do here what he had done in London? He did not know whether he could face that long process again, nor subject Jacob and Angelica to the turmoil during it.

Perhaps he should let go of this house and return to London.

"Mr. Martindale," said Dora, curtsying at the doorway of the library. "Lady Theresa to see you, sir. Said it was private, she did." The girl's eyes were wide with curiosity.

He could not complain about a little inquisitiveness though, since the girl was excellent with Jacob. In fact, he was considering hiring her as nursemaid since Jacob seemed more amenable to her gentle coaxing than Bobby Turner's bluff commands. "Send her in," he said. "And leave the door open!" He had no wish to accidentally compromise Lady Theresa into marriage, especially when he was unsure of her motives in visiting so frequently and befriending Angelica. He had met his share of curiosity seekers, as well as marriage-minded young ladies. He would satisfy neither.

"Mr. Martindale," she said, sailing forth, hand extended.

He stood and shook hands and offered her a seat. Instead, she restlessly paced to the window and gazed out over the landscape, the view overlooking the stables and rolling hills behind. She turned and clasped her hands in front of her.

"You have a problem," she began, without preamble.

He stayed silent, regarding her steadily, taking in her neat, absolutely correct mode of dress and her angular figure. She certainly did not look like the normal husband-hunter, in his experience. "Do I?"

"You do."

She glanced at the open door and walked toward it, but he said quickly, "I asked that it remain *open*, my lady."

She whirled and faced him, her lips primmed into a straight gash across her face. "Now see here, Mr. Martindale," she said, her tone stern. "I am not now nor will I ever be in the market for a husband, and if I were, I can assure you I would not seek to entrap him in that manner. I would think that my personal recommendations are not so . . . so lacking that I would need to resort to such means."

He felt himself color at her straightforward assessment of his fears. How had she inferred that from his simple words? "I . . . I assure you, my lady . . ."

"Never mind," she said, waving off his faltering apology and pacing over to a table. She restlessly turned over a gilt-edged book and stared at the title. "I know there are ladies who will resort to such means, and you don't know me from Adam, so what should I expect? I know I have been audacious and unusual in my approach to your family." She looked up directly into his eyes. "You interest me. Jacob and Angelica interest me. But I am concerned."

"Oh?"

"Yes." She glanced again at the door, but did not cross to it. Finally, she moved toward James and sat down. He sat opposite her.

Lowering her voice and leaning forward, she said, "There's talk in the village. Cruel talk. I don't like to admit it, but St. Mark-on-Locke is afflicted with the usual number of gossips, backbiters, and vicious minds. In London when one meets with such people, one can exclude them from one's circle, or at least keep one's distance. That's impossible in a village the size of St. Mark."

She spoke, he thought, from experience, and he gazed at her curiously. He had heard tell of a broken engagement, but he would never pry.

"I fear my own staff is the worst," he confessed. He clutched his head and thrust his fingers through his hair. "I don't know what to do but go back to London where at least I have narrowed my staff down to those whom I can trust."

"That is closing yourself and your children off from society. Would you," she said carefully, glancing down at the floor, "care to stay at Meadowlark if you could find peace?"

"I like the house," he said, glancing around him. "It reminds me of the house I grew up in. I was raised in the country and miss it profoundly. I'd like my children to have that same experience, but I'm afraid things are not such with my family—my father, in particular—as to allow visits there." He was silent for a minute and patted down his tousled hair. Sighing, he finally said, "Yes. Yes, I would like to stay, but I won't have Jacob subjected to the petty cruelty of small minds. He deserves better than that, as does Angelica."

"I agree completely!" she exclaimed, hitting the arm of her chair. "And I would help, if I may."

She told him much he didn't know, and it was worse even than he feared. The housekeeper he had let go, Mrs. Hurst, had spread her vile poison among the villagers; now with the stableman let go, it would likely spread to any who hadn't already heard. He appreciated Lady Theresa's honesty, but it seemed to him that the outlook was bleak.

He came, sometime in the half hour they spoke, to trust her motives. "Whatever you think we should do, my lady, I'll go along with. I'm willing to place myself in your hands."

"Sir, if you said that to a husband-hunting lady, she would be booking the parson." When he chuckled she smiled back at him and said, as she stood and extended her hand, "I look forward to the challenge, Mr. Martindale."

He stood and took her hand to shake. She had removed her gloves, and her hands, large for a woman and with a capable look about them, were very soft and cool to the touch. He felt a fleeting moment of attraction but dismissed it. He liked women, so it should not be surprising to him, that sensation. He had been attracted to many women in his life, from chambermaids right up to duchesses, but it didn't mean anything but that he liked women.

He doubted she noticed or felt for him anything but a friendly interest. She had made her motives clear. She wanted to help Jacob and Angelica, and incidentally, him. He thought she might be relieving boredom, too, but gave her too much credit to think that was her primary motive.

"May I see Angelica now?" she said brightly, her voice oddly breathless. "I have some fabric I wanted her to look at. She is going to be thirteen soon and is growing quickly; she will need new dresses."

"I'll go find her."

Once he was gone Theresa let out her breath on a long sigh. The touch of his skin against hers had been like an electrical spark on a dry day. His hand was warm and large, engulfing hers, and he had squeezed with just the right amount of pressure, like a hug that makes one tingle.

She hadn't felt that from a mere handshake since—

Since Paolo. Paolo and the debacle that followed were consigned to that territory of rarely remembered memories. He was a Spanish diplomat's son and she met him in London the spring after her mother died. She had not even intended to go to London that year, but her father had been traveling and she was at loose ends, so though she still had a few more weeks in half mourning, she had gone to stay at her aunt's house in Mayfair, to join in what limited activities were suitable.

And then she had met Paolo. She was twenty-five and he twenty-two, but she fell for him with all the desperate infatuation of a lonely girl with her first love. And he had seemed to feel the same. She had suggested marriage to him, he'd acquiesced, but then deserted her, running back to Spain and the girl to whom he was affianced. She hadn't known about Señorita Vasquez and the understanding between them that had existed since their early childhood.

The worst part was, to be fair, she had to acquit him of the worst kind of chicanery. He had been kind and gentle and had listened to her talk for hours about her fey, adorable mother and how much she missed her. She had been the one to suggest marriage, to ask him, in point of fact. He had been gallant, he had been evasive, but she had heard enough to send an announcement to the papers.

She had been wrong. He fled London, she feared, to avoid having to tell her to her face that they couldn't be engaged, would never marry. He had an arranged marriage to a distant relative in his near future.

She had been a fool.

After, all of London had tales of his conquests, and it appeared that she had been just one of many. Ladies of all types and ages and appearances claimed he had made love to them, offered them marriage, seduced them with his dark good looks. She supposed she would never know the truth, what she had meant to him, how much of what the other women said was true.

She had been so sure she was his one and only love. What did that say about her perspicacity as a woman that she could be so misled, mostly, it seemed, by her own desires and needs?

On that bleak thought she was interrupted by Angelica and forced to put a smile on her face. She put Paolo from her mind and focused instead on the girl in front of her.

* * *

She spent much of the next two days with the Martindale family, assessing their strengths, watching them, and listening to their conversation.

Mr. Martindale was not the problem. He was presentable—handsome, actually, with gorgeous eyes and—

She restrained her wayward thoughts. He was presentable and had a good family history, being the younger son of the Viscount St. Boniface. He was intelligent, likable, and canny, though frightfully naïve about people. He expected people to judge him based on his actions and integrity. Unfortunately, sometimes being good, kind, hardworking, quiet, and gentle made others feel inadequate by comparison. One jealous or bitter person could spread buckets of poison, and folks were ever willing to listen to the worst about a person.

She would have to work around that determined naïveté, she decided.

It came down to the children, Jacob in particular. Maybe someday the world would understand more about what happened in the mind to create a child like Jacob, silent, withdrawn, sometimes totally focused on one object—like her bird-adorned hat—and at other times content to just stare off into the sky for hours. But until that day, an enlightened day when those whose mind did not work as everyone else's were not seen as evil, subterfuge was called for.

Not that she minded subterfuge. She was afraid she was often far more devious than people knew, even those closest to her. In Angelica she saw a possible confederate, for the girl was as crafty and cunning as herself at that same age, she thought, and as willing to manipulate people.

How to enlist her aid?

Bribery usually worked.

Five

"What do you want, Angelica?"

Theresa and her young friend strolled by the banks of the stream on the Leighton property while the girl visited. It was not quite Midsummer Day—it was actually the first day of summer—and the air buzzed with bees visiting the wildflowers along the stream.

"What do you mean?" Angelica asked, pulling a long stem of grass and chewing on the end.

"Very simply, what do you want? You could tell me what you want from life, a philosophical outlook. Or you could tell me what you want this minute . . . like lunch!" She laughed. "Or, you could tell me what you want soon, an amber necklace, or an amethyst ring. When I was your age I longed for an amethyst ring. My mother found out." She put forward her hand and showed the delicate filigree ring with a pale amethyst, the purple glowing in the midday sun. "She designed this for me."

Angelica gazed at it. "I wish my mother had lived."

"I wish she had too." Theresa put her arm over the girl's shoulders as they strolled, the long grass swishing around their skirts, daisies brushing their fingers. In just a few days she had come to care for the child. "She must have loved you very much to name you 'Angelica.' It's a very pretty name."

"My governess told me she named me for the candied herb because she had low tastes and liked sweetmeats."

"And how did she know that?" Theresa said acidly. "I cannot

suppose the wretched woman was there at the hour of your birth. No family engages a governess for a newborn infant."

Angelica looked startled. "I guess that's true. Do you think Mother named me just because . . ."

"Because she loved you and you were her angel."

"Oh."

There was silence for a few minutes. The air was warm and still, laden with the scents of grass and clover. They were supposed to be out gathering herbs and wildflowers for their Midsummer Eve wreathes. Theresa began to gather daisies, piling them near the stream bank, and Angelica followed her example.

"Does your father never talk about your mother?"

"No. I think it's just because she died so long ago." She found some pinkish daisies and gathered a handful, putting them with the others. "And he worries about Jacob all the time and doesn't think of anything else."

Bitterness laced her voice. Theresa would bet that if the girl could wish for anything it would be more time with her father. But that was something she could not promise the child. However, maybe James Martindale would stay and they could work on that part of their lives a little more.

"Ah, here is what I have been looking for," she said, distracted as she found the herb most important to their Midsummer wreathes. "This is St. John's Wort. Of course, since Midsummer Day is also St. John's Day, it's very important to weave in this particular plant."

They gathered the delicate green herb, protecting the yellow blossoms, and put it with the daisies and grasses they had already gathered. Together they sat down in the long grass by the stream, and Theresa showed Angelica how to plait the grasses into a wreath, working in the daisies and St. John's Wort.

"What will we do with them?" the girl asked, holding hers up and examining it critically.

"In the country St. John's Eve, or Midsummer Eve, as I still call it, is very important, and can have great affect on the crops even. The evening of the twenty-third of June, on a high hill, a great fire will be set and folks will stay up all night. These wreathes will be hung on doors and over stables." Theresa worked quickly, her long fingers whipping the grass into plaited circlets with delicate fronds of daisies and the all-important herb worked in.

"Why is it so important?"

"Magical things happen that night. And one man in the village will jump over the Midsummer fire flames. How high he jumps will be how high the crops grow."

"What a lot of rubbish!"

"Profane child." Theresa laughed, tossing one wreath up into the air, where it spun for a moment, framing the sun.

"But isn't this all very . . . heathenish?"

"That's why the Church insists we celebrate St. John the Baptist's Day, rather than Midsummer. But the old ways last, especially among the most superstitious. My mother believed in the old ways." Theresa stacked her wreathes in a pile, and said, "I will send William back to fetch these. We have made far too many to carry. I suppose we should go back for luncheon."

"May I carry mine?" Angelica said, gazing down at her thick circlet of grass and daisies.

"Certainly."

They started back along the stream bank, the lush grass thick and the stream sluggish.

"So what do you want?" Theresa asked, glancing sideways at her young friend. "Say, this summer?"

"I want a pony," she said quickly. "A white one. And I want to ride!"

"Have you never learned to ride?"

"No. Father's afraid if I learn, Jacob will want to, and then he'll be in danger because he has no sense."

"Is that true?"

"That Jacob has no sense? Sometimes he acts that way, but . . . I don't know. I wonder."

"You wonder if he just causes trouble to get attention?"

The girl looked up at her swiftly. "Do you think so?"

"It's possible. I did that on occasion. So, what would you do in return for a white pony and riding lessons?"

"Do?"

"Nothing in life is free . . . or very little anyway," Theresa said. More of her cynical philosophy. She really must be more careful that she did not create a world-weary child. Misanthropy was very unattractive. "I don't mean that. Love is free. I know your father loves you both. You never need to do anything to earn that love, either."

Angelica reflected on that for a few moments and nodded, as if she accepted that statement. True or not, Theresa hoped it was at least what she needed to hear.

"I would do anything for a white pony!" Angelica put her pretty, lopsided wreath on her head and hugged herself, dancing in the long grass, her white dress whirling around and her long hair streaming out.

Theresa caught her breath. The child was breathtaking, her expression joyful in the sun-filled meadow. She suddenly laughed and danced with her, whirling, arms spread wide, face turned up to the sun, feeling the joy of childhood once again. She and her mother had done this, Lady Leighton, fey and unpredictable, dancing wildly like a Gypsy.

Finally they both fell down, breathless and laughing in the long grass, staring up at the sky while their breathing returned to something like normal. It was said, Theresa reflected as she gazed dizzily up at the sun, that if you stayed out all night on Midsummer Eve you could end up with the talents of the immortal bard, or you could just end up insane, or you could be taken away by the fairies. Lady Leighton was rumored to have spent that one Midsummer night among the fairies. She was "fairy-touched," magical but fearsome, too, in her supernatural powers. She had gained a reputation as a healer and good-luck charm. For her to visit a household was said to bring instant good luck. Money would arrive when it was most needed. A creditor would send a notice that a bill had been mysteriously paid. It was magical! So though the most superstitious feared her, a visit from her was still coveted and she was never insulted by anyone.

Oddly, few caught on to Lady Leighton's subtle probing, her delicate way of finding out what was plaguing a troubled family. The old reverend knew, but he was from the previous century, and his respect for Lady Leighton's position in society kept him silent. The countess wanted no credit when she helped someone, so she would do things in secret and shrug when someone mentioned it. She had not purposely set out to become a fairy godmother to the village of St. Mark, but it had happened anyway. She had become a good-luck charm.

A good-luck charm. Theresa sat up and stared off at the misty hills. The village had been without such a talisman since Lady Leighton's death five years before. Maybe it was time they had one again. Maybe it was time Midsummer Eve worked its magic.

James Martindale stomped back up to the house from a loud confrontation with the farm manager. A desire to do things a new way was met with stubborn refusal and an oft-repeated phrase he was coming to loathe. " 'Tis not the way it's aught been done."

He had negotiated in the lease for the rights to farm the immediate acreage, though the far fields were rented out. But Puget, the farm manager, only said that since he was not the owner he had no right to change how things had been done for generations. The man didn't care that the land was producing poorly. He didn't care that the topsoil was being systematically blown into the stream by overtilling. Things had always been done one way, so that was how it should stay. If Mr. Martindale were the owner, he would have no choice but to comply, he said.

He slammed into the house, threw his boots at his distraught valet, and demanded luncheon in the library, where he would not be disturbed. The butler was saying something to him, but he didn't listen, storming in his stocking feet into the library.

He should have listened. There in the library was Lady Theresa with both Jacob and Angelica. His first instinct was to turn and leave, but the lady looked up from her book and smiled, and he was caught.

Her nose was red; so was Angelica's. They looked sunburned, but happy.

"Mr. Martindale," she said, standing. "I brought this book on the history of St. Mark-on-Locke and was showing it to the children. If you do decide to stay, I thought they should know more about their home."

Jacob was sitting cross-legged on a chair and he had in his arms a rag doll. He hugged it to him and rocked back and forth.

"If I have to deal with Puget again I swear I will leave this . . ." He stopped before he swore, took a deep breath, and sat.

"You're in your stockings again, though I suppose that's an improvement over muddy bare feet."

"I thought I would be alone. I thought you and Angie were still out, and that Dora would have Jacob."

"Puget is one of the best managers in the area, Mr. Martindale. What problem are you having with him?"

Oddly, explaining it all to Lady Theresa and the children, and having them laugh at his troubles, calmed him. When his luncheon came he was able to share it out to the children—Lady Theresa said that she and Angelica had already dined, but his daughter gladly took another sandwich—and eat his own share washed down by liberal tankards of ale. He hadn't realized he was so hungry.

"Where did you get the doll, son?" he asked, watching Jacob cradle the rag baby as he ate cress.

"I brought it," Theresa said. "It was what I used to play with when I was a child, and I remember how soothing I found it."

"He is not a baby, my lady."

"No, but comfort is comfort. One never outgrows certain needs."

He let the subject drop.

"I wonder if you would like to go into town one day soon, Mr. Martindale. With me. I thought if I introduced you around, it may break the ice a little. Make you more acceptable."

He eyed her thoughtfully, drained the last drop from his tankard, and pushed it away. "I do need to speak to Mr. Dartelle. He is acting as my man of business in St. Mark, while I am away from the city. He has some messages for me, I believe."

"Shall we say Friday?"

"Friday it is," he agreed, wondering at her secretive smile.

"May I also ask to take Jacob for a ride tomorrow?"

He hesitated. "I don't think . . ."

"I'm perfectly able to care for him. I'll have Dora come with us, if you like."

"Papa, let him go," Angelica said. "Jacob should see some of the neighborhood as I have. And Lady Theresa knows everyone."

A look passed between his daughter and the lady, and James glanced between them uneasily. But he could find no fault with the plan—other than that it was odd for Angelica to come down on the side of any treat for Jacob that didn't include her—and said, "I suppose, if you take Dora with you."

"Good. I'll call tomorrow at one, then." She knelt in front of Jacob. "Jake, you and I and Dora are going to go for a ride tomorrow, after you sleep tonight, that is. We'll have a grand time and I'll show you where I got that cress from. We can gather some for your dinner. All right?"

Miraculously, his eyes never leaving her mouth, he nodded.

Six

Theresa combed out her long hair and stared blankly in the mirror over her vanity table. She realized that the vague feelings of dissatisfaction she had felt since coming home from the Season had disappeared, and the Martindales were responsible. Angelica had quickly become a friend. The sullen attitude the girl displayed with her father and others was never present when they were alone.

And little Jacob . . . something about the boy haunted Theresa. He had an unnerving habit of staring directly into one's eyes, as if he were reading one's soul. That was just fancy, no doubt, but she knew deep down that he understood far more than he ever let on. Whether the secrets of his own soul would ever be unlocked, only time would tell. And even if he always remained an enigma, that did not mean that he could not be communicated with and cared for.

That was one of the things she appreciated about James Martindale. Love for his son was present in every interaction between them, ever minute of every day. Society said he was a fool, and so he chose to eschew society in favor of family. He had taken the more difficult road and walked it without complaint.

She put down her brush and picked up the stalk of vervain she had brought back from the meadow. This time of year some of the wild herbs were said to be at their most potent. Trefoil and rue, roses and vervain . . . all were said to be able to bring dreams about future lovers, future romance. She twirled the purple-flowered herb between her fingers, smiled at her fancy, and crossed to her bed.

Carefully, she put the vervain under her pillow and lay down, pulling the light covers up. Her mother would be proud of her, Theresa thought as she snuffed the candle.

"I'm here for Jacob," Lady Theresa said, not getting down from her brass-ornamented gig.

James, in the lane in front of the house speaking to his groundskeeper about a fence for the stew pond, looked up at her on her high seat in her gig and wondered at the two spots of color on her cheeks. "Will you come in for a moment? One of the grooms can take care of your horse."

"No, I think not. If you can have Dora and Jacob meet me out here, I'll wait."

Her evasive behavior was such a deviation from the day before that James wondered at it. "All right," he said. "I think Jacob is looking forward to this. Last night he clutched that doll you gave him so tightly I couldn't remove it when he went to bed. He slept with it."

Talking about his son did the trick; she eagerly met his eyes.

"Really? I do so want him to enjoy himself today. We're going to visit a man who has broken his leg, old Mr. Gudge, but then we're going to my secret watercress bed. Jacob does love cress!"

James sent the groundskeeper to the house to ask the butler to send Dora and Jacob out, and then strolled over to the gig. He laid one hand on the painted body and gazed up at Theresa. There was something different about her this day but he could not imagine what it was. She looked away hastily, but he had already noted how truly fine her gray eyes were, large and luminous. She must have slept well the night before.

Unlike him. He had been disturbed by the strangest dreams all night, of a bonfire and people leaping and dancing around it. He remembered the Midsummer festivals of his youth; it was likely just that memory plaguing him.

But that didn't account for the other dreams, of chasing a mystery woman through the forest, trying desperately to catch a glimpse of her, only to have her disappear with just a fleeting glance at a handsome ankle and a wisp of dusky curls fluttering on the night breeze. He shook his head, dispelling the disturbing image.

"Lady Theresa, I'd like to visit and meet your father. I fear I have been sorely remiss in that aspect, but there was so much to do at first. Would he be home this morning if Angelica and I visited?"

"He will," she said. "I thought perhaps I would take Jacob home with me; we could meet there for luncheon, about two? Would you care to do that?"

He felt a flood of warmth and gratitude that this odd young woman had befriended them. "We would be delighted, if you're sure it's not putting you out at all."

"No," she said. "Father and I would love to have company."

The two spots of deep pink appeared again on her high cheekbones. He had thought her plain at first meeting, but had begun to see how fine her bone structure was, and how lovely her eyes.

At that moment Dora, thrilled at her new position as nursemaid to Jacob and with her elevated status—going for a ride in Lady Theresa Barclay's gig!—approached with her young charge's hand firmly held in her own. Jacob was nervous at first and pulled back at the sight of the open gig.

Theresa jumped down and led Jacob around to talk to her horse. James couldn't hear what she said, but he could see that she had a way of hunching down and gazing directly into Jacob's eyes. His son reached up and petted the velvety nose of the mare, and when they came back to the side of the carriage, happily clambered up into the gig and onto Dora's lap as Lady Theresa, with James's help, climbed up and took the reins.

"We'll meet you at two then," she said brightly, with a brisk snap of the reins.

He watched her competent handling of the mare and the steady gait of her horse, and tried not to worry. But why did he have the feeling that something was up that he should know about?

Theresa guided the gig expertly down the country lane. A side glance told her that Dora was afraid of the high, open vehicle, but was doing her best to conceal her fear, for Jacob's sake or perhaps her own.

"I've never had an accident," she said gently.

Dora, clutching tightly on to Jacob and the edge of her seat, said, "No, my lady."

"Do you know Mr. Gudge, Dora?"

"Yes, ma'am. He's my great-uncle."

"Wonderful. This will be a family visit for you, then."

"Oh, I don't know him to speak to him. Me mum calls him an evil old man and willna let me father visit."

Theresa bit back a smile. "I expect that is just because Mr. Gudge has a liking for ale and gin. It's how he broke his leg, though he won't confess it. But regardless, he's an intelligent old man. I like him."

They pulled up outside the cottage, a ramshackle home cobbled together with daub and wattle, some wood, and a dash of luck. Theresa jumped down from the carriage, took Jacob from Dora, and said, "Dora, if you would prefer to stay out here and wait, that will be fine."

"If you don't mind, my lady," she said. She held on to the side of the gig as she stepped down. "My pa would be that put out if he was to find out I'd gone into the old man's hut when he is not even allowed. And me mum would skin me alive."

"Well, we can't have that."

Theresa led her mare to a shady spot to crop grass and then took Jacob by the hand as she entered the man's cottage without knocking. They were old friends, she and Mr. Gudge. He had been game master of her father's estate, and there was not another person in the county who knew so much about rabbits and partridge, quail and voles.

Jacob hung back at first, but when she gazed directly into his eyes, his trust shone on his solemn face and he followed her with no more tugging backward.

"Mr. Gudge, I've brought a visitor."

The old man was at his ease in a chair by the window, using daylight to carve his wooden animal figures. Since he couldn't get about on his own just then, he was dependent on whatever she chose to bring him, and she chose not to bring him spirits. At first he had been in a foul mood because of it, but he had steadily improved, and the apothecary had been surprised when last he had visited the old man to find him almost healed, though he was not a bit better, to hear him tell it. She suspected his malingering was brought about by an unexpected enjoyment of the attention his invalidism had attracted. Perhaps he would soon have reason to have a miraculous recovery.

"Who have you brought to plague me, then?" he said querulously.

"This is Master Jacob Martindale. Jacob, this is Mr. Gudge."

The two sized each other up for a few long minutes in the dull light of the odorous cottage. Gudge stuffed some tobacco from an oilskin pouch into a dark wood pipe and lit it from a taper set near the fire, but his eyes never left the boy's face. Jacob's consideration was equally silent.

Theresa watched the old man's eyes. She could read the flickering thoughts, almost, as if they were writ on a page. He was intrigued. Because he was a miserable old cuss, folks dismissed Gudge as lacking in intelligence, but the opposite was true. He could not abide fools and so drove most people away, since, in his own words, most people were fools.

But he had loved Lady Leighton with a devotion no one suspected but Theresa. They had mourned together when she died. Ever since, she had been sincerely attached to him as a reminder of her mother, and how that lady's spirit lived on in those who loved her.

Theresa reminded him of the girl she had brought to visit the last time and then said, "Jacob is Angelica's brother, the son of Mr. James Martindale, new tenant of Meadowlark Mansion."

"Ah. That so."

The two, boy and old man, stared at each other for a moment longer, then Gudge took another knife up from his side table and a block of wood, and handed them to Jacob. "See what you can make outta this, boy," he said gruffly, staring directly into the child's eyes.

Theresa left the two to sit alone for a while as she made tea, some sandwiches for the old man's luncheon, and soup for his supper. She unpacked some more dainties, washed dishes, and put them away. Folks in the village would be amazed to see her doing such menial chores. She could just hire him some help, but she knew he would hate that. Soon, he would be on his feet again and able to do for himself. Until then, she would do his chores.

She called out the window for Dora to bring her a pail of water from the well, and tidied the last of the crumbs and leftovers away, putting them into a pail and handing them to Dora to give to Mr. Gudge's pig in the hut behind the cottage.

Housework done, she came back to the two, who carved in silence.

Jacob, his narrow face intensely focused, carved with quick strokes that took Theresa's breath away, so frightening was it to see his deft hands flash and move, the blade like quicksilver. But in another moment he was done and held up his handiwork to the light.

Theresa gazed, astonished, at the marvel he had wrought in the hour they had been there. It was a tree, but it roiled with life: squirrels—clumsy but clearly squirrels—chased each other in circles on the trunk and birds, some in flight, attached to the tree limbs by just the most tenuous tip of their wings. The leaves practically fluttered and danced, there was such life in the little carving. It was crude, but there was a mysterious power to it.

She let her breath out. "Amazing," she sighed. "Jacob," she continued, taking his face in her hands and staring into his eyes, "that is a lovely piece of carving. Would you like to take it for your papa to see?" He nodded. "Okay. Run along outside for a moment while I talk to Mr. Gudge alone."

He handed the old man back his knife and gazed at him for a minute.

"You're welcome, lad. Come back anytime."

Jacob bounced out to show Dora his tree, and her glad cries and exclamations could be heard through the open window.

"You have made a friend."

"He's all right," he grunted. "Silent. That's always a good thing in a child."

"However, some in the village don't like him. They're afraid of him because he's different."

"Pack of fools, the lot of them."

"Some. Some just easily led. And some believe whatever they're told." She told him about Mrs. Greavely, Dame Alice and the housekeeper, Mrs. Hurst, and the groom who said Jacob had "the evil eye."

He snorted through her story, and then gazed at her shrewdly. "An' what do you want from me, eh?"

"I'll tell you what I want, and I'll tell you what I am prepared to do to get it."

A half hour later she left the cottage, singing an old tune. Time to collect cress in her secret spot with Jacob and Dora, then go home to luncheon and to see James Martindale again. Why that should give her such a trill of happiness she would not examine, in light of her dreams the night before, dreams brought on by vervain under her pillow, or something much more insidious.

Seven

"Can Jacob and I please stay with Lady Theresa for the night?"

James Martindale, interrupted in the middle of his work in the library, frowned at his daughter. She had never expressed any interest in going anywhere or doing anything with her brother, and now, suddenly, she was his champion. He should be happy at this turn of events. Angelica had been better behaved and happier since the moment Lady Theresa had trundled into their lives. Their luncheon the day before at the Leighton home had been refreshingly informal, for all the awesome history of the turreted home. Lord Leighton was a good man, quiet, gently humorous, with a twinkle in his eyes when he spoke to Jacob that warmed James's heart.

They were a worthy family and good friends.

So why should he complain if Lady Theresa wanted to invite Jacob and Angelica to stay the night? It was Midsummer Eve, and Angelica had explained that the Leighton farmhands always staged a bonfire ritual that was all in good fun.

But it would be his first night ever away from both of his children at once, and it made him uneasy.

"Will Dora be able to go with you to look after Jacob? I would not have all the burden on Lady Theresa's staff."

"Of course Dora will come."

"Then . . ." James was having trouble saying it, but Angelica was bouncing in front of him from foot to foot, her pretty green dress with gold velvet ribbons—courtesy of Lady

Theresa's talented seamstress—fluttering about her legs. "All right. You may go."

"Three cheers for Papa!" Angelica said, taking Jacob's hands and dancing around in a circle with him. He pulled away from her and retreated, clutching his hands behind his back and staring, eyes wide. She immediately stopped, stooped just as Lady Theresa might, and said, "It is all right, Jake, I am just happy. We are going to visit Lady Theresa, you and me and Dora. You will like that, won't you?"

He nodded slowly, and James felt a pang as he watched his silent and mysterious son. He knew Jacob better than anyone, and yet still, most of what went on in his boy's mind was a puzzle. Sometimes the child could not bear to be touched, and one had to know just by the look on his face. Lady Theresa seemed to have found the key to Jacob's heart much faster than anyone. He ought to be grateful, he supposed, but he found that he was a little jealous. It would not stop him from letting Jacob experience all the lady had to offer, though. He thought she was good for him, and that *did* please him.

"All right," he said, clapping his hands together. "We should get your things together and take you over to Lady Theresa, then."

Theresa sat at the table in the breakfast parlor and gazed out the window in the curved west turret wall. She should be planning the children's evening. She had received a message from Meadowlark Mansion that James Martindale would bring the children over himself later in the afternoon. Her plan was about to take flight, and she was pleased.

And yet another night of dreams—even without that cursed vervain under her pillow—had left her uneasy. This was not the product of any herb; her own mind had conjured these dreams.

At first in her dream James Martindale, handsome and self-assured as he always was, was behind her, holding her against him and whispering words she could not quite hear. She turned in his arms and he kissed her, gently, and then the dream drifted into hazy imaginings she could not now remember. But then later they sat on the stream bank near her cress bed, and he was holding her hand and telling her that as much as he liked her and appreciated her kind offer of marriage, he could not see attaching himself to a woman of her age.

She was no fool; she knew from whence the dream had come. Sometime during the week or so she had known him, she had become attracted to him. He was handsome but she wasn't a child, her head turned by a pretty face and smooth manner. This was not like Paolo. She had been so lonely after her mother's death, and Paolo's gentle attentions had been a balm to her wounded heart. She had been grasping for happiness, but looking back, she could see how bad a match they would have made.

This was different. Every time she saw James she noted something new to admire. He was gentle, and she admired that trait in a man. As far as she could tell he was rigidly moral, following his own strict beliefs about how a man should act; she could never respect any man who did less.

If he was occasionally hasty in temper, it was no more than her own outbursts of frustration or pique.

But it was what his behavior said about his heart that attracted her. He would sacrifice anything for his children's benefit, no matter how misguided some might think him. Many would criticize him and believe he was harming his daughter by keeping his son in the household. It was even possible that that was the truth. Many worthy suitors might be repelled by the odd, silent younger brother. But James Martindale was doing his utmost to balance the needs and rights of both his children. Angelica might feel herself ignored, but Theresa had seen the love in James's eyes when he looked at his daughter. It was there, naked and exposed, for anyone with the will to see it. He loved her with all his heart and would do whatever he could that was consistent with his other child's good, to benefit her. Theresa had never met, among the many widowers who had courted her of late, anything to compare with his behavior toward his children.

But she was completely realistic. She had no reason to think him looking for a wife or even open to that possibility. He was consumed with making a home for his children. In her mind the right wife would only enhance—

Wife?

Theresa pulled herself up. She had long ago decided that she was not wifely enough for any man. She could not be less than she was, nor would she hide her questing mind and biting intelligence from anyone, and those characteristics, in her experience, were not what a man looked for in a wife, nor were they designed to make a marriage happy and easy. And besides, she had everything she could want without marriage.

"Tuppence for your thoughts, my dear," her father said, coming up behind her and putting his hands on her shoulders.

She put her right hand over his left. "I am afraid I have not the change necessary to give you my thoughts *and* what is left over after their worth is paid."

He chuckled and sat down beside her at the table. "So, we are to have company this Midsummer Eve," he said. "Remember how your mother would prepare? 'Twas like Christmas for my darling."

Theresa put her head on his shoulder. "She would have wreaths on all the doors and mummers to play fairies. She loved this time of year."

They were silent with their memories for a few minutes.

"I wish I were more like her," Theresa said, straightening.

"Do you think yourself so different, then?" Lord Leighton had a quizzical expression on his lined face.

"Well, yes. Completely different. I am so pragmatic . . . not the least bit romantic or fluttery."

"No, you are not the least bit romantic."

Disconcerted by her father's secretive smile, Theresa said, "You must admit I am very unlike Mother."

"Unlike her, and yet so like her. Do not ask me to explain,

for you will not understand. So, what time are we to expect our guests, and what do you have in store for them?"

She let him change the subject, but she did wonder what he meant.

Twilight fell late, as it was now just past the summer solstice, when day stretched long into evening. On a high hill overlooking the ancient, turreted Leighton house, Theresa, with Angelica on one side and Jacob on the other side and trailed by Dora, watched a man from the stable—traditionally, to honor the saint whose day it would be, it had to be a fellow named John, so it was old John, the senior groom—set fire to a huge pile of sticks and logs. A flame flickered, and then a blaze danced from one log to another, fueled by lamp oil liberally spilled on the tinder. The flames, gold and red and orange, capered wildly against the indigo and kohl sky.

Jacob, his eyes wide, quivered. Theresa whispered to Angelica, "We must keep close to your brother tonight. This is all so new to him, and I am not sure how much he understands."

The girl nodded. "But we must stay out long enough for the plan to work."

"Until after midnight. I told enough people. We are sure to have a few villagers creeping up here to watch."

The fire blazed and danced, the flames eloquently flickering against the dark, star-jeweled sky. Theresa, with the children and Dora, held hands and danced around the fire, then they took some of the wreaths, liberally laced with herbs and flowers, and tossed them on the blaze. The next day the ashes would be spread on the fields to ensure a good harvest.

Dora, her eyes wide, said, "My lady, does the vicar approve of these paganish goings-on?"

"We are just honoring St. John. Nothing pagan about that."

"I suppose not," she said, doubt in her tone. "But the wreaths and the dancing . . . I don't know what me mum will say!"

"Then don't tell her," Theresa said.

The girl looked startled, as if such a thing would never cross her mind.

Angelica, as if she had been taking part in such mad events her whole life, twirled and shouted to the dark sky, head back, long hair streaming out behind her. Jacob held tight to Theresa's hand and she did not let go, happy that he trusted her. His eyes wide, he watched his sister. On his face was an expression Theresa had never seen there: Jacob was smiling.

She made a memory of that moment: Angelica in the darkness, free, happy, and young, Jacob smiling and reaching out his free hand as if he were taking everything in through all of his senses. If she never had children of her own—and she did not expect to—this would have to suffice, this night and these children.

Her senses heightened, Theresa was aware just when some of the villagers arrived to watch. Like a mummer in the plays her mother used to put on, she felt the tightening in her belly that told her the performance of her life was about to take place.

It had started, the Midsummer madness.

Eight

It was Midsummer Day, St. John the Baptist's feast day. The second stage of her plan must now begin.

They were all sedately going to town in the barouche, children dressed immaculately, Theresa for once not driving. This was no time to emphasize her unseemly independence. She needed to draw on all the dignity of her position in the community this day.

"First, Mrs. Parsifal's cottage, Anthony, and then the church," she said to the driver.

With the stop first to her old friend's home they would not be in time for the St. John's day service, but the vicar would still be there. That was all she needed.

She glanced from right to left. Angelica, sitting on her right, was dressed sweetly in a white muslin gown with a tidy spencer against the morning chill and dampness. Jacob, on her left, was perfectly turned out in breeches and jacket, his dark hair, so like his father's, damped into place. Dora was with them, of course, facing them, her eyes wide at the treat of riding in a barouche. She was going to visit her mother while they were in the village. That was Theresa's doing. She did not want to involve the naïve and scrupulously honest Dora in her scheme any more than she had to; it didn't seem right, somehow. Angelica, she trusted, could be as devious as need be. Her scruples did not extend to involving a child in her scheme, she noted dispassionately, but then, she had known immediately that the girl was a very special child. And Jacob was her brother, after all.

When they finally did reach St. Mark-on-Locke, after their visit to Mrs. Parsifal and dropping Dora off at her parental home, they were just in time to find the vicar in the church, putting away his vestments. They could see him through the open side door of the church, laying his religious accoutrements away with reverence and a methodical hand.

Vicar Jamison was an old friend of Theresa's; he had even had an affection for her at one time that could have blossomed into something more if she had not been so far out of his social sphere. But there lingered a preference, and a gentleness in his treatment of her. It would be sorely tested over the coming weeks, but Theresa knew his heart and that she could explain to him her methods and her madness. There was no one kinder than he.

Theresa helped the children down from the carriage and approached the gate at the end of the path to the churchyard. He greeted them just as he closed the side door to the church.

"Lady Theresa, who do we have here?" he asked. He walked down the stone pathway, toward the gate where they stood waiting.

"Mr. Jamison, this is Miss Angelica Martindale and Master Jacob Martindale. They are Mr. James Martindale's children, and are the new tenants of Meadowlark Mansion."

"Yes, I met Mr. Martindale." Jamison gravely shook hands with both children, paying particular attention to Jacob, who was silent, of course, but whose eyes were devouring the man in front of him.

"Angelica, will you take care of your brother for a moment while I speak to Mr. Jamison?"

As the children walked hand in hand into the church garden, she took the vicar aside; he gazed at her with a question in his eyes.

"So, how was the service this morning?" she said, her voice lilting with mischief.

"'Twas very interesting. Higher attendance than usual, but I fear most were here to speak to their neighbors, rather than give thanks and worship."

Theresa bit her lip uncertainly and examined the handsome, black-haired man in front of her. She had never imagined herself in love with him, though he had made plain his feelings for her, but she did hold him in a great deal of affection and respect, and she would not abuse a longstanding trust and friendship between them.

However, if he were a willing participant in her scheme—

"Jacob Martindale . . . have you heard anything about him?"

"I must admit, folks were talking. Mostly about your 'heathenish' Midsummer Eve celebration."

"Ah, so word got around. How did they know anything about it," she exclaimed innocently, "when it was meant to be a private affair, with just our family, the children, and our staff attending?"

"Oh, I don't know," he answered. "Could it be that you spoke of it with such mysterious mutterings that some of the local lads just had to check it out to see if there was any . . . er, unseemly behavior?"

"Good heavens," she said, genuinely startled. "Is that what they thought?"

The vicar colored. "I'm afraid so. They were disappointed, and I will not be surprised if they begin to embellish the story over a pint. You can be sure I will vigorously dispute such embellishments." He took her arm and they strolled after Jacob and Angelica. "But much of the talk was about young Jacob Martindale. Theresa, what do you have in mind? What are you up to?"

She gazed off after the children. "Jacob is . . . different. No one is quite sure what is wrong with him, but he is silent and sometimes withdrawn. On occasion, he cannot bear to be touched and freezes up into a state almost like catatonia."

"Poor child."

"But he is so full of love," Theresa said. Under a spreading tree she stopped her friend with a hand on his arm. "You can see it in his eyes sometimes. Mr. Martindale is a wonderful father; he will not farm that poor boy out to some family of keepers like he is a . . . a wild beast. You must have heard the talk from fools like Dame Alice and ill-tempered gossips like Mrs. Greavely. Why do people shun Mr. Martindale rather than honor him?"

"Folks are afraid of anything different."

"Then 'folks' ought to think for themselves rather than being blinded by idiotic prejudice and superstition." She looked away. "I'm sorry; I should not be battering you. I came to ask your help, or at least your silence."

"I will do anything to help that boy that is consistent with my pledge to God."

"Don't worry, Andrew, I will not ask you to dance around my Midsummer night fire or any such thing. Let us walk through the graveyard. I have something to ask of you."

In the butcher shop a while later, Theresa huffily reflected on her old friend's words. The best she had been able to pry out of him was an agreement that he would not actively counter her plans, but he was not pleased and had told her why. It just illustrated how little he understood the villagers' deeply superstitious nature. She supposed it was understandable, coming from a man of God; he had to condemn much of that old way of thinking as pagan nonsense.

But her mother had understood and made use of the old ways. Surely there was nothing wrong with it when the end result was a better life for all involved. Today, though, she would rely on the truth to try to improve the Martindales' position in the community.

She entered the butcher shop with Angelica and Jacob to find Dame Alice there—her husband was very particular about his meat and no one could see to it but his wife—with her other friend, Miss Tratt. There was a very interesting tug of war between Mrs. Greavely and Miss Tratt over friendships, with the end result being that they shared the same group of friends, but were never in their company at the same time. Theresa had known Dame Alice would be there; her schedule was unchanged through three decades. But the presence of Miss Tratt was a pleasant surprise.

Dame Alice, at the sight of Jacob, drew back, but Miss Tratt, curious and eager, stepped forward.

"Lady Theresa, how nice to see you," she said, her eyes wide with curiosity.

"And you, Miss Tratt. May I introduce to you Miss Angelica Martindale and Master Jacob Martindale."

The spinster shook Angelica's outstretched hand and turned to Jacob. Theresa saw something change in the older lady's eyes. She touched his head gently and said, "Master Jacob, it is a pleasure to meet you."

She was rewarded by a fleeting smile, a rarity on the small boy's lips.

"He likes you," Theresa said, genuinely amazed.

Miss Tratt, tears in her gooseberry eyes, said, "He is very much like my nephew's son, Lawrence. That child was the sweetest baby in the world, but they sent him to the country to live with a slatternly woman and he . . ." She turned away, sniffed delicately into her handkerchief, and turned back, clearing her throat. "Welcome to the village, children." She fished in her reticule and found a couple of paper-wrapped sweets. She handed them each one and gave Jacob another affectionate pat on the head.

Dame Alice, hesitant still but braver in the face of her friend's rare endorsement of anyone considered a newcomer, stepped forward and said, "Yes, welcome."

That was the height of her courage, but it was a step forward, Theresa thought.

She spent an hour in different shops, and in every one she found people to talk to. Her topic was the great improvements Mr. Martindale was making to the land, and what a boon it would be to have someone buy the Meadowlark property and really take an interest in it. At the draper's she spoke of Mr. Martindale's service to the military during the war, how, when a supplier of cloth for flags and uniforms was caught in a scandal for vastly overpricing his wares, Mr. Martindale stepped in and gave Wellington ells and ells of cloth to clothe the poor tattered foot soldiers. For nothing!

At the genteel tea shop, newly opened, she and the children stopped for luncheon and she engaged the proprietor, a Mrs. Smythe-Blessing, in a conversation about Mr. Martindale's illustrious family, the Viscount St. Boniface, his father, and his eldest brother, the Baron Wyethorpe. She rambled quietly as the children stuffed themselves on cream cakes, about how modest Mr. Martindale was and how he would never mention his distinguished family ties.

Of the people she spoke to during the morning some were silent, some disbelieving, but enough were interested and encouraging for Theresa to be satisfied with the day's work. But at long last she guided the children to the livery, where Anthony would be waiting with the barouche. They started down the lane to the inn stable and a man stepped out and spat on the ground in front of them.

"S'truth, but he's an odd duck, ain't he, milady?"

"Are you addressing me?"

"I am. Even a commoner can address a queen, eh?"

She looked him over. He was acceptable-looking and neatly dressed, which made his bitter expression and sneer all the more shocking, somehow. One generally associated rudeness with the ill-kempt and dirty. She decided to ignore him and held tightly to the two children's hands as she searched for a sign that her carriage was being brought around.

"That is the man Father let go," Angelica whispered.

"Yer coach'll be here soon." The fellow spat on the ground again. " 'E's evil, y'know," he said, pointing one stubby finger at Jacob. "I seen with me own eyes that look he gave the mare, an' then she miscarried. He done it. Give it the evil eye."

"Angelica, take Jacob around to the front while I see what is keeping the carriage," Theresa said, her voice tight with anger. She was not afraid of the groom, as there were others near enough that he would try nothing foolish. As Angelica hurried around the corner with her brother, Theresa said, "You will stop your foolish talk immediately. If I hear you maligning that poor boy again, I will . . ."

"You'll what, milady? 'Ave me dismissed? They're lucky to get me here, an' they know it. But that there boy caused me to lose a soft job, an' interfered with a promising bit o' fun with Dora. So I be thinkin' the Martindale brats oughta consider a new home, back in London, where they belong."

A promising bit of fun with Dora? Theresa opened her mouth to ask him what he meant, but she would not lower herself to speak with this man. She turned and strode toward the stable, calling out, "What is keeping my carriage?"

A scared-looking groom, probably threatened by the other man to hold back the carriage, led the team forward; Theresa's driver followed, swearing at him in colorful language. When he saw his mistress, he stopped abruptly.

"Pardon, milady," Anthony said, "but this dolt swore there was something wrong with the strapping, and would not send the carriage out until he had inspected every harness. I told him . . ."

"Never mind, Anthony," Theresa said through clenched teeth. "The children are waiting."

Though she tried to talk normally over the journey home, she feared that she failed, judging by Angelica's worried glances. She returned the children and Dora to Meadowlark Mansion.

Theresa did not descend from the carriage, but as the children headed toward the front door, she said, "Dora, may I ask you something?"

The girl turned back. "Yes, milady?"

She gazed down into Dora's innocent blue eyes. How could she frame this question delicately? "Have you ever had any trouble with any of the staff here, say, one of the grooms?"

The girl colored a bright red and tears welled up into her eyes. "I didn't do nothin' wrong, milady, honest. It was that Bill Johnson; he . . . he tried to kiss me, an' only let me go when young Master Jacob wandered into the stable an' saw what he was doin'."

That explained much, Theresa thought; it explained the original accusation of the "evil eye." The man had figured to discredit Jacob if he said anything, not knowing, perhaps, that the boy was silent. And now he was angry at losing his job, and all over nothing. And yet he had chosen the most insidious manner of persecuting the child.

She glanced back at the girl to find her crying.

"Whatever is wrong, Dora?"

"I'm going to be sacked now, an' all 'cause o' that rotter, Bill Johnson."

"Don't be ridiculous," Theresa said briskly. "Why should you be let go because of an evil fellow like that man? Tell Mr. Martindale I shall be waiting for him tomorrow morning. I am going into St. Mark with him, if he remembers. We can go now, Anthony," she said, more loudly, to her driver.

It seemed that her plan was necessary after all, and since it was already set in motion, she had nothing to regret.

Nine

James Martindale dressed unusually carefully the next morning. He remembered the care which Lady Theresa always displayed in her clothing and accoutrements, and he did not want to appear less than polite in return. Her opinion of him mattered, if only for his daughter's sake.

Angelica did nothing but talk of the lady day and night. It could easily get annoying, except she also had lost much of her sullenness, just by Lady Theresa's involvement in her life, and she voluntarily took charge of Jacob now. It would be churlish not to befriend the lady who was responsible in return.

And so he did not regret the planned trip into St. Mark, even though he had met the two men whom he considered the principle residents, the vicar and the solicitor. He suspected the visit had more to do with her plan to make his family acceptable to the villagers, but it behooved him to get to know Lady Theresa better, for if he did decide to stay at Meadowlark, Angelica would no doubt insist on continuing her burgeoning friendship.

He pulled his phaeton—a sensible one, not a garish high-perch phenomenon—up to the Leighton home; when a groom came to hold his horses he jumped down just as Lady Theresa came out to meet him. He felt an odd spurt of joy at the sight of her. She was handsomely dressed in a quiet country way, and her movements were tidy, too, economical, with no show or flounce like some of the young ladies he had met in London. He had been much sought after by some of the more desperate London belles. Even though he did not go out much in company, he was hunted down like a reticent fox by fathers and brothers by the score. His wealth suddenly made him respectable, even though his money was gained through trade. He might not be suitable for a duchess or an earl's daughter, but the feminine offspring of barons and knights, squires and even viscounts found him closely enough allied with the aristocracy to burn off the stench of the mill.

But Lady Theresa was the daughter of the eminent Lord Leighton, earl and widowed man-about-town. It was a sobering thought; he greeted the lady politely, but kept that reserve in his tone that he feared he had lost in her company. It would never do to get too familiar. He had started by thinking that she was a husband-hunter. Ridiculous and vain, he thought now, looking back at it. He would not now make the mistake of letting her think him a fortune hunter or social climber.

"Lady Theresa," he said, taking her hand and helping her up into the carriage.

"Mr. Martindale," she returned, folding her hands on her lap as he climbed up into the driver's position.

There was silence while he negotiated the tricky exit from the property along the winding lane and through the stone pillars that demarcated the Leighton property. When the silence stretched as they rode along the well-kept road toward St. Mark-on-Locke, he glanced over at her. Tension was indicated in her stiff posture and rigidity.

"My lady, I . . ." He faltered to silence, but then frowned and started over. "I would be sorely remiss if I did not tell you of the improvement I have seen in Angelica's manners since she has been spending more time with you. I thank you for it. Her mother would be proud."

She was smiling when he stole another glance, and she chuckled. "You might not be so pleased with me if you knew her behavior was encouraged by selfish concerns. I told her that if one is polite, one is more likely to get what one wants from people."

He laughed out loud, and it felt good. For the first time he noticed the long hedgerows that hemmed in the lane and the birds that jumped from limb to limb within them. A butterfly crossed their path. "Perhaps it will become a habit for her."

"That is my hope," she said primly. She looked over at him. "You spoke of her mother. What was Mrs. Martindale like?"

"Mary was the daughter of the man who took me into his business and taught me everything. I did not think of marriage at first, though . . . well, she later told me that she fell in love with me very quickly." He rolled his shoulders, embarrassed by that confession, and not sure why he made it. "She was intelligent, quick-witted, handsome, older than I by several years. Some called her stout, but she was a pretty woman and carried it well. I took her home once and I am afraid my father and brother hurt her deeply. They were insulting about her antecedents and behavior, which was forthright and honest, but not genteel. I have not been back since."

"I understand your anger at your family," Lady Theresa said. "They should have been more kind. But shouldn't Jacob and Angelica know their grandparents?"

"My mother died before I married Mary. And my father . . . he would not understand about Jacob."

"You have fought many battles for your little boy. I honor that."

He cast a sideways glance at her, grateful for her forbearance and gentle reply. "You're the first person I have allowed this close to the children who didn't tell me what I should do about them. Everyone has an opinion. Most think I should send Jacob away and Angelica to a school."

"Of course Jacob should stay with you, and Angelica shouldn't go to school yet unless she wants to. Do you truly know what she wants?"

"To stay with me and Jacob."

"How do you know that?"

"I remember what it was like to be sent off to school," he said, grimly staring at the road ahead. They came out of the shade of the hedgerow into the sunshine.

"You had a bad experience. But are you sure Angelica will not feel differently?"

"What has she said to you?"

"About school? Nothing. But I don't think you should assume her feelings based on your own experiences."

"I have been doing that, haven't I?"

"Yes. It's natural, I suppose, to see our children as extensions of ourselves, but they are such different creatures, aren't they? I always marvel at how different children can be from their parents."

"What should I do?"

"She's an intelligent girl; I would just ask her, if I were you. But you must do what you think right."

He gazed over at her for a moment, still primly sitting, feet together, hands clasped. "You who have no children are very good with them. How is that?"

She frowned and shook her head. "Before this I would not have said I was especially good with children. I haven't had much to do with them. But it seems to me that if you remember your own childhood, you can deal with them very well."

"And you haven't forgotten your own childhood."

"How could I? I had the best of mothers and fathers; it was a happy time."

"Tell me about your mother?"

And she did for the half hour it took to go the rest of the way into town. He smiled at some of her tales, and began to see how the daughter was a melding of the mysticism and delightful quirkiness of the mother and the solid, kindly goodness of the father. Her faults, he opined, were a tendency to interfere in people's lives, and perhaps that she thought she knew best in most situations. But those could not be considered dire faults, could they?

The village of St. Mark, he had noted on his previous visits, was laid out in a roughly triangular pattern, with a large village green in the center, where a well took pride of place. The Locke, a river that was sluggish in midsummer but from what he had heard, turbulent and quick in spring, ran behind one row of shops. They passed over it, the fishy odor wafting up to them in the open phaeton, and entered the village.

He noticed her tense as he drove the carriage into the yard of the Goose and Feather, but he thought nothing more of it when they strolled out to the first row of shops and he glanced around, orienting himself.

"Ah, there is Mr. Dartelle's office."

"But you are not going there yet," she said. "Let us just stroll about the village. After all, if you do buy Meadowlark Mansion, you should know the village and its people."

"Why do you care if I buy Meadowlark or not?" he asked, taking her arm and strolling with her up one walk near a row of neat shops. He wasn't sure why he asked, nor what he hoped she would say, but what she did say was a disappointment.

"I just would like to see that house better cared for. An absentee landlord is never a good thing. Once the owner died and it passed into the hands of distant relatives, there was no one to care for the house. That's a shame."

What had he expected her to say, he chastised himself. That she liked him and wanted him to stay? Absurd.

They went to several shops, and stopped at a tiny, quaint tea shop, where the proprietor, a Mrs. Smythe-Blessing gave them personal service and watched them avidly from her chair in the corner.

"Why is she staring at us?" he whispered to Lady Theresa.

"Perhaps it is just that you are a very good-looking man!"

He let out a great shout of laughter, and realized that it was not the first time in her company that he had laughed so heartily. Before meeting her he couldn't remember the last time he had laughed. "My lady, that is the most absurd thing I have ever heard."

She grinned. "Is it absurd that you are good-looking, or only that a woman of Mrs. Smythe-Blessing's discriminating taste should find you so? I assure you, she has excellent taste."

He watched her eyes, the silvery light in them glittering

with laughter. For one heart-stopping moment he realized with a sickening lurch that he would quite like to see that light and those eyes often, every day, even. His fault was a tendency to take life too seriously. The blows he had been dealt had left him cautious and serious. But in her presence he felt buoyed, like a weight was lifted from him.

She shared his concerns and gladdened his heart.

He pushed away such thoughts. He knew the differences in their station, and he knew that though eligible, his fortune and his name were tainted with the stain of trade. He was a cloth manufacturer and a merchant. It was a sobering thought.

"Do you think we shall have rain soon?" he asked, sitting back in his chair and taking a sip of his tea. He damned himself as a cold-natured idiot as he saw the silvery light die in her eyes, but things were how they were. Better he not start thinking of her in that way, as an important part of his daily life. Even aside from their differences in situation, he would likely kill that joyousness in her nature, as he had just killed her smile.

"I think we shall. The clouds are building today," she replied.

They left the tea shop and continued their slow perambulation of the village, finally stopping at the butcher shop so he could thank Mrs. Butcher, Lady Theresa said, for the excellent preparation of the beef tongue he had enjoyed so much.

They climbed the three deeply grooved stone steps up to the shop; conversation stopped as they entered. Seven pairs of eyes were fixed upon them. He felt Lady Theresa tense, and she took in a deep breath, as if she were preparing for battle. She fixed her attention on one woman, an older, stout lady dressed in black and gray.

"Mrs. Greavely," she said sweetly, "I would like to make known to you Mr. James Martindale."

"Mrs. Greavely," he said, nodding to her. "Good day to you, ma'am."

Her stern manner thawed just a fraction, and she said, "Good day, sir."

Tension broke in the butcher shop and Mr. Butcher himself came forward, wiping his hands on his apron and bowing obsequiously to James. They had an odd conversation about beef tongue and his preferences in meat cuts, something of which he rarely thought. He felt as though he had passed some test of which he was not even aware. Conversation resumed, though there was a great deal of whispering and pointing. He supposed he was a novelty in so small a village. He and his family had only been in residence a month or so. But he occasionally heard Jacob's name and a sharply indrawn breath.

The bell over the shop door rang loudly and an old man stumped in.

"Mr. Gudge," Mrs. Greavely said with a gasp. "I thought you were still laid up with a broken leg?"

"I was until just a day ago."

The tiny shop was getting crowded, and James was just about to turn to leave when the old man caught his arm.

"Say, you. You Mr. James Martindale?"

"Mr. Gudge," Lady Theresa said. "I was just about to introduce you. Mr. Martindale, this is Albert Gudge; he used to be my father's game master, but Papa pensioned him when his . . . uh, heart began to give him trouble."

"You mean I began to drink too much and became a danger carrying a gun," the old man said.

The lady's eyes widened and she fell silent.

Gudge turned to James. "Sir, milady visited me with that boy o' yourn. I broke m'leg and had no will to get up outta my chair afore that, but that boy o' yourn . . . he's a special lad. We sat an' we carved, an' he . . ." He broke off and swiped a hint of moisture out of his eye. "I like 'im," he said loudly, looking around the shop as if daring anyone to contradict him. "He be a special lad."

Stunned and touched, James took the old man's outstretched hand. "Are you responsible for that interesting carving he gave me last night, then, the tree with the woodland creatures?"

"Not responsible. Just handed him a knife an' a block o' wood, and he done it."

"He did that himself?"

"He did. Natural genius with a block o' wood, is that boy. If I might, I would like Lady Theresa to bring him again. Or . . . if *you* had a mind to visit an old man . . ." He trailed off and looked embarrassed. He ducked his head and touched his cap, then scuttled out, throwing one last glance and word over his shoulder. "Lady T., you bring that there boy anytime you're of a mind."

Babbling conversation broke out in the clean, white-painted shop.

"He was sober. I don't think I've seen Albert Gudge sober in . . ."

"His leg was just fine. He limped, but it has healed, and I thought he was an invalid for life . . ."

"It's that boy, it's that Jacob Martindale. I heard this morning that Harriet Parsifal has just inherited over two hundred pounds—can you imagine?—and she didn't even know it was coming! And that after a visit from the boy!"

Lady Theresa took James's arm and bustled him out of the shop while his brain whirled with the things he had heard, the babbling gossip, some of it involving his son, it seemed.

"Lady Theresa, what is going on? What was that all about?"

"Just village gossip," she said feverishly, guiding him toward Mr. Dartelle's office.

He grasped her arm, stopping her. "What is going on?"

She stopped then, and drew herself up. She was tall, eye to eye with him. "Why, nothing at all, Mr. Martindale. Folks are just surprised to see Mr. Gudge looking so good. He broke his leg in a fall some time ago and has not been able to walk since." She shrugged and repeated, "People are just surprised."

He had to be satisfied with that, and allowed her to guide him to Dartelle's office, where he had business to conduct.

"I will meet you at the livery stable, sir. I think we have done enough . . . uh . . . well, I think you have *met* enough of the villagers for now."

Her color was high and he was suspicious, but he could not imagine what she would be hiding.

Dartelle was a portly, prosperous-looking man in his late forties. His hair was thinning on top, and his chins were multiplying, but for all that he was pleasant-looking. He greeted James with a vigorous handshake and they got down to business. When it was accomplished, James frowned and sat back in his chair.

"Mr. Dartelle, I have just come from meeting some of the villagers."

"May I hope that you will be thinking of offering for Meadowlark Mansion? Did they make you feel welcome in our village?"

"Yees," James said, drawing it out, doubt lingering as to what his recent experience really meant. "Do you know a Mrs. Harriet Parsifal?"

"The widow Parsifal; indeed I do." He sat back in his chair, resting his hands on his paunch and steepling his fingers. A stray beam of sunlight in the dim office glanced off his balding pate.

"Did she recently come into an unexpected inheritance?"

"She came into an inheritance," he said cautiously. "But it was hardly unexpected. She has known about it for some time, but she is not one to talk, you know. How, if I may ask, did you come to know about it?"

"It is being talked of in the butcher shop. But it is clearly being spoken of as unexpected, as though she had no idea it was coming and it was some sort of miracle."

Dartelle shrugged. "Misunderstanding, merely. Things get twisted in the telling, you know. One person whispers, another mishears . . . happens all the time."

"I suppose," James said, reluctant to let go of the mystery.

He toyed with a seal on the desk, turning it over and over. "If someone had not named my son in conjunction with it, I would not be even mentioning it. But someone said something about Jacob, and a visit to Mrs. Parsifal before she learned of the inheritance."

"Preposterous," Dartelle said, sitting up sharply, his chair clunking down on the wood floor. "Widow Parsifal knew about the inheritance before you and your children even came to St. Mark."

There was no arguing with such certainty, so what he heard must be gossip or misunderstanding only. James stood and extended his hand. "Thank you, Dartelle. I will see you again soon. I am still thinking about buying Meadowlark. My concern is my children, but they seem to be getting along much better, thanks to Lady Theresa."

The other man stood. As he took James's outstretched hand and shook, he chuckled and said, "That lady is a spark, Mr. Martindale! If she is sponsoring you, you are assured of acceptance in this village. Old family, sir, and an honored one."

James was tempted—so very tempted—to ask questions concerning the lady's single state. It was a mystery to him how a woman with charm, family, and money could have remained in her single state. It had to be by choice; there could be no other explanation. Or there could, he supposed, be some tragedy there of which he knew nothing. But he would not expose her to gossip by asking Dartelle.

He left with more questions than he had had when he arrived.

Ten

The days drifted on. More and more, James left the management of Meadowlark and its fields to Puget, even though he insisted on his own way, still, in some things. But summer in Somersetshire was too pleasant a time to spend it on toil only.

There were idyllic days with all four of them taking jaunts about the countryside. He wondered, had he been blind before? How else could he explain his failure to see Jacob's ability, which was considerable, to learn new skills? He was a natural hand with animals, and had an artistic side James had never thought to encourage before.

But Lady Theresa did. She brought him a gift of an art set full of paper, charcoal, pencils, and watercolor paints. His work was wild and imaginative, primitive in a way, but becoming more skilled day by day.

And Angelica! How could he take in the change in his sullen, unhappy, pasty-skinned girl? She was golden now, too tanned for fashion, but a brown, happy child with laughter in her eyes.

They sat on the banks of the stew pond one sunny, brilliant day. There had never been such a sky. It was blue, with soft puffs of cloud floating like paper sailboats across a cerulean sea. Jacob sat under a tree, watching an oblivious stoat nosing and nuzzling under the tree for acorns just feet from him. James lay, hands behind his head, on the turf.

Lady Theresa and Angelica were playing some kind of wild game, racing up and down the sloping green, a gauzy wisp of fabric stretched between them. Angelica was laughing and golden, her brown hair streaming out, glinting with sunlight. She raced to Theresa and threw her arms around her waist and the two tumbled, laughing, to the ground.

And James had never been so happy. Not even when he was newly prosperous and marrying Mary, as guilty as he felt about that. He had loved Mary, but she had loved him more and he always knew it.

This was different, this family they had created, Lady Theresa, Angelica, Jacob, and himself. Would it ever be complete again without Lady Theresa? His breath caught as the two stood and walked back toward him, arms about each other's waists.

Angelica was laughing at something the woman was telling her. Her eyes glowed and for one moment he could see the beautiful young lady she was becoming.

Normally absolutely correct in dress and grooming, Lady Theresa's hair was coming out of its restricted bun, wisps curling about her angular face, softening it, and she had lost her hat. She wore no gloves and her gown was an old one, soft and worn from use. She looked unexpectedly young and carefree.

Would she marry him if he asked?

The thought made his mouth go dry and he sat up, watching them as they approached and both collapsed at his feet, exhausted and pink-cheeked. He needed to think. Where had that question come from?

It must be just the product of the gratitude he felt toward her for her kindness to his children. Yes, that was likely it. It couldn't possibly be that he was falling in love.

She threw herself back in the grass and smiled up at him, her lips rosy and her cheeks pink from exertion and summer sun. An unaccountable urge to kiss her caught him by surprise. But that, too, was merely the urge of the moment. He couldn't *possibly* be falling in love.

Theresa didn't deny it. It came to her unexpectedly one day when James Martindale came to lunch with her father. He had some farming questions for Lord Leighton, he'd said, and the two men were closeted for hours together.

When they came out of her father's study, they were earnestly discussing something and she looked up from the hem she was sewing. Her father clapped the other man on the shoulder and they laughed; in that instant she knew. She loved him. She loved his fine, true heart and his goodness. She adored everything about him.

He had kind eyes; sometimes there was worry in them as he watched his silent son, and then at other times there would be laughter in them at some jest witty Angelica had made. But always she could trace the fine lines just beginning to soften the edges and see the light of love in them when he gazed at his children. She adored that about him.

But what had first touched her was that he was so considerate in almost everything he did. She shivered and he brought her a shawl; she licked her lips and he retrieved a cold drink for her. She had never had anyone take care of her as he did. She had always been the caregiver and it warmed her to know someone was watching out for her comfort.

She had fallen in love day by day, hour by hour, moment by moment. And now it was too late to retrace the steps, some tiny, some huge, and go back from love. It wasn't possible. Her heart was committed.

It was difficult, that day, to maintain her composure through lunch, sitting at the same table with the two men she loved more than any other in the world, with her new knowledge singing in her brain. Couldn't they see it, feel it emanating from her like a misty aura around the moon on a still, humid night? She thought that anyone with eyes would be able to see it clinging to her, floating around her, radiating from her like energy, like the aureole depicted in old paintings of the saints.

And yet—

Alone in her room later that night, she admitted to herself that she was no more sure, even knowing she had fallen in love with James Martindale, if marriage would be the right thing for her, even if he should ask her, and a far-fetched imagining *that* was! She still had no reason to think him interested in her in any other way but as a friend to his children and a valuable introduction to the village.

Perhaps she was mistaking friendship for love.

Except she had never wanted a friend to kiss her before. And she longed for, dreamed of, *needed* James Martindale to kiss her.

No, it was not just friendship, though that was there, too. It was love. How very unexpected, and in a way, unwelcome. Though she would not for anything take back knowing James and his children, what should she do now that she had fallen in love?

July dwindled to a handful of days. James had visited the village on his own, and found the people friendly; often they inquired after his children, especially Jacob. He was even invited to their homes, and always they would ask him to bring his children, *especially Jacob*. Angelica did not mind; she was very good about caring for Jacob on those visits, even going off with him to visit an invalid in the family, or, on one memorable occasion, a sick cow.

What strange people the folks of St. Mark were, James began to think.

He still had the feeling that folks were gossiping about him, but he had become accustomed to it. It was just their way of assimilating this stranger into their midst, he thought.

He would have been oblivious to any other nuances in their treatment of him and his family if it hadn't been for Bill Johnson, the groom he had fired for his vicious lies about Jacob.

Fortunately he did not have his children with him that day. He was just waiting for his horse to be brought out from the livery stable after a morning spent conducting business with Dartelle, the solicitor. He had not driven the phaeton, since he was alone. Johnson brought the horse to him, but did not let go of the reins even when James grabbed hold of them.

"What is it, Johnson," James said through gritted teeth. He tried not to show the man how much he despised him, but it was difficult.

"Look down yer nose at me, I know you do. But yer the one willin' to buy folks round here with barmy tales 'o his bein' a good-luck charm."

James stood absolutely still for a moment and stared at the man, a well set-up fellow, though his teeth were yellowed and his beard stubble marred his healthy looks. "What are you talking about?" he asked slowly.

Johnson did not answer for a moment, and then said, "You don't even know, do ya? It mus' be that frustrated bag, Lady T. Her ma was another such . . . fairy bedazzled, like."

James shook his head to clear it. "I have no time for this. Let go of my reins or I will whip you all the way back into the stable."

Johnson snarled and jerked on the reins, causing the horse to rear. James switched at the groom with his crop, but then bent his efforts to calming his horse.

Johnson, holding his bare arm where the switch had cut a strip of red, grunted. "Mr. High Muckety-Muck. We'll see how yer like it when those whut think yer son fairy-possessed start thinking he's devil-possessed! An' I'll make sure they do!" He whirled and stalked back into the stable.

That was when he understood, finally, what had been before him for weeks.

If Lady Theresa had been home he would have gone directly to confront her, but she was gone for the day to a friend's lying-in, and would not likely be back until late the next day. He was an impatient man and wanted confirmation of his suspicions immediately.

So though he shrank from precipitous action normally, he obtained directions from Mr. Butcher and started down a country road, watching for the tumble-down cottage he had been told housed old Gudge. It was more mud than mortar, more sticks than stones, just as he had been warned. He looped the reins of his mount over a low branch and, hesitant now, approached the dwelling.

He tapped on the door. "Mr . . . . uh, Gudge? Are you home?"

"Out back!"

James circled the building to a hesitant garden haphazardly cut into the ground behind the precarious cottage. The old man was sitting on a wooden chair with a hoe in his hands, and he was scrabbling with the implement in the dirt. A few straggly seedlings were coming up. He dumped a pot of water on some and set the hoe aside.

Standing with an obvious effort, he hobbled forth to greet James. "Howdy do, sir?"

James didn't quite know what to say, nor how to start.

"Kin I offer you an ale, sir? I bin tryin' my best to stay away from the gin and rum, sir, but a bit o' ale never hurt a body." He led the way into his cottage.

Following, James stooped his head as he entered the ramshackle cottage. Gudge limped over to a shelf and took a crockery jug down, and two tankards of pewter.

"Lord Leighton gave me these here tankards when my service to him was done. He were a good master, but I'd become a danger, an' kind as he is—good man through an' through—he pensioned me off. He visits me time and again, not like Lady Theresa does, mind, but more'n an old coot could expect." As he spoke he had filled the two tankards with ale and set one with a bang down in front of James.

"Take 'em outside, we should," he said, glancing around his cottage. "Nowhere for a gent like you to sit in here."

Outside they settled on a bench under a craggy tree. Gudge's cottage was in a pretty spot overlooking the valley close to the Leighton home. It was, in fact, still on Leighton property, James surmised. He took a sip of the ale, found it surprisingly refreshing, but then set it aside and turned to the old man.

"Mr. Gudge, I don't quite know how to ask this without sounding either impertinent or mad."

"Well, now, you got me attention, anyways."

"Your leg . . . it was broken?"

He nodded. "I were drunk as a lord, an' comin' home from the inn. Fell off the road, strange as that sounds, an' landed in a ditch over a log. Bones ain't what they used to be. Broke it in two places."

James thought for a moment. "When you came into the butcher shop that time and we spoke, I heard some whispering after . . ."

"Always whisperin' in a village, sir, forgive me interruption."

The old man seemed anxious and shifted on the bench. He squinted off into the distance over the rolling green hills. James frowned and watched him for a moment, then said slowly, "Mr. Gudge, I was accosted today by Bill Johnson, a fellow I fired from my employ for telling tales about Jacob."

"Bill Johnson," Gudge murmured, nodding sagely. "Bad lot. Got a gal in the family way an' refused to marry her. All the Johnsons hereabouts are a bad lot."

Refusing to be led away from the topic, James said, "What I am concerned about is what he said, that Jacob is being spoken of as . . . as 'fairy-charmed' or some such nonsense. And it reminded me of the whispers in the butcher shop. They attributed your sudden health and a woman named Mrs. Parsifal's windfall of money on a visit from Jacob. And it puts me in mind that lately, everyone wants my son to visit and touch sick animals and people . . ." He trailed off. "Mr. Gudge, man to man, who started this rumor? And why?"

"Now don't go a-blamin' her. She were only doin' what was best, an' she knows the folks round here. She were counterin' a lot o' superstitious nonsense 'bout the boy havin' the evil eye. Some folks might not listen to Bill Johnson, but that housekeeper you let go, Mrs. Hurst, she's bin spreading her own poison, and folks whut would not believe Bill will believe her."

Digesting his speech for a moment, the truth dawned on

James in a rush. He started up from the bench. "Theresa? *Theresa* started this idiocy?"

Uneasily, the old man coughed and shifted, and then said, "Well, yes, but she were only doin' what she thought best. Folks round here believe in such things."

But James had heard enough. He barely said good-bye to the old man; he left abruptly, galloping away on his horse. Theresa still would not be home and he must wait a full day to see her. Until then he would hold his temper and wait for her explanation.

Though how she would explain making of his son a rabbit's foot, he did not know. He had thought better of her. He tried to rein in his disappointment, but he had a horrible feeling that the joy of the summer was gone for him.

Eleven

Lady Theresa, accompanied by her maid, could barely summon the energy to control her mare, so it was lucky that the horse knew her own way home. She was so very tired and sad. Helen, her good friend from childhood, had given birth to her child the night before, but it was, tragically, dead. Theresa thought, looking back, that Helen had suspected it, because whenever her husband would speak of their coming child, their first to be carried the full nine months, she was silent and occasionally tearful. She may have known she was carrying a dead child; after all, there must have been no movement, and there should have been some.

She was just able to hand the reins of her gig over to old John, who took one look at her and stayed silent, not even asking after the baby, which he normally would do. She had already sent her maid ahead with the order to prepare her bed and a cup of hot tea, and she trudged wearily up to the house alone, her eyes dazzled by the angle of the setting sun and the tears that would not abate.

When she heard the voice, she was not sure who it was at first, an error that could only be explained by her exhaustion.

"So, you're home at last, back from your latest round of meddling!"

She halted, shaded her eyes, and stared. "James!" she blurted, forgetting her usual careful address. She felt a little spurt of happiness that he should be there to greet her, but then his tone rather than his words sank into her weary brain. "Is something wrong?"

"It is. Unless you can explain to me why you made my son into some kind of human lucky charm, a rabbit's foot to be rubbed when people need a shot of good luck!"

She stared, unable to take in what he was saying. She was so very tired from the devastation she had witnessed, a young family blighted by tragedy, and she could not comprehend this accusation. Tomorrow. She would talk to him tomorrow. "Go away, James," she said, plodding past him.

"No. You will explain now, if you please!" He caught her arm and spun her around.

She lashed out at him, slapping his hand, tears dried in her sudden fury. "Let go of me, if you please! I said, tomorrow. I'm tired. You have no idea what I have . . ."

"No!" His voice was bitter with accusation. "This is your doing and I will have an explanation! Was it a joke? A hoax? Did you think it was humorous to pull one over the eyes of the villagers? Even at the expense of my poor son?"

"I wasn't making a joke of Jacob. That you could even say that . . ." She broke off, no words being adequate to express her anger.

"But what do I really know about you? You have already confided your cynical tutoring of my daughter, teaching her to manipulate others with sweet behavior. Clearly you follow that philosophy. Jacob and I have been your cats' paws."

She gazed at him, trying to understand his anger, trying to know what to say, but it was no use. She had seen such sadness, felt such grief; she had no more emotions to feel. She was numb, and didn't care what he said or what he did. "Think what you will. You are now welcome in our village, are you not? People are kind to Jacob, aren't they?"

James thrust his face into hers and she instinctively recoiled.

"Because they think he's a bloody talisman! They want him to ensure the harvest, rub their afflicted feet, bring them an inheritance!" His face was red and he looked like he was going to fall down in an apoplectic fit. "I had begun to think the people of St. Mark mad! Everyone we visit wants Jacob to come; they want him to rub their mare's belly or touch poor old Aunt Mehitabel's boil! It is disgusting, the way you have used that poor child!"

"Don't speak to me that way," she said, trembling. Her limbs were near collapse, her hands shaking as if palsied. The day had been a nightmare, and it continued.

Old John came charging out of the stable with a pitchfork in his hands. "You, get out o' here. If'n I'd known you wus gonna terrorize the mistress, I'da run ya off!"

James stalked away to where his horse stood, calmly surveying the scene. "Lady Theresa, I would ask that you keep your distance from my children in future. If you had some explanation, or if you were sorry . . . But I don't need their brains poisoned with your nonsense, and I must now find a way to undo the hideous damage you have done to my son by making him some kind of superstitious spectacle for backward villagers."

Theresa found the energy to run all the way up to her room, not even stopping for her father, who begged to know what was going on. But once in her room, secure with the door locked, the tears still didn't come. She was utterly spent and fell into a deep sleep, not to awaken until late the next day.

"Why doesn't Lady Theresa come around anymore?"

James looked up from his desk and frowned at Angelica's question. "We've disagreed on some things, and I feel it is in your and Jacob's best interest not to see her again."

"You're just being hateful," Angelica said, stamping one foot. "You just don't want me to have any fun."

"That isn't true, and you know it."

"Then what have you disagreed about?"

"It is adult business."

"In other words, something stupid."

"Go to your room," James said, bending back over his papers.

"No, not until you tell me . . ."

"Go to your room," James thundered, rising from his desk and planting both hands on the surface.

Jacob edged into the library and stared at his father. Angelica stalked back, took his hand, and said, "Fine, we'll go away and leave you alone the way you want it. The way you've always wanted it."

Together they left the room. But Jacob threw one long, puzzled look over his shoulder that left his father shaken.

James sank back into his chair and buried his face in his hands. His anger hadn't abated, but his natural good sense had taken over or come back, whichever was the best description. He thought back to that evening, several days before. He should have seen how tired Theresa was. Perhaps he should give her another chance at explaining.

What explanation could possibly make up for the mess, he didn't know. But still—

Tomorrow. He would do it tomorrow.

But the next day left him unsure. He sat in the breakfast room and ate toast, chomping through piece after piece, barely aware that he was eating.

Angelica, who normally took her breakfast in the nursery with Dora and Jacob, edged into the room, the sullen look still on her face. It changed a bit, muted by indecision.

"I'm sorry I bellowed at you yesterday, Angelica. I apologize." James set the toast aside and swung around in his chair, putting his hands on his knees and staring at his daughter. She was a pretty child now that her complexion had cleared some and her frame had filled out from the stick-thinness of the London days.

"I know why you're angry," she said, coming forward. She stood in front of him and stared into his eyes. "It's Jacob. It's the trick Lady Theresa played on the villagers."

"You're right," he admitted, surprised into honesty by her perspicacity. "I don't like it. It's just as bad as when they thought he was a bad omen, don't you see that?"

"But she said it would take a long time for people to accept him. Maybe never. This was like a shortcut."

"I don't take shortcuts."

"But sometimes they make life easier, Lady Theresa says. Lady Theresa says that some people are . . . are hidebound and impossible to change, and that you're justified then in tricking them into something for their own good."

"That's a dangerous way to live your life, Angelica." He tried to put his thoughts into words, struggling with concepts he knew were deep within him, but that he had never needed to voice. "Come here," he said, pulling her onto his lap like he used to when she was a little girl. He hugged her, smelling her hair and her child essence. He had forgotten how good it felt to hold his children. Though Angelica was a child no longer. This summer was likely the last time she would seem so. "Maybe Lady Theresa was trying to help, but then, when some of these people don't have good luck, or if something happens—a cow Jacob touched dies or a person gets sicker—then they could blame him. That will make things much worse."

She thought about it and nodded. "I suppose that's true."

"But beyond that, Angelica, how we live our lives every day makes us who we are. If we trick the people around us into doing things, even for the right reasons, how are we better than folks who trick people for the wrong purposes, to hurt them? And where is the line? Humans are selfish; we can so easily fool ourselves into thinking we're doing things for some good purpose, when it's self-interest at work."

She frowned.

"Look, when you were a little girl, you used to ask for treats for Jacob just because you knew you would get them yourself. You didn't really care about Jacob, just about getting something for yourself. But I would wager you thought you were doing it for him, at least some of the time."

There was silence for a minute, and then his daughter leaned her head on his shoulder. "But I miss Theresa, Papa. And Jacob does too."

"So do I," he said, realizing it was true. Days were darker. Hours were longer. He set Angelica away from him. "I have to go out," he said, making up his mind. He had to give her another chance to explain herself. He wouldn't believe she was careless and unthinking, not when she had done so much good. And he had to explain his own side of things.

Twelve

Theresa stood, arms wrapped around her gaunt frame, hugging herself, staring out the open window across the misty meadows of Leighton. Strings of low fog caressed spikes of bearded purple iris and cornflowers like fingers, waiting to pluck them. When she was a child her mother had told her the mist was magical; if you could feel its touch on your skin it was a blessing from the fairies. And yet, she felt no temptation to go out in it that moment. If Angelica had been there she might have, but not now.

It had been a long few days without Angelica and Jacob . . . and James. Theresa had kept herself busy, but the emptiness in her heart could not be "busied" away.

She had never seen James so angry, and she couldn't pretend that she didn't know what it was about. Somehow the innocent deception she had perpetrated on the folks of St. Mark had gotten out of hand. She had expected it to be a mild diversion, to last just long enough so people could see that Jacob was just a quiet boy, a little different from others but not some evil harbinger of doom.

She had thought that if they could just get over their initial aversion, they would come to accept him as he was. Instead, an hysteria had arisen, and many swore now they had seen Jacob charm the animals. What a muddle.

"There's someone to see you, my dear." Her father approached her from behind and put his arms around her, giving her a brief hug and releasing her.

That in itself was odd. He was a reserved man. All of the

outward signs of parental love she had ever experienced had come from her mother. When Lady Leighton died she had felt so horribly alone. It was only in the last few years that she had reached out to her father, making him submit to her embraces.

"Someone to see me?" she repeated.

"Mr. Martindale."

"I don't wish to see him."

"Don't be a fool," her father replied.

"What?" She turned and stared at him, wondering at his unwonted harshness.

"Don't be a fool." His eyes were kind, even if his words were harsh. "I have never seen you so sad—or at least not since your mother died—as you have been since your argument with Mr. Martindale. Yes, I know about it," he said at her surprised exclamation. "Don't you think old John talks to me? I don't know what it was about . . ." He held up one hand as she began to speak. "And I don't want to, but you miss him and his children."

"I do."

He put his hands on her shoulders and stared into her eyes. "My dear, I've noticed a change in you this year, even before you met Mr. Martindale. I don't think this life is enough for you anymore."

"What are you saying?"

He squeezed her shoulders and released her, his arms falling back to his side. He stepped back from her. "Perhaps it's time for you to move on with your life and take some risks. You haven't been up to that challenge. It was all right as long as you were happy, but I think you need more in your life than just me and this house."

"Are you trying to get rid of me?" Her voice was strange, clogged with tears. She wrapped her arms around herself again, squeezing, fighting back the weepiness that she despised.

"No. I will miss you if you leave."

"Where would I go?"

"Theresa, my dear, I know you have fallen in love with Mr. Martindale."

She stiffened. It sounded so bold and foreign coming from her father. A lady did not admit to feelings before the gentleman. "But I can't just tell him that and say, 'So, let's marry.' Can I? And I don't think he feels the same for me."

"He's here now. Go and fight it out, whatever your ridiculous argument was. I think you might be surprised . . ." He shook his head and stopped. "Not my place. I cannot speak for him. *Should* not speak for him. Go," he said, turning her around and shoving her gently toward the door. "Go and talk to him. He's waiting in the morning parlor."

James heard her come in and turned from his perusal of the view. His first thought was that she looked even more gaunt than usual and pale. Not the laughing, happy woman of a few days before by the stew pond.

And he remembered the evening of their confrontation, when she had been coming from her friend's home. She had been distraught, it seemed to him. Previously she had spoken of her friend's situation as a happy one, but childbirth was risky.

"I neglected to ask you the other evening, how does your friend do? Is she well?"

"She lost the baby," she said, and then turned her face away. "Their little boy was born dead."

"Oh, my God, Theresa, and then I badgered you . . ." He moved forward without thinking, and before he knew it she was in his arms. "I am so sorry," he whispered into her hair, rubbing her back with one hand. He felt her shudder, her whole body convulsing, but when she lifted her face and moved away from him her eyes were dry.

"You didn't know," she said, her voice soft.

He gazed at her and took in a long breath.

"How are Angelica and Jacob?" she blurted out, twisting her hands together.

"Fine. Just fine." He frowned. "No, that's not true. Angelica misses you horribly and Jacob has withdrawn again. I try so hard, but he doesn't respond to me sometimes. He shrinks away when I try to touch him."

"You want so much *from* him and *for* him. I think he senses that and it frightens him. Just relax in his presence and let him be who he is."

"Do you think that will help?"

"I know it will. You've done it before, you know, without effort. He loves you so much, even though he can't say it."

"You have such a natural way with him," James whispered. "The children have missed you. I've missed you, too."

"Have you?" Her voice was soft and breathless.

He had to keep himself from moving back to her and taking her in his arms again. But it had been so natural before; it wouldn't be that way again. And there were problems.

"But I cannot condone what you did. You made my son into a talisman, some unnatural fairy charm. It is wrong. Either people accept him the way he is or they can go to hell."

She smiled, not the reaction he was expecting.

"You may be right," she said, with a rueful tone. "But let me at least explain my reasoning. You must know, first, that I would never do anything to purposely hurt either Angelica or Jacob."

"I know that," he said. "I was angry the other night, and I was wrong to imply that you would."

Her expression softened, and his heart thudded. She had felt, in his arms, as if she belonged there, and that was an alarming thought.

"Thank you. I have never had a man apologize to me before. What a novelty!"

He laughed. She always managed to make him laugh.

But then her whimsical smile died and she turned away. "I have been realizing how foolish I was. You were right and I was wrong. Jacob deserves more than just to have people want to use him."

"I know your intentions were good . . ."

"But hell is paved with good intentions."

"Johnson said that."

"No, he rephrased it, merely. It is an old aphorism."

"Good God, a bluestocking!"

She laughed, a burbling sound that rose from her like a bubbling stream. "Would you sit, James? I hate standing and speaking of serious things. I'd like to explain."

His name on her lips sounded right and he took in a deep, shaky breath. There was something between them, this unlikely woman and himself. Guided by her motion, he moved to a sitting area by the window, a bow window overlooking the garden path. He waited for her to sit and took the chair closest to her.

"My mother told me this story. Once, there was a young girl who married a very handsome gentleman, an eminent peer of the realm. She didn't know him very well, but he was kind and soon she found that she had fallen in love with him, and he with her. But the people of his village didn't understand her well because she was dreamy and odd, and she sometimes pretended to hear voices and see visions, just for fun. People began to speak of her as if she were possessed. It was rumored that one Midsummer's Eve she stayed out all night, and everyone knows that dancing with the fairies on Midsummer's Eve leaves a person fairy-charmed. Or mad.

"But then one day she visited a farm where the child was sick and there was no money for the apothecary to visit, nor for medicine even if he did. The family was proud and the young wife knew they would never accept charity, not even to save their child. It was a hard kind of pride. So she invented a distant relative for them and had the town's solicitor deliver to them an 'inheritance.' She enjoyed so much giving these people the money anonymously—and saving that child's life, perhaps—that she did other things, and accidentally a legend was born. She became a good omen."

James nodded. He thought he saw now how that had inspired her to use the same methods for Jacob. "That lady was your mother. Did she ever regret what happened?"

"No. Eventually people came to love her for who she was, and I think most folks eventually understood that she was behind folks' good fortune, but not in any supernatural sense."

"And you thought to do the same with Jacob?"

Theresa leaned forward. "Only at first! I thought to use Harriet Parsifal's inheritance and Albert Gudge's healed leg, just to make people open their hearts to Jacob as Mr. Gudge did. I knew once they got to know you all, they would love you."

James considered how best to say what he needed to say. He cared too much for her to want to hurt her. "Did you never consider that if things had gone wrong, they would blame Jacob? It could have turned very bad."

"I realize that now," she said, gazing out the window. "It was wrong to try to recreate artificially what had occurred naturally with my mother. How could I have been such an imbecile?"

"Theresa," he said, leaning toward her and taking her hands in his. "I know you did not do this cavalierly."

"Do you? I don't. I didn't even think of the consequences, James! I just went ahead and did it."

"At least you did something! I can see now how wrong I was from the start to separate my family from the villagers. It only encouraged people like Bill Johnson and Mrs. Hurst in their vicious lies. If I had joined in village affairs from the start instead of isolating us, things might never have gone so far wrong."

"You were only trying to protect your children."

"I should have asked for your aid. Why did you enlist Angelica's help?"

"She is very intelligent and . . . well, devious enough. It was wrong of me. Please don't blame her; I actually bribed Angelica to go along with the fiction."

"Bribed her? What did you promise her?"

Theresa grimaced. "A white pony and riding lessons. She so wants to ride, James, but you won't let her because you worry about Jacob wanting to ride, too. But I think Jacob *could* learn to ride. He has been so much better lately, don't you think, and . . ."

He did the only thing he could, under the circumstances. He pulled her to her feet, wrapped his arms around her, and kissed her.

Thirteen

Theresa thought of all the poetry she had ever read, all the romances describing in ecstatic detail a first kiss. It did not begin to compare. James was clearly a master of the craft, if she was to judge impartially.

But then she was terribly, beyond redemption, partial.

He was kissing her! Kissing. Her.

He stopped. She stared at him for a long moment. Doubt creased his forehead and he took a step backward.

"I'm terribly sorry."

"Are you?" She clasped her hands together at her breast.

"Yes. I mean, I'm sorry if you didn't like it, but you looked so adorable and I was tempted beyond caution."

"Adorable?"

"Yes. You were pleading Angelica and Jacob's case, and the only way to shut you up was to kiss you."

"Shut me up?"

"So I could tell you . . . I love you." Beads of sweat trickled down his forehead, down his cheek and neck, and soaked into his neck cloth.

"You love me?"

"I do. Very much."

"Oh."

"Have I shocked you?"

"No. Not at all."

Suddenly the door behind them shot open and shuddered against the paneled wall. "For God's sake, James, ask her to marry you!" Theresa's father glared at them both. "Couple of forlorn idiots," he said as he whirled around and left the room. He could be heard muttering as he strode off down the hall.

"Will you?"

"What?" Theresa stared at James.

"Will you marry me?"

"Of course."

"Of course?"

"What else am I to say?"

"Do you love me?"

"Well, of course. I wouldn't want to marry you, else."

"No?"

"Oh no, I have only *ever* wanted to marry men whom I loved."

He laughed out loud and took her in his arms. "And has that happened so very many times?"

"Only once before." She watched his face. It was time to tell him about Paolo.

"Oh?"

She told him about Paolo, how she was grief-stricken after her mother died, but Paolo had made her feel that someone could love her. James held her as they talked and rocked her against his shoulder. She felt cocooned in love, surrounded, padded, protected. But not from life, just from ever feeling again that there would never be anyone who could love her for herself. Life would still buffet her around from time to time. She had only to look at her friend Helen to know that a husband's love did not protect one from all the world's pain.

But there would always be someone there to share that pain.

She was going to marry! She looked up at him anxiously. "Is all of that all right? Paolo? The whole mess?"

"Poor Theresa; his defection must have hurt you badly. How could I fault you for having loved before? I did. Mary was very special and precious to me."

"Your capacity for love was what first attracted me," she confessed. "Oh, James! I have loved you for so long!"

"Have you? Truly? I am a merchant, just a rather successful sales clerk, in essence. I was afraid it would sink me in your eyes."

"I could never think less of a man for choosing to provide for his family."

He released her finally, and they stood, awkwardly. What *did* one say?

"Let's tell your father and the children," he said.

That was what she wanted to hear!

The windows of Meadowlark Mansion glowed in the setting autumn sun. Jacob, head bent over his drawing pad, sat at the edge of the stew pond—unfenced after all, since he could at last be trusted not to throw himself in—and sketched the ducks that paddled among the reeds. Dora sat at his side, throwing bits of bread to the birds.

In the lane James led a lovely white pony by the bridle and looked up at a laughing Angelica mounted on her silver-ornamented sidesaddle. Theresa stood to one side and watched her husband—her husband!—with his . . . *their* daughter.

The wedding had been simple, performed the old-fashioned way, after the calling of the banns by Vicar Jamison in the village church on three consecutive Sundays. The wedding breakfast had been in the village green, with the entire population invited.

James's openhanded generosity had gone a long way toward helping the Martindales assimilate into village life. But the rumors of Jacob's "powers" had been refuted, too, and the slow transformation back into just a silent little boy had been started.

Mrs. Parsifal, encouraged by Theresa, had acted surprised that anyone had "misinterpreted" her tying of Jacob's visit and her windfall together. How strange people were, she was heard to say. As if a little boy could affect fate in such a way. Why, her kinsman had been dead for months and the will written long before that; no magic charm had brought her the money.

Mr. Gudge, resplendent in his best suit of clothes at the wedding breakfast, had admitted that he had been lazy and curmudgeonly, not invalided. Anyone who had thought differently was a fool. 'Twas easy to see, he said, that the boy was just a quiet, decent lad, with an uncommon talent for drawing and carving. Nothing supernatural about that. And if he froze up now and then when folks tried to hug him, well, it just showed the child had uncommon good sense, for people were entirely too grabby, in his opinion.

And so now, a month into her marriage, Theresa was well on her way to contentment. James, after walking the pony a ways, let Angelica go with just a groom to guide her around the property.

He joined his wife and wound one arm around her waist. Nuzzling her neck, he whispered, "Shall we creep off into the bushes for a bit of naughtiness?"

"Behave, Mr. Martindale," she whispered back.

"Do you really want me to?"

"No."

"Good."

They stood for a while, watching as Angelica walked the pony, and then, with the groom's instruction, cantered. She was learning every moment. Theresa leaned her head on her husband's shoulder.

"To think," she said suddenly, looking up at him, "if you didn't have children, I might never have met you."

"What do you mean?"

"Well, you moved here for your children's sake, true?"

"I suppose. Though I always wanted to move back to the country anyway."

"And then it was only Mrs. Greavely's unkind comments about Jacob that urged me to break with courtesy and visit you in such an outrageous manner. And then, when I found Jacob about to go into the pond and I grabbed him, well that certainly made things more informal between us from the beginning."

"So, I have my children to thank for my wife?"

"Mmm, yes. But it was your love for them, a father's love, that first impressed me with what a kind and good man you must be. You were awfully frosty at first, and you thought I was looking for a husband; admit it!"

He laughed. "That seems so long ago. It didn't take me long to realize that a woman of your stature would not need to 'hunt' for a husband. You must have had gentlemen begging for your hand."

"Not a one like you, James. I could never have loved anyone the way I love you." She gazed up into his eyes and touched his cheek, gently.

"It's a miracle, and I thank the heavens every day."

He encircled her in his arms and she leaned back against him, content and filled with the spirit of love. She had a family. She had James. Whatever came now, good or bad, she had love to surround her.